Drowned Ammet

The people of Holand are bitterly crushed by their tyrannical ruler, whose armies of spies, informers, secret police, and cruel rent collectors terrorize the countryside.

Mitt has grown up with the idea of joining the Freedom Fighters and avenging the wrongs done to his father. But when his part in the plot to kill the wicked ruler goes wildly wrong, he finds himself on the run—and the only place to hide is in the midst of his enemies.

This is the second book in the best-selling Dalemark Quartet by acclaimed author, Diana Wynne Jones.

Diana Wynne Jones's early childhood was disrupted by World War II. From her point of view, the world suddenly went mad and she was transported first to Wales, then to the Lake District, where she lived in the house that belonged to the children in Arthur Ransome's books, and thence to a nunnery in York. Back in London briefly, she discovered, at the age of eight, that she was going to be a writer. This was not a decision: it was more as if someone tapped her on the shoulder and told her so. After this, her family moved to a village in Essex full of bizarre personalities, where she started writing books to read out to her sisters. There, just before she went up to Oxford to study English, she met her future husband who encouraged her to attend the lectures of both C. S. Lewis and J. R. R. Tolkien, and she lived in Oxford for many years after that. In 1976 she moved to Bristol with her husband and three sons and she has lived there ever since.

Drowned Ammet

Other books in the Dalemark Quartet

Cart and Cwidder

The Spellcoats

The Crown of Dalemark

The Dalemark Quartet

Drowned Ammet

Diana Wynne Jones

OXFORD
UNIVERSITY PRESS

For my mother

OXFORD
UNIVERSITY PRESS

Great Clarendon Street, Oxford OX2 6DP

Oxford University Press is a department of the University of Oxford.
It furthers the University's objective of excellence in research, scholarship,
and education by publishing worldwide in

Oxford New York
Auckland Cape Town Dar es Salaam Hong Kong Karachi
Kuala Lumpur Madrid Melbourne Mexico City Nairobi
New Delhi Shanghai Taipei Toronto

With offices in

Argentina Austria Brazil Chile Czech Republic France Greece
Guatemala Hungary Italy Japan Poland Portugal Singapore
South Korea Switzerland Thailand Turkey Ukraine Vietnam

Oxford is a registered trade mark of Oxford University Press
in the UK and in certain other countries

First published by Macmillan London Ltd 1977
First published by Oxford University Press 2000
First published in this paperback edition 2001

British Library Cataloguing in Publication Data available

ISBN 978-0-19-275278-9

3 5 7 9 10 8 6 4

Typeset by AFS Image Setters Ltd, Glasgow
Printed in Great Britain by
Cox & Wyman Ltd, Reading, Berkshire

Part 1

Free Holanders

1

People may wonder how Mitt came to join in the Holand Sea Festival, carrying a bomb, and what he thought he was doing. Mitt wondered himself by the end.

Mitt was born the day of the Holand Sea Festival, and he was called Alhammitt after his father. Perhaps the first sound Mitt heard as he burst bawling into the world was his parents laughing about both these things.

'Well, he took his time,' said Mitt's father, 'and chose his day all right. What does this make him? A man of straw, born to be drowned?'

Milda, Mitt's mother, laughed heartily at this, because the Sea Festival was something of a joke. On that day, every autumn, Hadd, the Earl of Holand was required by tradition to dress up in outlandish clothes and walk in a procession down to the harbour carrying a life-size dummy made of plaited wheat. The dummy was known as Poor Old Ammet. One of Hadd's sons walked after him carrying Poor Old Ammet's wife, who was made entirely of fruit, and her name was Libby Beer. The procession that went with them was both noisy and peculiar. When they reached the harbour, they said traditional words and then threw both dummies into the sea. Nobody knew why this was done. To most people in Holand the ceremony was just an excuse to have a holiday, eat sweets, and get drunk. On the other hand, everyone would have thought it horribly unlucky not to have held the Sea Festival. So Milda, even though she was laughing until her dimple was creased out of existence, bent over the new baby and said:

'Well, I think it's a lucky birthday to have had. He'll grow up a real free soul, just like you—you wait! That's why I'm calling him after you.'

'Then he'll be common as dirt,' said Mitt's father. 'Just like me. You go into town and shout "Alhammitt" in the street, and half Holand will come to you.' And they both laughed at the thought of the common name they were giving their baby.

Mitt's early memories were full of his parents' laughter. They were very happy. They had the good luck to rent a small-holding on the Earl's land in what was known as the New Flate, only ten miles from the port of Holand. It had been reclaimed from sea-marsh by Earl Hadd's grandfather and grew lush emerald grass, big vegetables, and corn in narrow yellow stripes between the dykes. Dyke End holding was so fertile and the market of Holand so near, that Mitt's parents had plenty to live on. Though Earl Hadd was said to be the hardest man in Dalemark, and other farmers in the Flate were always being turned out of doors for not paying their rent, Mitt's parents always had just enough money to go round. They laughed. Mitt grew up running carelessly along the paths between the crops and the dykes. It never occurred to anyone that he could drown. When he was two, he taught himself to swim by falling into a dyke when his parents were busy. Since no one was there to help him, he had to help himself. He struggled to the bank and got out, and his clothes dried in the stiff breeze as he ran on.

The sound of that breeze was as much part of his early memories as his parents' laughter. Apart from the hill where Holand stood, the Flate was flat as a floor. The wind blew straight across from the sea. Sometimes it came storming in, laying the grass over, chopping the sky

4

reflected in the dykes into grey V's, and hurling the trees sideways so that their leaves showed white. But most days it simply blew, steadily and constantly, so that the dykes never stopped rippling and the leaves of the poplars and alders went *rattle-rattle* up and down the banks. If the wheat was ripe, it rustled in the wind, stiffly, like straw in a mattress. The constant wind sighed in the grass and hummed in the chimney, and kept the sails of the big windmills always turning, *creak-thump*, *creak-thump*, to pump the water to the dykes or grind the flour. Mitt used to laugh at those windmills. It was the way their arms pawed the air.

Then one day, shortly after Mitt had taught himself how to swim, the wind suddenly dropped. It did that sometimes in early summer, but it was the first time in Mitt's life that he had known the Flate without wind. The sails of the windmills creaked and stood. The trees stopped moving. There was blue sky in the dykes, and trees upside down. Everything went quiet, and unexpectedly warm. Above all, there was suddenly an extraordinary smell. Mitt could not think what was happening. He stood on the bank of the dyke nearest the house with his ears tipped to the silence and his nose lifted to the smell. The smell was cow-dung and peat and trampled grass, mixed with smoke from the chimney. But that was only in the foreground. Beyond that was the smell of fresh things growing—cow-parsley, buttercups, a hint of may, and, strongest of all, the heavenlike scent of willows budding. While, at the back of it, there and not there, so that Mitt almost missed it, was the faint boisterous bite of the distant sea.

Mitt was too young to think of it as smells, or to realize that the wind had simply stopped. He thought it was a place. It seemed to him that he had got an inkling of somewhere unspeakably beautiful, warm and peaceful, and he wanted to go there. Yes, it was a land. It was not

5

far off, just beyond somewhere, and it was Mitt's very own. He set off at once to find it while he still remembered the way.

He trotted to the end of the dyke, crossed the foot-bridge, and continued trotting, northwards and inland. He passed all the places he knew, impatiently—they were obviously not his land—and trotted on until his legs ached. Even then he was still in the New Flate, lush and green, with its dykes, poplars, and windmills. Mitt knew his land was different from the Flate, so he was forced to toil on. And, after a mile or so, he came out into the Old Flate. Here it was different all right. The ground was wide and treeless and covered with pinkish marsh-plants. In some places, long lines of rushes and green scum showed where there had once been dykes and farms, but now it was all flat and blank. Nothing seemed to be alive there but mosquitoes and plaintive marsh birds. In the wide distance, it was true, there were one or two islands of higher ground with trees and houses on them. The roads to them crossed the pink waste on causeways, raised up like the veins on an old man's hand. Otherwise there was nothing, until, away on the edge of the distance, there was what Mitt took for a line of clouds, but was in fact the beginning of the land above sea-level, where Holand joined Waywold.

Mitt was a trifle daunted. This was not the kind of land he had in mind. His vision of his perfect place faded a little, and he was no longer sure this was quite the way to it. Nevertheless, he set forward bravely into the dismal landscape. He felt he had come too far to turn back now. After a while, he thought he saw something moving, out in the marsh. He set his eyes on the movement and waded towards it. It was extremely dangerous. There were snakes in the Old Flate. And if Mitt had walked into one of the scummy pools, he could have been sucked down into it and drowned. Fortunately, he had no idea. And, even more fortunately, the moving things he could see were a troop of the Earl's soldiers combing the Flate for a runaway revolutionary.

Mitt could see they were soldiers before long. He stood on a clump of rubbery plants, with the marsh sucking and gobbling around him, and wondered whether he ought to go near them. When people in the New Flate talked about soldiers, they talked as if soldiers were something to be afraid of. There was a causeway quite near Mitt. He wondered if he ought to climb up on it, out of the soldiers' way. While he was wondering, a muddy horse heaved itself on to the causeway from the marsh behind it. The young officer on its back reined in and stared at the sight of such a very small boy standing all alone in the middle of the Flate.

'What on earth do you think you're doing?' he called to Mitt.

Mitt was rather pleased to have company. 'I'm looking for my home,' he told the officer chattily. 'I come a long way, too.'

'I can see you have,' said the officer. 'Where is your home?'

'There.' Mitt pointed vaguely northward. He was busy examining his new acquaintance. The gold on the officer's coat took his fancy. So did the officer's face, which was very smooth and pale and narrow, with a nose that went out much more sharply than any noses Mitt had known before, and a mouth which Mitt somehow thought of as clean. Altogether Mitt felt he was a person worthy of knowing about the perfect place. 'It's all quiet, with water,' he explained, 'and it's my place where I'm going to, but I can't find it yet.'

The officer frowned. His own small daughter had been found marching out into the Flate only yesterday, saying she had a house on a hill that was hers and she had to find it. He thought he knew the signs. 'Yes, but where do you live?' he said.

'Dyke End,' Mitt said impatiently. It was unworthy of the officer to ask such things. 'Of course. That's where I come from, and I'm going to my home.'

'I see,' said the officer. He waved at the distant soldiers. 'Come here, one of you!'

The several troopers who came running at his shout were somewhat astonished to find not a full grown revolutionary but an extremely small boy. 'He shrunk with the wet,' one suggested.

'He says he lives in Dyke End,' said the officer. 'One of you take him home, and tell his parents to take more care of him in future.'

'Dyke End's not my home. It's where I *live*!' Mitt protested.

Nevertheless, he was taken back to the New Flate almost dangling from the hand of a huge trooper in the Earl's green uniform. Mitt was sullen at first, disappointed and vaguely humiliated. And he was deeply disillusioned about the officer. Mitt had told him a valuable secret, and the officer had barely even listened. But the trooper was a cheerful man. He had children of his own, and it had been hot, wet work, hunting the revolutionary in the windless Flate. The trooper was pleased to have a rest. He was very jolly to Mitt and, before long, Mitt cheered up and chatted happily about how far he had walked, and how he thought he would like to be a soldier, too, when he grew up, and a sea-captain as well and sail the Earl's ships for him.

When they came to the New Flate, people came to doors and gates to stare at Mitt trotting along with his hand stretched above his head in order to reach the great warm hand of the trooper. The stares were unloving. Earl Hadd was a hard man, and a vindictive one. The soldiers

8

were the ones who carried out the Earl's harsh orders. And lately, the Earl's second son, Harchad, had taken command of the soldiers, and he was even harder than his father, and a good deal more cruel. But since, all over Dalemark, an earl in his earldom had more power than a king, in the times when there were kings, Harchad and his soldiers did exactly as they pleased. Therefore soldiers were hated heartily.

Mitt understood none of this, but he saw the looks. 'Don't you look like that!' he kept crying out. 'This is my *friend*, this is!'

The trooper became steadily more uncomfortable. 'Take it easy, sonny,' he said every time Mitt cried out. And, after a while, he seemed to feel the need to justify himself. 'A man's got to live,' he told Mitt. 'It's not work I enjoy, but what can a poor boy off the harbour edge do? When I get my bounty, I aim to take up farming, like your dad does.'

'Did you fall in the harbour?' Mitt asked, fixing on the only part of this he understood.

They came to Dyke End. Mitt's parents had missed Mitt about half an hour before, and they were by then in a panic. Mitt's father received him with a great thump and his mother hugged him frantically. Mitt did not understand the reason for either. The vision of his perfect land had faded by then. He was not sure what he had gone away to do.

The trooper stood by, very stiff and correct. 'Boy was found out in the Old Flate,' he said. 'Said he was looking for his home, or some such story.'

'Oh, Mitt!' Milda cried joyously. 'What a free soul you are!' And she hugged him again.

'And,' said the trooper, 'Navis Haddsson's compliments and would you keep more of an eye on him in future.'

9

'Navis Haddsson!' exclaimed both Mitt's parents, Milda in considerable awe, and Mitt's father with surprise and resentment. Navis was Earl Hadd's third and youngest son.

'Big of Navis Haddsson,' Mitt's father said sarcastically. 'Knows all about bringing up boys, I suppose?'

'Can't say, I'm sure,' said the trooper, and he made off, having no wish to get into an argument with such a thickset and aggressive person as the elder Alhammitt.

'Well I think it was very kind of Navis to send us our Mitt back like that!' Milda said, when he had gone.

Mitt's father spat in the dyke.

All the same, Milda remained extremely impressed by the kindness of Navis. She told people about it whenever her husband was not by to resent it, and most people she told were impressed too. Earl Hadd and his family were not, as a rule, kind to anyone. After that, Milda took a great interest in Navis for a while, and found out everything about him that she could. There was not very much known. The Earl's eldest son, Harl, and his second son, Harchad, were the Earl's favourites and the ones people heard most about. But about the time Navis sent Mitt home, Navis was enjoying a little more of the Earl's favour. The reason was that three years or so before, the Earl had chosen Navis a wife, as he had chosen wives for his other two sons. Milda heard that Navis and his wife adored one another and went everywhere together. Then Navis's wife gave birth to a daughter. That was the reason the Earl was pleased with Navis.

The Earl valued granddaughters. He did not like girls in the least, but he needed granddaughters because he was an extremely quarrelsome man. Granddaughters could be married off to other earls and lords, who would then become Hadd's allies in his quarrels. But so far, only Harl's wife had had a daughter. So when Navis's wife, too, had a

10

daughter, Hadd was delighted with them. Milda learnt that Navis's wife was expecting a second child shortly, and Hadd was gleefully expecting another marriageable granddaughter.

The baby was born the following month. He was a boy, and Navis's wife died having him. It was said that Navis was so stricken with grief that he could not be bothered to find a name for his son. The nurses were forced to ask Earl Hadd to think of a name, and Hadd was so annoyed at not having a granddaughter that he called the boy Ynen, which was the name of a lord he particularly disliked. Hadd was consoled later on that year when Harl's wife and Harchad's both had girl babies. As for Navis, he gave up his commission in the Earl's army and fell into total obscurity. It was soon quite impossible to learn anything about him or about his children, Hildrida and Ynen.

Mitt did not quite forget his perfect land. He remembered it, though a little fuzzily, next time the wind dropped, but he did not set off to look for it again. It was plain to him that soldiers only brought you back again if you went. It made him sad. When an inkling of it came to him in silence, or in scents, or, later, if the wind hummed a certain note, or a storm came shouting in from the sea and he caught the same note in the midst of its noise, he thought of his lost perfect place and felt for a moment as if his heart would break. But then he would shake off the feeling and laugh with his parents.

It seemed to Mitt that the three of them could laugh at anything. He remembered laughing with Milda one evening during a rainstorm. Mitt was trying to learn his letters. He found them so difficult that he had to laugh. Then the door came clapping open in a gust of rain, blowing everything in the house to the end of the room, and there stood Mitt's father, soaking wet and laughing, shouting above the gale that the cow had calved. At that, the door came off its hinges and fell on Mitt's father. And they all laughed till they ached.

The very funniest thing happened when the calf had grown into a young and gamesome bull. Mitt and his parents were all in the pasture, trying to mend a place where the dyke-bank was giving. The bull stood watching them, rather interested. Life was a little dull in the pasture. Then Hadd's rent-collector climbed over the fence and stalked irritably over to the dyke.

'I've been all the way to the house,' he said. 'Why couldn't you—?'

The bull, with a look of pure mischief in his merry red eye, lowered his horns and charged. He would not have dreamt of harming any of the family, but the rent-collector was another matter. And, in a misty, bullish way, he may have noticed that the family was not altogether pleased to see the rent-collector. Anyway, up went the rent-collector in a graceful arc, moneybag and all, and down he went again, moneybag and all, into the dyke, where he gave out a truly tremendous splash. He came up. He swore horribly. He floundered to the bank and tried to get out. The bull was there to meet him, and simply prodded him back in again. It was the funniest thing Mitt had ever seen. It never occurred to the rent-collector to cross the dyke and get out on the opposite bank where the bull could not reach him. He kept floundering up, clutching his moneybag. And prod, prod went the bull, and the rent-collector was sitting in the dyke again. Over and over again, with the rent-collector, floundering, reeling, sitting down *splash*, and squawking 'Can't one of you control this beast!' and Mitt's parents leaning head to head, too helpless with laughter to do a thing about it. It was Mitt, laughing as hard as anyone, who at last hooked

12

his finger in the ring on the bull's nose and let the raging rent-collector scramble out. And the rent-collector was not pleased.

'I'll teach you to laugh, boy!' he snarled.

He did. Next time he came for the rent, he asked double. When Mitt's father protested, he said, 'Nothing to do with me. Earl Hadd needs the money.'

Probably Hadd was short of money. The rents were put up all over the Flate. Rumour said that there were riots in the town of Holand, and the Earl needed to pay more soldiers to deal with the rioting. But only at Dyke End was the rent doubled. That was the rent-collector's private revenge. And there was nothing Mitt's parents could do about it. Theoretically, they could have gone to law and accused the rent-collector of extortion. But the rent-collector was the Earl's official, and judges always upheld the Earl's employees against ordinary people—unless, of course, you gave the judge a big enough bribe. Mitt's parents had no money for bribes. They needed more than they had to pay the rent-collector. They had to sell the bull.

Next quarter, they sold the mule. Then some furniture. And by that time they were in a vicious circle: the more things they sold from the farm to pay the rent, the less they had to make money with to pay the next quarter's rent, and the more things they had to sell. Mitt's parents stopped laughing. That winter, Mitt's father took to spending most of the week away in the port of Holand, earning what money he could there, while Milda tried to run the farm with what help Mitt could give. It was desperately hard work. Milda's pretty face acquired a seam of worry down one side—a sort of pucker where her dimple had been. Mitt hated that pucker. He did not remember how his father looked at that time. He remembered a curt, bitter voice, and his father's square

13

back plodding away from them down the causeway to Holand to find work.

He could not have found much work. He spent longer and longer away in Holand, and brought very little money back, but what he did bring enabled them to drag on at Dyke End for the following summer. But Milda on her own was a poor, forgetful manager. Mitt did all he could to help, but they lost money steadily. There were still a few times when Mitt was able to lie on his back by the dyke, looking up at the rattling leaves, and think yearningly about his perfect land. As times grew harder, he seemed to want it more and more. He longed to set off again to find it, but of course he was older now and he knew he had to stay and help his mother.

Then quarter day came round again, and there was no money at all. It did no good for Milda to beg the rent-collector to wait a day or so. He came back the next day with the bailiff and three of the Earl's soldiers, and Mitt and Milda were turned out of Dyke End. A short while before Mitt's sixth birthday, he helped his mother pack their few belongings into a handcart and push it into Holand to join his father.

2

Mitt always hated to remember that first winter in Holand. His father was living in one room in a big tenement block down by the harbour. Mitt and Milda joined him there. The tenement had perhaps once been the house of a wealthy man. Outside, on its greenish, peeling walls, there were the remains of pictures—once fine paintings of garlands of flowers and people out of stories, sheaves of wheat and bunches of fruit. But they were so old that Mitt could not quite tell what they were, and, anyway, the inside of the building was what he saw most. The large rooms had been chopped into as many small ones as possible, so the house was crowded as full as it would hold of people. It was filthy. The buckets on the dark stairs stank. Bedbugs lived in all the walls. They came out at night and bit, viciously. What with that, and the strangeness, and the noise of all the people, Mitt could not sleep very well. He lay awake and listened to his parents quarrelling as they had never quarrelled before.

Mitt could not understand what the quarrels were about. It seemed as if his father was not pleased to have them with him in Holand. 'Hanging round my neck!' he put it. He wanted them to go back to Dyke End. When Milda shrieked at him that there was no rent, he cursed her for laziness.

'Why should I work my fingers to the bone to keep you in idleness?' Milda screamed at him. But, after a week of quarrelling, she found a job in a workroom which made

15

fine embroidered hangings, and she was there, sewing, from early morning until light failed in the evening.

After this, the quarrels Mitt's parents had became even harder for Mitt to understand. His mother kept saying to his father, 'You and your Free Holanders! *Free* Holanders! There's no such *thing* as freedom in this place!' Mitt had no idea what that meant.

Mitt was shocked and shattered by the town of Holand itself. He hated the dirt and the noise and all the people. His job for the day was to carry their bucket to the waterfront and tip it in the harbour. As Milda said, the one advantage of living in that tenement was that you did not have to go far to get rid of your rubbish. Mitt hated the smell on the greasy waterfront, where fish-scales glimmered on the flagstones like sequins on a dirty dress. The crowded harbour appalled him. There were tall ships with many masts and pennants flying, merchant ships, ships of the Earl's fleet, loading and unloading going on most of the time. In between were small boats, packed and bustling, rowing boats, cutters, jollyboats, and a good hundred fishing-boats. Mitt was always glad when the fishing-fleet sailed out, because the crowded water seemed a little emptier then.

After Mitt had brought the bucket back to the door of their room, he was all on his own once Milda had found work. He had nothing to do but keep out of the way of the other children. He hated them most of all. They were town children, shrewd, nimble, and knowing. They made rings round Mitt. They jeered at him for not understanding town ways. They made him look a fool, then ran away laughing.

Mitt hid from them, usually, in the dark holes and corners of the house or the waterfront. But one day, he felt he had had enough of that and ran away instead, up the hill from the harbour, into the better part of the town.

Here, to his surprise, the streets were cleaner, and became wider and cleaner still as he went upwards. The air smelt almost fresh. There was a tang in it of the sea, and an autumn smell from the Flate. Better still, most of the houses were painted and, unlike the tenement, the paint was fresh and bright and Mitt could see what the pictures were about. He walked slowly, looking at trees and fruit, red swirls and blue flowers, until he came to a particularly fine tall house, where the painting was in gold as well as other colours. On one gable, a stiff sort of lady in a green dress held out a very purple bunch of grapes to a stiff man on the other gable, whose hair seemed to be solid gold. Mitt much admired them. They reminded him a little of the figureheads on the fronts of the big ships. And, perhaps because of the fresh air smell, they made him think of his perfect land.

He was standing lost in admiration and daydream, when a servant of the merchant who owned the house came out with a stick and told him to be off. He called Mitt a guttersnipe and said he had no business to be there. Mitt ran away, terrified. As he went, he looked back and upwards. And there, on the very top of the hill was the Earl's palace, larger, whiter, brighter, and with more gold paint than any other house in Holand. Mitt felt it was squashing him. He felt like a pip in a cider press.

That was the last time for many years that Mitt remembered his perfect land. Holand quashed it out of his mind entirely and left him simply bewildered.

When Mitt's birthday came, a few days later, and with it the Sea Festival, that was bewildering, too. Everyone had a holiday, so there were more people about than ever. Mitt watched the Festival procession, hoisted on to the shoulders of a kindly man called Canden, who seemed to be a friend of his father's. Down the street came a boiling and a bubbling of brightly-clothed people. There was terrific shouting and yelling, and ribbons, fruit, and flowers on everyone. Some had silly hats. Images went by on sticks—heads of cows and horses, with hats and ribbons on, too. Big boys went tearing in and out of the procession, shouting and swirling wooden rattles. It was noise, noise, noise. Every so often came a group of people playing the traditional tune on traditional instruments. There were pipes called scarnels, which sounded just like their name, and triangular stringed things you played with a horsehair bow. They were cruddles, and they sounded just like their name, too. And the groups of musicians were so far apart from one another that it was only by accident that they played the same part of the tune as the rest. Then *drub, drub, drub*, came people banging at horsehair drums and drowning out even the scarnels. In the midst of it, Mitt glimpsed a straw dummy, fantastically looped with cherry-coloured ribbons, riding along in somebody's arms.

'Look,' said the kindly Canden. 'There's Poor Old Ammet. That's Earl Hadd carrying him.'

'What's he going to do with him?' Mitt asked anxiously. He had never heard of Earl Hadd doing anything good with anything.

'Throw him in the harbour of course. For luck,' explained Canden.

Mitt was horrified. Earl Hadd must be quite heartless. He thought of Poor Old Ammet being tipped into the harbour just like the bucket of muck Mitt tipped in daily, and Poor Old Ammet sinking, soaking, drowning, his ribbons getting spoilt. 'Doesn't he float?' he asked tensely.

'Not too often,' Canden said, quite unaware of Mitt's state of mind. 'Mostly he falls to pieces and sinks in the harbour, or just outside it.'

'He doesn't!' Mitt said frantically.

There was another friend of Mitt's father's standing

beside Canden. He was called Dideo and his face was a mass of tiny lines. Mitt thought Dideo's eyes looked like two shiny fish caught in the net of his skin. Dideo said, 'He doesn't always fall to bits—Old Ammet. If the tide's right, he goes out on the tide in one piece. Or they say he does. Floats for miles. And those in a boat that can find him and pick him out, have a lucky boat ever after, they say.'

If anything, Mitt found it even more distressing to think of Poor Old Ammet floating, floating, all on his own out to sea. He tried to change the subject. 'Who are those boys with rattles?'

Canden glanced at the procession, where boys in red and yellow trousers were having great fun whirling their rattles under the noses of cruddle-players. 'Boys from the Palace. All them in the procession come from the Palace,' he told Mitt, and turned to Dideo again. 'I've never seen Old Ammet float. He goes down almost as quick as Libby Beer.'

'Would they let me run about with a rattle?' Mitt interrupted desperately.

'No. You're born a nobody,' said Dideo. 'He does float,' he said to Canden. 'You've not been in Holand long enough to know, but he was picked up once, a good ten miles out, by the old *Sevenfold*, and I heard every man on that ship made a fortune afterwards. That was the only time I ever knew it happen, though,' he added regretfully. 'I was about Mitt's age at the time.' Here he looked up at Mitt and, finding him inexplicably white and tearful, nudged Canden.

Canden took Mitt down and peered at his face. 'What's the matter? Would you like an Ammet of your own?'

'*No!*' said Mitt.

Nevertheless, he arrived in front of a stall where dozens of tiny straw Ammets were for sale. With them came another friend of Mitt's father's, a man with a dour, blank face, called Siriol, who stood by without saying anything while Canden and Dideo bent over Mitt, doing their best to please him. Would Mitt have this Ammet here? Or how about this one with blue ribbons? And when Mitt firmly refused to have anything to do with Poor Old Ammet in any colour ribbons, Canden and Dideo tried to buy him a wax model of Libby Beer instead. But, real and enticing though the wax fruit looked, Mitt did not want Libby either. She was thrown into the sea just like Poor Old Ammet. He burst into tears and pushed her away.

'But they're lucky!' Canden said, quite mystified.

Dour-faced Siriol picked up one of the toffee-apples from the other end of the stall and stuffed it into Mitt's damp fist. 'There,' he said. 'That'll please you best, you see.' He was quite right. Mitt forgot his distress, somewhat, in the difficulty of getting his teeth through the toffee into the apple underneath.

There was some mystery about these friends of Mitt's father's. Mitt knew his mother did not care for them. He heard her objecting to them every night when his parents quarrelled. Her objections seemed to mount steadily through that winter, until around the new year, when Mitt heard her say, 'Oh, I give in! Only don't blame me when the soldiers come for you!'

It must have been about a week after Milda said this, in the very heart of winter, when Mitt woke up suddenly in the middle of the night. A red light was flickering on the ceiling. He could hear crackling and distant shouting, and smell smoke. One of the big warehouses on the waterfront was clearly on fire. Mitt could see it, when he raised himself on one elbow, blazing into the sky and down into the dark water of the harbour. But what had woken Mitt was not that. It was the slow shuffling outside the door of the room. The sound made Mitt's back prickle.

20

He could hear Milda trying to light the lamp, whimpering with haste and annoyance because she could not get the wick to burn. Then the light came at last, and Mitt saw his father was not in the room. Milda ran through the room with the lamp, making lurching shadows as she ran, and tore open the door.

Canden was on the other side of it. He was clinging to the door-frame to hold himself up. Mitt could not see him well, because Milda was holding the lamp all wrong, but he knew that Canden was either hurt, or very ill, or both. He could see it in Canden's face. He had a feeling that the part of Canden which was behind Milda and the doorpost was the wrong shape. It did not surprise him that Milda gave a dreadful strangled scream.

'Eeech! What——? I knew it would go wrong!'

'Harchad's men,' said Canden. He sounded disgusted. 'They were there waiting for us. Informers—that's what they were. Dideo, Siriol, and Ham. They informed on us.'

After that, Canden gave a quiver of indignation and slid down the doorpost to the floor. Milda knelt down to him, hugging the lamp and whimpering. 'Oh ye gods! What do I *do*? What can I do? Why doesn't somebody help?'

After that, doors began cautiously opening and shutting up and down the stairway. Ladies came in nightgowns and old coats, with more lamps, or candles. There were troubled whispers and soothing words, while Milda rocked about on her knees, moaning. Mitt was too appalled to move. He did not want to look at Canden, or his mother, so he lay and looked at the ceiling instead. The bustling ladies thought he was asleep, and, after a while, he must really have gone to sleep. Canden was not there in the morning. But he had been there. He had left a stain on the floor. And Mitt's father was still not there either.

Mitt knew both of them were dead. Nobody told him, but he knew. What he did not know and wanted to be told was what had happened. He wanted to know why ladies in the tenement came and told Milda, 'I should lie low, if I was you. You don't want to get yourself arrested, too.' Milda stayed away from work for a while, sitting very still by the window. Her face was so drawn in by worry that the seam where her dimple used to be looked more like a puckered scar than a line. Mitt hated her face like that. He crouched beside her feet and asked to be told what had caused it.

'You're too young to understand,' said Milda.

'But I want to know,' said Mitt. 'What's happened to Dad?' He asked at least forty times before he got an answer.

'Dead,' said Milda. 'At least, I hope that's what he is, because they all say it's better to be dead than have Harchad after you. And I shall never forgive them that did it to him—never, never, never!'

'What did Siriol and Dideo and Ham do?' Mitt prompted her.

'Leave me be, if you know so much!' Milda said irritably. But Mitt went on asking, and in the end Milda told him as much as she knew.

It seemed that when Mitt's father had found it so hard to get work in Holand, he had felt so bitterly against the Earl that he had joined a secret revolutionary society. There were a lot of them in Holand. The Earl's son Harchad had spies and soldiers hunting out these societies night and day, at all times. But when he found one and marched the members off to be hanged, there was always another to take its place.

The one Mitt's father joined was called the Free Holanders. It was composed mostly of fishermen who felt there should be more justice and better living for the ordinary people of Holand. Their ambition was to have the whole city rise against the Earl, and, as far as Milda knew, they had never done much except talk about it. But when Milda and Mitt had been turned out of Dyke End, Mitt's father was so angry that he had tried to stir the Free Holanders to action of some kind. Why not set fire to one of the Earl's warehouses, he said, to show the Earl they meant business?

Canden and the other younger Free Holanders were delighted by the idea. It would hit Hadd where it hurt, they said—right in the moneybags. But the older members, particularly Siriol, Dideo, and Ham, were clean against it. If they fired a warehouse, they said, the Free Holanders would be hunted down by Harchad's men, and how would that help the city to rise and overthrow the Earl? The society split in half over it. The younger members went with Mitt's father to fire the warehouse. The older members stayed at home. And when the younger ones reached the warehouse, Harchad's men were waiting for them. All that Milda knew beyond that was that someone had managed to start a fire even so, and that no one had come back from it except Canden to say that Siriol, Dideo, and Ham had informed on them. And Canden was dead, too.

Mitt considered all this. 'Why did Siriol and them inform, though?'

The crease of worry down Milda's face drew into a tighter seam. 'Because they were frightened, Mitt, like I am now.'

'Frightened what of?' Mitt asked.

'Harchad's soldiers,' Milda said, shivering. 'They might come banging at this door any moment now.'

Mitt considered what he knew of soldiers. They were not so frightening. They brought you home when you were found wandering in the Flate. 'How many soldiers are there? More than everyone else in Holand?'

In spite of her misery, Milda smiled. To Mitt's relief,

23

the crease on her face turned into a dimple again for a moment. 'Oh, no. The Earl couldn't afford that number. And I don't suppose he'd bother to send more than six or so to come and take *us* away.'

'Then,' said Mitt, 'if all the people in this house, or all the people in Holand, all got together, they ought to be able to stop the soldiers, oughtn't they?'

Milda was forced to laugh. It was quite beyond her to explain why everyone in Holand lived in dread of soldiers, and even greater dread of Harchad's spies, so she said, 'Oh, Mitt, you're a real free soul, you are! You don't know what fear means. It seems such a waste, when Hadd and the Free Holanders have done for us between them, it does really!'

Mitt realized that by talking in this sturdy way he had managed to comfort his mother. He had sent the hateful crease of worry out of her face twice. Better still, he had made Milda comfort him by calling him a free soul. Mitt was not sure he knew what a free soul was—it never occurred to him that his mother had no idea either—but he thought it was a splendid thing to be. By way of earning it, he said stoutly. 'Well, you're not to worry any more. I'll make it all right for you.'

Milda laughed and hugged him. 'There's my Mitt!'

3

Miraculously, no soldiers came for Milda and Mitt. It seemed as if Dideo, Siriol, and Ham had contented themselves with getting rid of the younger half of the Free Holanders, and had not bothered to include wives and families. All the same, Milda and Mitt had a hard time of it for a while. When, after a week or so, Milda dared to go back to work, she found her place had been taken. Mitt was furious.

'It's the way things are in this town,' Milda explained. 'There's hundreds of poor women willing to work their fingers into blisters. And the rich people have to have their curtains ready on time.'

'Why?' said Mitt. 'Can't the poor people get together and tell the rich ones where they get off?'

That was the kind of question which made Milda call him a free soul. Mitt knew it was, so he made a point of asking such things. It was a great comfort to know he was a free soul who did not know what fear was, while Milda was out trudging from workshop to workshop. Mitt himself, hungry and miserable, spent the days hanging round the back doors of counting houses, or on the edges of boat-builders' yards, hoping to be sent on an errand. Few errands came Mitt's way. He was too small, and there was always the crowd of bigger, quick-spoken city boys to jostle Mitt aside and run the errand instead. And of course they jeered at Mitt too. But Mitt would tell himself that *he* was a free soul, he was, and wait patiently on. It helped him greatly.

25

At night, Mitt had horrible dreams. He dreamt repeatedly that Canden was coming shuffling to the door again. Then the door would open, and there would be Canden, hanging on to the doorpost and slowly falling to pieces like Poor Old Ammet in the harbour. 'All dead,' Canden would say, as pieces dropped off him, and Mitt would wake up trying to scream. Then Mitt would lie and tell himself sternly that he did not know what fear was. In the middle of the night that was not always so easy to believe. But sometimes Milda woke up when Mitt yelled. She would tell Mitt stories she had learnt as a girl until he went back to sleep again.

Milda's stories made good listening. There was magic and adventure and fighting in them, and they all seemed to happen in North Dalemark in the time when there were kings—though there were earls in the stories, too, and ordinary people. Mitt puzzled about the stories. He knew Holand was in South Dalemark, but this North Milda talked about seemed so different that he wondered for a while if it was real.

'Do they have kings still in the North?' he asked, to see what Milda would say.

But Milda knew disappointingly little about the North. 'No, there's no kings any more,' she said. 'I've heard they have earls in the North just like we do, only the earls there are all freedom fighters like your dad was.'

Mitt could not understand how an earl could be anything of the sort. Nor could Milda explain.

'All I can say is I wish there *were* kings again,' she told Mitt. 'Earls are no good. Look at Hadd—us poor people are just rent on two legs to him, and if we do anything he doesn't care for, he claps us in prison, or worse.'

'But he can't put everyone in prison,' Mitt objected. 'There wouldn't be anyone to catch his fish for him or sew his clothes.'

'Oh, you are a free soul, Mitt!' Milda exclaimed.

Mitt was not sure when or how it happened, but in the course of these talks he had with Milda in the night, it began to be understood between them that Mitt was one day going to avenge his father and put right all the wrongs in Holand. It was an accepted thing, even before Milda found work. She found work fairly soon, in another sewing-house, because the one thing she could really do well was fine embroidery. They managed to pay the rent on their room in time to prevent the landlord turning them out. But they were still short of food. Milda spent the rest of her week's earnings on a new pair of shoes.

'To celebrate,' she said. 'I just happened to see them. Aren't they pretty?'

Mitt would have been very hungry indeed had not Siriol, the dour-faced informer, sent round his daughter, Lydda, with a basket of sea-fry. Lydda was a fat, meek girl of twelve. She showed Milda how to cook the fry, and she much admired Milda's pretty new shoes. Perhaps she described them to her father. At any rate, Mitt and Milda had a square meal, and there were still enough fish for breakfast. Milda put them out on the window-sill of their room to keep fresh. The ants came out of the wall in the night and ate them up. When Mitt opened the window to fetch in breakfast, all he found was some tiny scraps of bone. He was looking miserably at them, when Siriol came clumping up the dark stairs in his clogs and came into the room without being invited.

'Lost your breakfast, I see,' he said. 'You'd better come round to mine and have some. And best thing I can see, Milda, is for him to sail with me in future. I was thinking of taking an apprentice.'

'Well—' said Milda.

'Free Holanders look after their own,' said Siriol.

Knowing what he knew about Siriol, Mitt was speechless.

He had to stand there and let Milda do the refusing for him. But to his astonishment, Milda smiled gratefully at Siriol, thanked him over and over again, and agreed that Mitt should sail with Siriol.

'I don't need breakfast,' was all Mitt could think of saying.

'Be round at my place in half an hour,' Siriol said, and clumped away again.

Mitt rounded on Milda. 'But he informed!' he said passionately. 'What did you want to go and agree for?'

Milda shrugged, with the crease in her face very deep and bitter. 'I know. But we have to live. And maybe you'll see your way to getting even with him if you keep close to him.'

Mitt was mollified by that. And it made a great deal of difference that he had a job, too. Siriol was very scrupulous. Mitt had an apprentice's share of the takings, so that when the catch was good he earned nearly as much as Milda. That almost made up to him for the kind of job it was. He did not like fishing. He did not like Siriol. He hardly knew which he disliked most.

Fishing was a mixture of boredom, hardship, and frantic bursts of work. Siriol was sour and surly, and insisted that everything should be done exactly right. Mitt very soon learnt that he was not allowed to make a mistake. The first day, he forgot to coil a rope as Ham had shown him. Siriol picked up the end of the offending rope—which had a knot in it—and hit Mitt across the back with it. Mitt glared at him.

'Do it,' said Siriol. 'Do it right. Or else. You'll be glad to know how one of these days.'

Small as Mitt was, he shared watches with big, slow Ham, who was Siriol's partner. He learnt to patch the much-patched sail, to mend nets, and to gut fish. Siriol and Ham taught him to steer, at first by day, which was simple, then to find his way by night, by the stars, or in pitch dark, by the feel of the wind and the water, and the pull of the sails. They taught him to smell bad weather before it was near enough to hurt. Mitt also learnt what chilblains were, and how it felt to be too wet and too cold for too long. And he learnt all these things, loathing them, until they were second nature, and learnt them so young that they were with him all his life.

One thing that surprised Mitt was that he was never in the least afraid at sea. He expected to be. When he first climbed gingerly down into the *Flower of Holand*, and she rocked, and he knew there were only salt-swollen old boards between him and sinking into the sea like Old Ammet, he had to tell himself very hard that he was a free soul who did not know what fear was. Then *Flower of Holand* went dipping out to sea with all the rest of the fishing-fleet, and he forgot all about it. Sailing was just a job, like Milda's sewing. And it was good to have a job and earn money, when the host of bigger boys hanging round the waterfront had no such thing.

Sometimes, on a fine day, when Siriol's boat went bluntly out of the harbour on the tide, rich people's pleasure boats would be putting out too, from the West Pool. The West Pool was a shallower mooring just beyond Holand, where the dues were so high that only wealthy people could keep boats there. Mitt enjoyed watching them. But Siriol and Ham had nothing but contempt for them. They spat in the water when they saw them.

'Rich men's toys,' said Siriol. 'Half out of the water in this little breeze! Put one of those in a gale, and she's under in five minutes.' Siriol's respect was reserved for the stately merchant ships. Let the *Proud Ammet* or the graceful *Lovely Libby* come nodding out of Holand, crowding up sail as she came, then Siriol's face would light up, and Ham's also. 'Ah!' Siriol would say. 'That's a ship for you!' And he would look round his thick and fishy *Flower of Holand* as if she disappointed him.

After a year of fishing, Mitt felt himself the equal of any boy in Holand. He did not grow much—probably because he had to work so hard—but he was as tough and quick-witted as any lad on the waterfront, and much quicker-tongued. He knew every bad word there was. He had a retort for everyone. Boys and girls alike treated him with respect now. Indeed, many of them would have liked to make friends with Mitt. But Mitt kept himself to himself. These children, or children like them, had made his life a misery when he first came to Holand, and he found he could not forget it. He preferred grown-ups. He cracked jokes on shore and on board that made big slow Ham guffaw and even Siriol smile. That pleased Mitt. It made him feel grown up and independent—a proper free soul.

It was just as well Mitt was independent. Milda had simply no sense of economy. It became a habit with her to 'just happen to see' something whenever she came home with her wages. One week it would be a huge iced cake, the next, a pair of pretty earrings.

'You have to keep up your self-respect,' she told Mitt when he protested. 'I'm being ground underfoot, I am, and if I don't keep my spirits up somehow, I shall just go under, I know I will!'

This was all very well, but if Mitt was out and the thing Milda 'just happened to see' cost more money than Milda had, she did not scruple to take Mitt's hard-earned money, too. Mitt had to hide his money, or they would have starved. He felt terribly put-upon and responsible. One evening, when he crawled home, tired out, to find Milda had bought a whole tub of oysters, it seemed like the last straw. She had opened the tub too, and left it in the sun under the window. It was already smelling rather queer, and the ants were swarming up the sides of the tub to investigate.

'What did you want to buy that for!' Mitt yelled.

Milda was injured. 'Oh, Mitt! I thought they'd be such a treat for you.'

'But there's thousands of them!' Mitt bawled. 'How are we going to eat all that lot? If you wanted oysters, I could have *got* you oysters—for nothing, from Dideo. Honest, you need more looking after than a kid! How am I going to pay Siriol out for informing, or do anything else, if you're going to carry on like this?'

'You sound just like your dad,' Milda said coldly. 'Let me tell you, those oysters were a bargain at two silver, and you ought to be grateful.'

'Two *silver*!' Mitt raised both his chilblained hands to the blotchy ceiling. 'That's no bargain. That's daylight robbery, that is!'

Mitt and Milda—and the ants—had oysters for supper and for breakfast, and after that they both felt unwell, although the ants seemed as lively as ever. Ham kindly helped Mitt throw the rest of the tub into the harbour.

'And she went and paid two silver for them!' Mitt groaned.

'Don't be too hard on her. She's used to better things,' Ham said. 'She's a lovely good woman, she is.'

Mitt stared at him. 'If I didn't feel sick as a dog already,' he said, 'I would after I heard you say that!' And he went back upstairs, muttering, 'Lovely good woman!' to himself in the greatest disgust. Of course he knew his mother was still young and pretty, in spite of that hateful crease on her face where her dimple should have been, and he knew she was not like those other ladies in the tenement who were always down on the waterfront, making up to the sailors whenever a ship came in, but for Ham to say *that*! Mitt had never noticed that Ham deeply

31

admired Milda. Ham was too slow and shy to let Milda know it. And Mitt's feeling was that all women were born stupid and grew worse.

Alda, Siriol's wife, was the worst of the lot. Mitt supposed he should be thankful that his mother did not spend all her money on arris, the way Alda did. Alda was usually too drunk to sell the fish Siriol, Ham, and Mitt had caught. She sat on a barrel at the corner of the stall, while Lydda stood dumbly behind the heaps of fish letting people have them too cheap. It pained Mitt to his soul. After all their trouble, out half the night pulling in fish in the drizzling rain, a rich merchant's housekeeper or a mincing man from the Palace had only to appear and point to a pile of sweet whitebait, and Lydda would humbly halve the price. It was not fair. The ones who could afford to pay the full price always got it cheap. But that was Holand all over.

At length, Lydda's spineless meekness was more than Mitt could bear. If the fish was to go cheap, he felt it should go cheap to the right people. He elbowed Lydda aside and tried selling the fish himself.

'Hadd, Hadd, haddock!' he shouted. 'Fit for an earl, and dirt cheap too!' When people stopped and stared, Mitt took up a haddock and waved it about. 'Hadd,' he said, 'ock. Come on. He won't eat you. You eat *him*.' He picked up an eel in the other hand. 'And here's an earl—I mean a Harl—I mean an eel—for sale. Who wants a nice fresh Harl for supper?' It was great fun, and it sold a lot of fish.

After that Mitt always sold the fish. Lydda weighed and wrapped it, while her mother sat on her tub chuckling at Mitt and breathing arris fumes over the customers. Mitt was often very tired. His hands were chapped and covered with little cuts from the fish scales, winter and summer, but it was worth it, just to be able to shout rude things about Hadd.

'You want to watch it, Mitt,' Siriol said, whenever he heard Mitt's sales talk. But he let Mitt go on. After all, there was always a laughing crowd round the stall, buying fish. Even the Palace lackeys sniggered as they bought.

Then one day, as soon as *Flower of Holand* was out of the harbour and no one could overhear, Siriol amazed Mitt by asking him if he wanted to join the Free Holanders.

'I'll have to think,' Mitt said. And he missed selling the fish that next morning, in order to hurry home and ask Milda what he ought to do, before she went to work. 'I can't join, can I?' he said. 'Not after what they did to Dad?'

But Milda went dancing round the room, her skirts held out and her earrings swinging, and her dimple deep and clear. 'This is your chance!' she said. 'Don't you see, Mitt? This is your chance to get back at them at last!'

'Oh yes,' said Mitt. 'I suppose it is and all.'

So Mitt became a Free Holander, and great fun it was, too. At first it was simply the great fun of being in the secret, with, behind that, the further secret that he was only in it to get revenge for his father. Mitt grinned to himself at both secrets all through long boring watches when he was alone at *Flower of Holand*'s tiller, and the stars wheeling overhead seemed to glimmer with sheer glee.

'Ah, shut up, he's useful!' Siriol said to Ham, when Ham protested. 'Who's going to bother with a lad who looks just like all the other kids? People think boys don't count. Look at the way he gets away with selling fish. He's safer than what we are.'

Taking messages for the Free Holanders was pure bliss to Mitt. He revelled in going unnoticed through the crowded streets. It was good to be small and ordinary-looking, so that he could get the better of Harchad's soldiers and spies. He would memorize the message carefully and slip off after selling the fish, mingle with the crowd in this street, watch a fight in that alley, loiter round the barracks, joking with the soldiers, and still go unsuspected. He was Mitt of the free soul, who did not know the meaning of fear. And the greatest fun of all was when he chanced to be in a street while soldiers stopped off both ends of it and questioned everyone in it about their business.

Harchad ordered this done quite often, as much to keep people properly subdued as to catch revolutionaries. In a tense silence, broken only by the clopping of soldiers' boots, his men would go from person to person, searching bags and pockets, and asking each one what he was doing in this street. Mitt delighted in inventing business. He loved giving his name. It was marvellous to have the commonest name in Holand. Mitt, with perfect truth, could call himself Alham Alhamsson, Ham Hamsson, Hammitt Hammittsson, and Mitt Mittsson, or any combination of those that he fancied. He enlivened boring hours of fishing by thinking up new ways to fool Harchad's men.

The only trouble about being a Free Holander was that Mitt did not understand what the meetings were about. Once the novelty wore off, they bored him to tears. They would sit in someone's shed or attic, often without a candle even, and Siriol would start by talking of tyranny and oppression. Then Dideo would say that the leaders of the future were coming from below. Below what? Mitt wondered. Someone would tell a long tale of Hadd's injustice, and someone else would whisper things about Harchad. And, sooner or later, Ham would be thumping the table and saying, 'We look to the North, we do. Let the North show its hand!'

The first time Ham said this, Mitt felt a shiver of excitement. He knew Ham could be arrested for saying it. But Ham said it so often that Mitt lost interest. He found he was using the meetings to make up sleep in. He never got enough sleep in those days.

Mitt felt this would not do. If he was to get his revenge on the Free Holanders, he needed to know what they were up to. 'What do they think they're doing?' he asked Milda. 'It's all looking to the North, or whisper, whisper, about Harchad, or tyranny and that. What's it *about*?'

Milda looked nervously round the room. 'Hush. They're getting at rebellion and uprising—I hope.'

'They don't get at it very fast,' Mitt said discontentedly. 'There's no plans at all. I wish you could come to meetings and see if you could make some sense of them.'

Milda laughed. 'I might—I bet they wouldn't have me, though.'

When Milda laughed, the crease on her face gave way to a dimple again. It was a thing Mitt always tried to encourage if he could. So he said, 'I bet they would have you. You could stir them up a bit and get them to come out with something. I'm sick of old tyranny and the rest!' And, since this made Milda smile broadly, Mitt did his best to keep her smiling. 'Tell you what,' he said. 'While I'm getting back at them for informing, I'd like to get back at old Hadd too. I'd like to give him what for, because of him trampling you underfoot all these years.'

'What a boy you are!' said Milda. 'You don't know what fear is, do you?'

After that, it was understood between Mitt and Milda that the mission of Mitt's life was a double one. He was to break the Free Holanders and rid the world of Earl Hadd. Mitt was sure he could do it. So was Milda.

Milda joined the Free Holanders too. Mitt was delighted. He had high hopes of it. Milda came to meetings and she talked as eloquently as anyone there. She loved to talk. She loved leaning forward over the secretive night-light and seeing everyone's listening faces shadowy and attentive. But the sole result was that Milda became as ardent a freedom fighter as anyone there. She talked revolution to Mitt whenever he was at home.

'Flaming Ammet!' Mitt said disgustedly. 'It's like being at a meeting all the time now!'

All the same, Milda's talk did make things clearer to Mitt. He was soon able to talk of oppression and uprising, tyranny and leadership from below, and feel he knew what it meant. And when he had leisure to think—which he sometimes did while *Flower of Holand* ploshed her sturdy way to the fishing grounds—he decided that what it amounted to was that there were two parts to Dalemark: the North, where people were mysteriously free and happy, and the South, where the earls and the rich people were free and happy enough, but where they made darned sure that ordinary people like Mitt and Milda were as unhappy as possible.

'Right,' Mitt said to himself. 'I reckon that sums it up. Now let's get busy and *do* something about it.'

But the Free Holanders seemed simply content to talk, and Mitt became increasingly annoyed by them. He was very pleased when another secret society actually killed four of Harchad's spies. Siriol was not. He told Mitt, with a glum sort of gladness, that things would be very much worse now. And they were.

Harchad imposed a curfew. Anyone found in the streets after dark was marched away and never seen again. Siriol forbade Mitt to carry messages during that time. Mitt did not quite understand why he should not.

Then a thief on the waterfront tried to rob a man. He knocked the man down and was taking his money, when he found a gold button with the wheatsheaf crest of Holand on it, hidden in the man's coat. The thief knew it was the badge Harchad gave all his spies, and he was so frightened that he jumped into the harbour and was drowned. Mitt did not understand this story at all.

36

'Well, if you don't, I'm not telling you,' was all Siriol would say.

Then Earl Hadd quarrelled with four other earls at once. Everyone in Holand groaned. Much as they detested Hadd, they almost admired him for being so very quarrelsome. 'Fallen out with Earl Henda again, has he?' the women in Milda's sewing shop would say. 'Honestly, I never knew anyone like him!' This time, however, Hadd fell out not only with Henda, but with the Earls of Canderack, Waywold, and Dermath too. And so powerful were these earls, and owned so much of South Dalemark between them, that there was some doubt in Holand whether Hadd could hold his own against them all.

'Bitten off more than he can chew this time for sure, the old sinner,' Dideo said to Mitt. 'Maybe this is where the Free Holanders get their chance.'

Mitt hoped so. But Harl, Hadd's eldest son, managed to put himself into Hadd's good books by suggesting a way to deal with the four earls. Harl, fat and indolent though he was, could sometimes be seen with his brother Navis and a crowd of beaters, servants, and dogs, walking over the Flate and shooting birds with a long silver-inlaid fowling piece. Harl was allowed to use a gun, being an earl's son. No one else was, apart from lords and hearthmen, because there had been so many uprisings in the South. Big ships carried cannon, as a protection against the ships of the North, but guns were otherwise banned. But, said Harl, why not give all the soldiers guns as well? That should make the four earls think twice before attacking Holand.

Hadd agreed that it would. And that put paid to the hopes of Mitt and the Free Holanders. Up went rents and taxes and harbour dues. The people of Holand admitted grudgingly that Hadd was up to everything, even while they groaned.

'It's not right,' said Ham. 'Give Harchad's men guns and they'll be ten times worse than they are now. But you have to admire Hadd. Fair play.'

But Hadd took other precautions, too. The Earl of Canderack, since most of the coast north of Holand was his, owned a fair-sized fleet he could send against Holand if necessary. Holand also had its fleet. But to be on the safe side, Hadd betrothed his granddaughter Hildrida to the Lord of the Holy Islands, north of Canderack. The ships of the Holy Islands were famous. As Siriol remarked to Ham, the Holy Islands fleet was probably the main reason why the North had not long since conquered the South and brought freedom to everyone. Milda, as she sewed with three other women at a great bedspread to be covered with blue and gold roses, thought of it from another point of view. One of the women said that Lithar, Lord of the Holy Islands, was twenty years old. And, another added, Hildrida Navisdaughter could only be about nine.

Milda remembered she had once been interested in Navis and his family. 'Then in that case I don't think it's fair at all!' she said warmly.

4

I t did not seem fair to Hildrida Navisdaughter either.
She thought at first she was in trouble. She and her
brother Ynen had gone sailing. They had been tired of
being told they were too young to go out in a boat alone,
and of being taken tamely up and down the coast by the
sailors the Earl employed to sail his family. Ynen had
wanted to sail a boat himself. So they slipped away and
borrowed their cousins' yacht. It had been splendid fun,
and very frightening too. Ynen had nearly laid the boat on
her side, just outside the West Pool, before he got used to
the wind. And they had twice found themselves nearly
aground in the shoals beyond. But they had managed. They
had brought the yacht back and not even bumped the jetty.

Then, as soon as she reached the Palace, Hildy was told
her father wanted to see her. Naturally, she thought he
had found out about the sailing.

Too bad for him! Hildrida thought, while she was
having a good dress put on and her windblown black hair
brushed. I shall be very angry. I shall say we're never
allowed to do *anything*. I shall say it's *my* fault, and I
shan't let him send for Ynen. And I'll tell him that it
doesn't matter whether we drown or not. It's not as if we
were important.

The lady-in-waiting who led Hildrida by her hand
through the lofty corridors to Navis's rooms, rather
thought Hildrida must have found out what was in store
for her. She had never seen her so white and stormy. The
lady-in-waiting was glad she was not in Navis's shoes.

Navis was well aware that his daughter had an awkward personality. He had taken refuge in a book. When Hildy was shown in, she found him sitting on the window-seat, with his calm profile outlined against the Flate beyond the window, and his eyes on a song by the Adon. She was exasperated. The ladies-in-waiting told her that Navis was still grieving for her dead mother, but Hildy found that hard to believe. To her mind, Navis was the coldest and laziest person she knew.

'I'm here,' she said piercingly, to stir him up a bit. 'And I'm not sorry.'

Navis winced a little, and kept his eyes studiously on his book. But, like the lady-in-waiting, he assumed that Hildrida had already heard about her betrothal, and he was heartily relieved. 'Then, if you're not sorry, I suppose you're glad,' he said. 'Whoever told you has saved me a great deal of trouble. You may run away and boast now, if you wish.'

Hildy was taken aback at not being scolded. But it seemed to her that her father was washing his hands of her, just as he always did, and she wanted to do battle with him instead. 'I never boast,' she said. 'But I could. We didn't sink her.'

Navis was puzzled enough to take his eyes off his book and look at Hildy. 'What are you talking about?'

'What did you send for me for?' Hildrida countered.

'Why, to tell you that you've just been betrothed to the Lord of the Holy Islands,' said her father. 'What did you think it was for?'

'*Betrothed?*' said Hildy. 'Without asking *me*!' It was such a bombshell that, for the moment, she clean forgot she had been sailing. 'Why wasn't I *told*?'

Navis found himself facing a blazing white daughter, out in the open, as it were, without a book to hide behind. 'I am telling you,' he said, and hastily picked up his book again.

'When it's too late!' Hildrida said, before he could find his place again. 'When it's done. You might have asked me if I minded, even if I'm not important. I'm a person too.'

'Most people are,' Navis said, rather desperately scanning his page. He wished he had not chosen to read the Adon. The Adon said things like *Truth is the fire that fetches thunder*, which sounded unpleasantly like a description of Hildrida. 'And you are very important now,' he added. 'You're forming an alliance with Lithar for us.'

'What's Lithar like? How old is he?' Hildrida demanded.

Navis found his place and put his finger on it. 'I've only met him once.' It was hard to know what else to say. 'He's only a young man—twenty or so.'

'Only—!' Words nearly failed Hildy. 'I'm not going to be betrothed to an old man like that! I'm too young. *And* I've never met him!'

Navis hastily got his book in front of his face again. 'Time will cure both those objections.'

'No it won't!' stormed Hildrida. 'And if you go on reading, I'll—I'll hit you and then tear that book up!'

Realizing that strong measures were necessary, Navis laid his book down. 'Now listen, Hildy. This is something that happens to all our family. Your cousin Harilla is being betrothed to the Lord of Mark, and what's-her-name—Harchad's daughter—to one of the—'

Hildy interrupted with a screech. Her father could call her Hildy all he liked—usually only Ynen did—but the thought of being lumped in with the dreadful girl-cousins was too much for her. 'Just you *un*-betroth me!' she said. 'And do it at once, or you'll be sorry!'

'You know I can't,' said her father. 'It's your grandfather's doing, not mine.'

41

'Then he'll be sorry, too!' Hildy proclaimed, and swept to the door.

Navis called after her. It was easier talking to her back. 'Hildrida! Don't make an undignified scene, there's a good girl. It won't do any good. I advise you to go to the library instead, and read about the Holy Islands. You'll find they're rather interesting.'

Hildy paused, with her hand on the doorknob. Islands were places surrounded by water, weren't they? Perhaps she could turn this bombshell to some advantage at least. 'I ought to learn to sail, oughtn't I, if I'm going to the Holy Islands?' she said.

'Yes, I suppose so,' Navis said. Rather relieved to find her no longer raging, he added consolingly, 'But you won't be going for some years yet.'

'Then I've got time to learn,' said Hildy. 'If I promise not to make a fuss, will you get me a boat of my own?'

'Er—if you like,' said Navis.

'I do like. But you must give the boat to Ynen, too, because he never gets anything,' said Hildy. 'Or I shall make a fuss to grandfather, and all over the Palace.'

By this time, Navis's one desire was to be left in peace with his book again. 'Yes, yes,' he said. 'If you run away like a good girl and don't make a scene, you and Ynen shall have the best boat money can buy. Will that do for you?'

'Yes, thank you, Father,' Hildy said, primly and bitterly, and swept out.

The Palace people kept out of her way. Even her cousins, when they saw Hildrida marching, white, upright, and staring like a mask out of the Sea Festival, knew better than to cross her path. They all knew Hildrida had inherited her temper from Grandfather Hadd himself. Only Ynen dared go near her, and he dared not say a word. Hildy swept to her own room. There, she collected all the

42

ornaments, from the gilded clock to the gold-painted chamber-pot, put them in a heap on the floor, and broke them with the poker. Ynen crouched on the window-seat, wincing at the carnage. He still dared not say a word, when Hildy flung aside the poker, somewhat bent, and went to sit by her dressing-table, where she stared long and earnestly at the thin white face in the mirror. She had left the mirror unsmashed on purpose.

'I am a person,' she said at last. 'Aren't I?'

'Yes,' said Ynen. 'What's happened, Hildy?'

'And not a Thing,' said Hildy. 'What's happened is I'm betrothed. And nobody told me, just like a Thing. Do you think I should sit quiet and not mind, and *be* a Thing? The girl-cousins are betrothed, too.'

'They'll make a fuss,' Ynen predicted. 'Have you been forbidden to go sailing?'

'No,' said Hildy. 'We're getting a boat out of it. You have to get between the islands somehow. I think I shall go to the library now.' And she got up and went. Ynen went with her. He was still mystified, but he was used to that. He knew he would have to be very patient and tactful if he was to hear more about this promised boat.

The library was very tall, and built of speckled marble, with a domed window in its high ceiling. Hildrida, looking very small, followed by the even smaller Ynen, marched across to the librarian. 'Give me all the books you have on the Holy Islands,' she said.

Rather astonished, the librarian went away obediently. He returned shortly with one big old volume and one small newish one. 'Here we are. Not too much, I'm afraid. I advise you to take the little book. It's easy, and it has pictures.'

Hildrida gave him a scathing look and took the big book. She marched to the nearest table and opened it. Rather helplessly, the librarian gave Ynen the small book and left them to it.

43

'This book is all pictures,' Ynen said dolefully. 'Read me yours.'

'Quiet,' Hildy said severely. 'I'm concentrating.' But she did not like to think of Ynen sitting humbly there with nothing to do, and, besides, the book was the difficult, old kind that is easier to read aloud. So she read:

'Indeed men say that the Holy Isles been of all places in the South marks the sole place where enchantment abides.'

'I like that,' said Ynen. 'What are marks?'

'The old name for earldoms. Quiet.

'Of legends that do there pertain, there is said by some to be a certain enchanted Bull which appears, no man can say how, now on one isle, now upon another. By some it is said that this Beast may grant wishes, and certainly to see it is deemed by all a great good fortune. Further, there may be heard in clear weather a strange piping among the islands, most piercing and pleasant to hear, though no piper can be seen, and which goeth like the Bull from island to island. This has been heard by many, and many good ships been foundered following the sound. Withal come the horses of the sea, and, it is said, at times the Sea himself in the likeness of an old fellow of the Islands, who will oft speak fair with those that meet him, but oftentimes be rough and violent. For this reason, the men of the Islands count themselves holy and favoured above others. And certainly the Holy Islands are a fair place, mild, fruitful, and full of fair havens.'

'They sound wonderful,' said Ynen. 'I'd like to go there.'

Hildy shut the book. 'You shall,' she said. 'You can come with me when I go. I think I shan't make an undignified scene after all. I'm important. There's no magic Bulls in Mark, are there?'

'I didn't know there were any anywhere,' said Ynen. 'When are we getting our boat?'

'I don't know. But Father promised,' said Hildy.

Later that day, their cousin Harilla learnt that she was

betrothed to the Lord of Mark and lay on the stairs, drumming her heels and screaming, while everyone near ran for smelling-salts and made a great to-do. Hildy managed to smile a little. It was a dry, stretched smile, but very dignified. And as, one by one, her four other girl-cousins learnt of their betrothals and promptly followed Harilla's example, Hildy's smile grew more and more dignified. She was still not exactly glad to be betrothed, but she did almost feel it was worth it when the yacht *Wind's Road* was towed into the West Pool.

Navis kept his promise lavishly. He had heard of the smashed ornaments, of course, but, knowing Hildrida's temper, he felt she had shown great self-control. *Wind's Road* was twice the size of the cousins' boat—Navis did not think his children were old enough to sail alone, so he provided space for a crew, as befitted the grandchildren of an earl—and she was sheer beauty, from the golden ears of wheat carved on her prow to the rosy apples decorating her stern. Her hull was blue, her cabin white and gold, and her canvas snowy. She carried two foresails, too, to Ynen's joy. In fact, Hildy felt that the look of pure bliss on Ynen's face almost made up for any number of betrothals.

5

That autumn, when the Festival procession poured, scraping and banging and colourful, down to the harbour to drown Poor Old Ammet, it was guarded by soldiers with the new guns. Mitt did not like watching it. Each Festival brought back his nightmares about Canden falling to pieces in the doorway. But the tenement was so near the harbour that it was hard to avoid watching. This year, Dideo came to lean out of the window between Mitt and Milda, with his netted eyes wistfully on those new guns.

'The stuff they use in those,' he explained, 'can blow a man up, used right. Years back, I used to sail with a man who could get the stuff, and we went after fish with it. You might call it unfair to the fish—but I know to this day how to make a bomb. And I was thinking that a bomb in the midst of Old Ammet could rid the world of Hadd, and give us uprising all over Holand in one moment.'

Mitt and his mother exchanged a long startled look over Dideo's gnarled hat. That was it! What an idea! They discussed it excitedly as soon as the procession was over and Dideo gone.

'If you were to get a bomb and throw it at old Haddock—you *do* throw bombs, do you?' said Milda. 'You could shout out that Dideo and Siriol set you on.'

'But I might not be heard,' said Mitt. 'No—I'd have to get myself taken. Then when Harchad comes to ask questions, I tell him the Free Holanders set me on to do it. But how can we get hold of some of that gun-stuff?'

46

'We'll get some,' said Milda. 'We'll think of a way. But you'll have to do it before you're old enough to hang. I couldn't bear to think of you taken and hanged!' She was so excited that she went out and spent the rest of her wages on fruit and sweets to celebrate.

Mitt looked at the bundles of toffee-apples as dourly as Siriol. He sighed. He saw he would have to put off throwing any kind of bomb until he had earned enough money to rent another farm for Milda. She would certainly starve if he was arrested and she left to manage all by herself. He thought he might have to wait until he was at least as old as Dideo.

It did not happen that way. A week later, Mitt came home from selling fish, smelly, slimy, and pinched with cold. He wanted only to go to bed. But, to his annoyance, his mother was entertaining a visitor. The visitor was a square, sober-looking man, with an air that reminded Mitt vaguely of something—or someone—else. He was wearing much more respectable clothes than most people wore on the waterfront, and, to Mitt's further annoyance, Milda had squandered her money this week on a bottle of Canderack wine for this visitor. Mitt stood in the doorway glowering at him.

'Oh, Mitt!' Milda said happily. She was looking very pretty, and the dimple was back in her face. 'You remember Canden?' Mitt did remember Canden—too well. He was still having nightmares about him after the Festival. He had to hold hard to the doorpost when he heard the name. Milda, quite unaware how Mitt was feeling, said, 'Well, this is Canden's brother, Hobin, all the way from Waywold. My son, Mitt, Hobin.'

The visitor smiled and came forward, holding out a square, useful-looking hand. Mitt shuddered, clenched his teeth, and put out his own fishy hand. 'I'm all covered with fish,' he said, hoping the visitor would not like to touch him.

But the warm, square hand seized his and shook it. 'Oh, I know what it's like to come in dirty from work,' Hobin said. 'I'm a gunsmith myself, and sometimes I think I'll never get the black off. You go and wash and don't mind me.'

Mitt smiled shakenly. He realized Canden's brother was a very nice man. But that did not alter the fact that he had a nightmare for a brother. Mitt went over to the bucket in the corner to wash, hoping that Hobin would go back to Waywold at once, and never be seen in Holand again.

That hope went almost immediately. 'Yes, I've got a tidy little house, up in Flate Street,' he heard Hobin telling Milda. 'Workshop below, plenty of room to live upstairs. Earl Hadd's done me proud.'

Mitt realized that Hobin had come to live in Holand. He was so dismayed that he called out, 'And who did Earl Hadd turn out of there, in order to do you proud?'

'Oh, Mitt!' said Milda. 'You mustn't mind him,' she told Hobin. 'He's a real free soul, Mitt is.'

Mitt was furious. She had no right to tell a stranger private things like that. 'Yes,' he said. 'Bit poor and common for you here, aren't we?' And, to make sure that Hobin would not want to visit them again, he wandered round the room swearing as hard as he could. He could tell that worried Hobin. He kept giving Mitt sober, concerned looks. It worried Milda, too. She apologized for Mitt repeatedly, which made Mitt angrier than ever. When Hobin at last put out his hand to say goodbye, Mitt turned his back and pretended not to see it.

'You didn't have to be like that, Mitt!' Milda said reproachfully, when Hobin had gone. 'Didn't you understand? He's a gunsmith! And you can see he was fond of Canden. If I can only get him to join the Free Holanders, then we can have that bomb—or a gun would be better. You could shoot Hadd from this very window, then!'

Mitt only grunted. He knew he would rather take a gun off a soldier in the open street than get one from Canden's brother.

To Mitt's acute misery, Hobin called again, repeatedly. It took months of visits before Mitt could forget Hobin had a brother who fell to pieces in his nightmares. When he did, he found he quite liked Hobin. Meanwhile, Hobin was firmly but kindly resisting all Milda's persuasions to become a freedom fighter. He agreed that the earls made life needlessly hard. He agreed that things were bad in Holand. He grumbled at taxes like everyone else. But he did not hold with freedom fighting, he said. He called Canden—sadly and a little severely—a boy who played with fire, and when Milda talked eagerly of injustices, he smiled, and said it depended on her circumstances. After a while, he took to scolding her kindly for buying him wine she could not afford.

Ham grew increasingly gloomy over that winter. Mitt could not understand why, until the spring, when *Flower of Holand* was gliding out on the tide one morning.

Siriol said, 'Your ma going to marry that Hobin?'

'*No!*' Mitt said indignantly.

'Good for the cause when she does,' Siriol said.

Ham sighed. 'Good for her, too,' he said nobly. 'Hobin's a good man.'

Mitt was furious. And when Siriol and Ham proved right, it made another grudge he bore them. Milda did marry Hobin. And all through the wedding, Mitt was muttering to himself that he would get Siriol and Ham for this, if it was the last thing he did. Probably will be, too, he thought. Since last Festival, he had been living as if there was nothing to look forward to, beyond the moment he somehow planted a bomb under Earl Hadd. The only good thing he could see in this wedding was that he would be living in reach of a store of gunpowder.

Milda and Mitt moved into the upper part of the house in Flate Street, some way west of the waterfront. It was a good house, though small and peeling. It even had a yard with a mangle in it, and a target on its dingy brick wall where, to Mitt's interest, Hobin tested the guns he made. Mitt had his own room for the first time for years, and, though he was far too proud to admit it, very lonely he was in it, too. Milda gave up her sewing and bustled round their four upstairs rooms, singing and laughing, and the crease of worry seemed to have left her face for good. It saddened Mitt. He had only been able to send that crease away from time to time, yet Hobin had banished it for ever. Hobin offered to send Mitt to school, but Mitt preferred to go on working. The Free Holanders would not find much use for a boy who was tied up at lessons all day. And, besides, Mitt felt that freedom fighting was almost the only tie left between himself and Milda.

It was then that Hobin showed a surprising strictness. 'You're a fool, Mitt,' he said. 'You've got a brain and you ought to learn to use it, not waste your time talking freedom with a bunch of boatmen who don't know what the word means. You'll wish you'd done otherwise when you grow to be a man.'

This kind of argument is always irritating. Mitt twisted about and did not answer. He wanted to say he was not going to grow up—he was going to kill Hadd instead—but with Hobin's sober blue eyes fixed on him, he did not like to.

'Well, if you *must* work,' said Hobin, 'you can do one job and one only. You can learn my trade from me, or Siriol's from him, or you can sell fish if you want. But you do no more than one.'

Mitt passionately wanted to go on selling fish. He enjoyed shouting out rude things about Hadd even more than he loved fooling Harchad's soldiers. Fishing—well,

50

he was glad of any excuse to stop doing that. On the other hand, he knew that he would have far more chance of getting his hands on some gunpowder if he was Hobin's apprentice. He shifted about, kept his eyes on the floor, and finally swallowed his annoyance enough to say grudgingly, 'I'll learn your trade then.'

'You did quite right, Mitt,' Milda said, and hugged him delightedly. That consoled Mitt somewhat.

But it was unexpectedly awkward when Hobin went with Mitt to Siriol's house to explain to Siriol and buy out the remainder of Mitt's apprenticeship. Alda threw both arms round Mitt and gave him an arris-scented kiss on both cheeks. Slow tears trickled down Lydda's face. 'I shall miss you on the stall, Mitt,' she said. Mitt was prepared for this. But what he had not been prepared for was the look of disappointment and resignation on Siriol's face.

'I should have thought of this,' Siriol said, and he got out the arris bottle and poured everyone a glass, by which Mitt knew that this was a special occasion. 'Yes, I should have thought,' Siriol said, when they were all sitting stiffly round the table. 'You got right on your side, Hobin, and Mitt's worth a better trade than fishing. But it's not easy for me—having no son of my own.'

Hobin looked uncomfortable. Lydda and Alda cried. Mitt sat squirming on his stool. 'It made me feel all slimy, sort of,' he told Milda afterwards. 'As if I was covered in fish-juice. *And* I can't abide the taste of arris.'

Siriol fetched the crumpled paper that Milda had signed on Mitt's behalf nearly two years back. At first he refused to take any money for it. Hobin insisted. Everything got more and more awkward, until Ham was called in to witness the bargain. Ham clapped Hobin on the shoulder, and wrung Mitt's hand until Mitt wondered if he would have the use of it again, and was generally so cheerful and

51

so pleased for Mitt that all the awkwardness vanished. Everyone had another glass of arris—Mitt poured his secretly into Alda's glass—and then he and Hobin came away.

'But I feel bad, I do, really,' Mitt told Milda. 'As if I owe it them to tell them we need the gunpowder.'

'Well, why don't you tell them?' Milda said. 'Dideo knows how to make a bomb. It wouldn't do any harm to get them to help.'

'You mean, bring the Free Holanders into it, really?' Mitt said. It seemed a very good idea.

Unfortunately, Hobin came in at that moment and caught the words 'Free Holanders'. Again he showed surprising strictness. 'I'm not having freedom fighting talk in this house,' he said. 'Silly cloak-and-dagger stuff! And don't get the idea I'm scared of Harchad, either. He knows I can go back to Waywold if I want. What gets me is the way those boatmen don't grow up. It's like a game to them, just like it was to Canden. Nobody's playing that silly game in my house!'

Mitt and Milda could only continue their talk in utmost secrecy, either in snatched moments, or when Hobin was out at the Gunsmiths' Guild. The upshot of their planning was that Mitt lied himself blue in the face to Hobin and managed to attend the next meeting of the Free Holanders. There he laid before them his suggestion: that he steal enough gunpowder for a bomb and plant it under Hadd when he next carried Old Ammet down to the harbour to drown.

The suggestion made a startled hush. Ham broke it by saying reproachfully, 'It wasn't because of the gunpowder I was glad for you, Mitt. I hope you don't think that.'

'Funny. I made sure you was expecting it,' said Mitt, who could seldom resist teasing Ham.

'Now, Mitt—' Ham began.

'Hush,' said Siriol. 'Learn to take a joke, Ham. Mitt, that's a risk. Horrible risk. You'd get taken.'

This was fighting talk from Siriol. He was really considering the idea. Highly delighted, Mitt made haste to assure Siriol that he had no intention of being taken. 'Suppose I was dressed up in red and yellow, like the Palace boys. They'd not know who I was until it was too late. I can run.'

'I know you can run,' said Siriol. 'Your ma never agrees, does she?'

'Ask her,' said Mitt. 'Only not when Hobin's there. She can sew the clothes, if we can get her the stuff.'

Siriol pondered, long and deep.

'Mitt looks just like any other lad I ever saw,' Dideo said persuasively. 'Half the time, I don't recognize him myself. And I would love to get making a bomb.' Indeed, all the other Free Holanders were loving the thought, too. They leant forward, murmuring eagerly across the nightlight.

'Boom!' said someone. 'Up goes Hadd. Lovely!'

'And all Holand rises to us!' said someone else. 'He can do it, Siriol.'

'Quiet!' said Siriol. 'I know he can do it. But he has to get away after. This is going to take careful planning.'

Mitt scampered home to Flate Street, wholly delighted. 'We did it!' he whispered to Milda, when she met him anxiously on the stairs. 'We're on!'

'And you're not afraid at all?' Milda whispered, wonderingly.

'Not a bit,' said Mitt. And it was true. He was looking forward to it. He felt dedicated.

The Free Holanders began to lay their plans, carefully and thoroughly as Siriol did everything. Mitt and Milda laid theirs. And all of them very soon realized that it would not be next Festival that Mitt planted his bomb. As Siriol said, they would need to study the road the procession took, and the way the soldiers were placed, to find out where and when would be the safest time for Mitt. And he had to look into escape routes and possible hiding-places for Mitt afterwards.

As Mitt had no intention of escaping, he never attended when Siriol talked of things like this. But, after the first week he spent as Hobin's apprentice, he knew that it would take him years, literally, to steal enough gunpowder to make Dideo a bomb. Hobin was only allowed enough gunpowder to test the guns he made. Harchad's arms inspectors called once a week to make sure there was no more. Sometimes they made surprise visits, to make doubly sure. They would weigh the powders and count the guns, and, unless their seal was on everything, Hobin was not allowed to work. They were a great annoyance to Mitt, though Hobin did not seem bothered by them. He would joke with them, almost as if they were friends.

Gunpowder, Mitt discovered, was made of three things, which Hobin mixed, very carefully, himself. One was charcoal, which Mitt never bothered with. Dideo could get that easily. But the sulphur and the saltpetre, were, as far as Mitt knew, impossible to get any other way than by stealing them. Mitt supposed they must be made somehow, but he never found out how. They were delivered in sealed bags by the inspectors, and locked away by Hobin. It was months before Mitt was allowed even to touch any. He had to spend his time instead melting lead and casting boring little bullets in a string of small sausage-shaped moulds. And watching, watching.

Hobin himself was the other great drawback to Mitt's plans. He was such a careful man, and so patient. Mitt suspected that, even without inspectors, Hobin would have kept all his things under lock and key anyway. And he was much in demand. There was scarcely an hour when there was not someone else in the workshop besides Mitt and Hobin. Troopers and captains came, bringing guns which had problems. Other gunsmiths came, to consult Hobin on difficult technical matters. Mitt discovered that Hobin had invented a way of making a gun shoot true, by putting a spiral groove up the inside of the barrel. That was why the bullets Mitt so boringly cast were pointed, and not round like the shot Harl used when he shot birds on the Flate. Twice, Hobin was actually summoned to Harchad to be consulted. By the time Mitt had graduated to carving butts and even weighing a little powder, he had grasped that Hobin was the best gunsmith in South Dalemark. Mitt was quite proud, and glad on his mother's behalf. But it did mean he had chosen the very worst man to filch from. Hobin had a name for honesty. He was respected in the Guild. And for a long time Mitt dared not do anything but pretend he was honest too.

Hobin was truly anxious for Mitt to learn, and to become what he called 'a decent citizen'. Mitt had to wear better clothes—which were certainly warmer in winter, but which he despised on principle. He had to wash when they came up from work. Once a week, he was forced to wash all over in front of the fire, in spite of his conviction that washing took the strength out of you. And every evening, Hobin produced a book. It was called *A Reader For the Poor* and it bored Mitt to tears. 'If you won't go to school, you must learn at home,' Hobin said, and he made Mitt read a page aloud every night after supper.

Mitt's only wonder was that he did not die of boredom in the first year. It seemed to him that he only came alive when he began to be able, at last, to take Dideo tiny packets of sulphur and saltpetre. Then it was even better than running errands for the Free Holanders. Mitt would lie to Hobin, as he told Milda, like a fishmonger's scales, and slip off into the streets with his packet, knowing that if he was caught with it on him, there would be trouble indeed. It was a marvellous feeling of danger, and marvellous to know he was getting somewhere at last.

He did not get on very fast, either as a gunsmith or a thief. Hobin was a patient man, but he sometimes grew irritated with Mitt. Mitt's mind was wholly on filching powders. He did not intend to be a gunsmith, so he attended to Hobin as little as he attended to the plans Siriol insisted on making about a hiding place for him after his bomb was thrown. Meanwhile, Milda had a baby, and another the year after. Mitt was rather astonished to find himself with two sisters long before he had a bomb. They were rather a nuisance. They would cry, and they would cut teeth, and they would take up Milda's time when Mitt needed her. But they would not believe they were nuisances. Whenever Milda dumped a sister in Mitt's arms, the baby would start to laugh and gurgle, as if Mitt liked her.

Mitt started to grow then. That astonished him, too. He was used to being the smallest boy in the street. Now he was one of the bigger ones, with long, long, thin legs. The woman who had stolen the red and yellow cloth to make Mitt's bomb-throwing clothes from, had to steal more, and Milda put off making them until she was sure Mitt would not grow out of them.

'All to the good,' Siriol remarked. 'If you keep on this way, you'll have changed so after a year's hiding that even Harchad's spies won't know you.'

The trouble was that Mitt needed a lot to eat, and Hobin became increasingly hard up. Hadd put the rents up again all over Holand. His guns had done very little good. Every other earl in South Dalemark had hastened to get guns, too. Hadd was forced to bargain for peace, and bargains cost money. Hobin, Mitt was glad to see, grumbled just like everyone else. He led a petition from the Guild of Gunsmiths, asking to be allowed to raise the price of guns. Hadd refused.

'Now don't you think there's some use to freedom fighting?' Mitt asked him.

'It only makes things worse,' said Hobin.

'No, see,' Mitt said persuasively. 'You could set all the earls fighting one another, then have an uprising, and the North would come and help us. They'd have to!'

'If the North did any such thing,' said Hobin, 'you'd find the earls would stop fighting one another and start on the North. And you'd find yourself on their side, Mitt. You couldn't help yourself. You're born a Southerner. The North knows that better than you do. It's history. It'll take more than an uprising to make things better in Holand.'

'The trouble with you is you're so patient!' Mitt said.

In spite of his patience, Hobin began to look a little worn by springtime. There were the babies and Mitt to feed. And Milda was still rushing out and 'just happening to see' expensive things, though these days it was mostly furniture. Hobin began to talk seriously of moving back to Waywold.

'We can't do that!' Mitt told Milda in a panic.

'I know. Not after I've trained you all these years,' said Milda. 'But he'd stay if only Hadd was gone. Run and catch Siriol.' And she broke a whole bowl of eggs to give Mitt an excuse to go out.

Mitt was lucky enough to catch Siriol just as he was boarding *Flower of Holand*. Siriol stood on the quayside and thought so long that Mitt wondered whether to suggest he would miss the tide. 'Ah,' said Siriol. 'Well. You better do it this autumn then.'

'This autumn it is!' Mitt agreed, and the muscles at the back of his legs jumped with excitement. 'And thank goodness! After three flaming years, I can't wait much longer!'

Part 2

The Sea Festival

6

There were great gales that spring. The sea broke the dykes in two places and, even in the harbour, boats blew this way and that and masts snapped. Siriol could not put to sea for a fortnight, and few people in Holand went out much because the wind in the street filled your face with sand and salt until you could barely see. Mitt was kept very busy. The old Earl of the South Dales died, and all the earls of the South began to gather in Holand to invest the new Earl, as the custom was. People asked one another whether Hadd would manage to quarrel with them all, or only half of them. Mitt thought Hadd must be determined to. Hobin was busy making and mending guns day and night. The Palace must have bristled with them. Mitt got little chance to look at any earls. He saw one windswept fine person, who looked as if he would very much rather have been indoors, but no one could tell Mitt if he was an earl or not.

'Down with him anyway!' Mitt muttered, and hurried back indoors.

Then a strange boat was sighted, beyond the shoals, beating her way to the harbour. There was intense excitement. The boat was said to be a Northerner. Mitt could think of nothing else.

'We'd best settle this for you before you ruin any more bullets,' Hobin said. He and Mitt put on pea-jackets against the gale and went out to look, along with most of the rest of Holand.

The ship was wallowing in the great waves outside the

harbour wall, black in the yellow stormy light. Though all her canvas was in and she was riding only on the rags of a storm-sail, Mitt saw at once that she was indeed a Northerner. She had the square rigging which few ships in the South used these days. People round Mitt shook their heads and said it was daft to go out in this gale with a little square-rigger like that, but then Northmen were all daft. And it was clear the ship was in bad trouble. For some minutes, Mitt doubted that she would make the harbour at all. Then she rounded the wall and it was clear she would be safe.

The harbour was lined with soldiers to meet her. Behind them, a lot of ordinary people had come out with knives and stones. And Mitt watched with the most extraordinary mixed feelings. He was glad the ship was safe. But how *dared* they! How dared they put into Holand harbour like this! The ship wallowed her water-logged way to the quayside. When some of the sailors on board saw the soldiers waiting, they dived into the harbour rather than be caught.

'What cowards!' he said to Hobin.

'They haven't a chance anyway,' said Hobin. 'Poor devils.'

The Northmen who stayed on board were taken prisoner as soon as soldiers could jump onto the ship. The crowd hid most of it from Mitt. But he had a glimpse of them being taken uphill to the Palace, a bunch of soaking draggled fellows with fair hair and brown faces, who all had a thicker, healthier look than anyone in Holand, even though they were plainly almost too exhausted to realize what had happened to them. Mitt's shaken thought was that they looked like people. He had expected them to look mysteriously free. But they held their heads low and shuffled along, just like anyone else taken by Harchad's men.

Their arrival caused quite as much excitement up at

the Palace. Everyone had been in a ferment there anyway, because of the investment of the new Earl. Feasts and fuss and arrangements had gone on for a week now. All the children were bundled out of the way and ordered to be seen and not heard—and not seen unless asked for. There was much excited peeping and giggling. To Hildy's scorn, all the girl-cousins decided that the new Earl of the South Dales was *terribly handsome* and spied on him whenever they could. They all wished they had been betrothed to him, and not to whoever they *were* betrothed to. Hildy herself thought Tholian looked rather unkind. She made the mistake of telling Harilla so.

'All right, Lady Be Different!' said Harilla. 'I'm not telling you my spyhole for that. Go and find your own.'

Hildy did not mind. Ynen and she were better than any of them at finding places where they could see what was going on. They watched a great deal of the feasting and music, until it was obvious that the Lord of the Holy Islands was not going to arrive.

'Why not?' Hildy wondered.

'I don't think he's anyone's hearthman,' said Ynen. 'His job is to keep the North's fleet out.'

Then it was learnt that one Northern ship at least had slipped through. Half the earls were convinced that it was the first of an invasion. The messages, the orders, and the bustling about made Hildy think of an ants' nest stirred with a stick, and there were more still when the soaking prisoners were marched in. The prisoners were questioned. It came out that two of them were nobly born—and not only that, they were the sons of the Earl of Hannart himself. The excitement was feverish. The Earl of Hannart was a wanted man in the South. Ynen reported to Hildy that, when he was a young man, the Earl of Hannart had come South and taken part in the great rebellion, just as if he were a common revolutionary.

The fate of the Northmen was no longer in doubt. They were all put on trial for their lives.

Now it is a fact that, if you are brought up to expect something, you expect it. Hildy and Ynen were used to people being tried and hanged almost daily. It did not worry them particularly that the Northmen were going to be hanged. Most of the Palace people said they had asked for it by putting into Holand anyway. But Hildy and Ynen were very anxious to catch a glimpse of the Earl of Hannart's sons while they were still alive to be seen. It was not easy to do. Hadd was afraid that some of the freedom fighters in Holand might attempt to set the Northerners free, and nobody was allowed near them who had no business to be. But on the last day of the trial, Hildy and Ynen managed to stand in an archway near where the younger son was being kept prisoner.

They saw soldiers come out. They saw their Uncle Harchad in the midst of them, and with him the Earl's son. When they came level with the archway, Hildy was astonished to see that the Earl's son was quite young—no older than Harchad's own son—just a big boy really. And when they were beside the archway, Harchad suddenly turned and kicked the Earl's son. Instead of glaring or swearing at Harchad, as Hildy herself or any of the cousins would have done, the boy cringed away and put one arm over his head. 'Don't!' he said. 'Not any more!'

Hildy stared after the soldiers as they marched the prisoner away to the courtroom. She had sometimes seen revolutionaries cringe like that. She had thought that was the way common people behaved. But that an Earl's son should be brought to behave like that shook her to the core.

'I wonder,' she said. 'Is Uncle Harchad very cruel, do you think?'

'Of course he is,' said Ynen. 'Didn't you know?' And

he began telling her some of the things he had heard from the boy cousins.

Hildy stared at him. Even though she realized Ynen was quite as shaken as she was, some of the things he said made her feel so sick and cold that she had to run at him with both arms stretched out and bang him against the side of the archway to shut him up. 'Oh be quiet! Don't you *mind*!'

'Of course I mind,' said Ynen. 'But what can I do?'

The prisoners were hanged the following day. Hadd gave permission for the Palace children to watch if they wanted. Ynen said he did not want to. Hildy was trying to decide whether, after what she had seen, she wanted to or not, when a message came from Navis. He forbade Hildy and Ynen to watch. Hildy found she was relieved.

But in some ways a dreadful thing you do not see is more dreadful. Hildy tried not to watch the clock, but she knew the exact moment when the executions started. When a groaning sort of cheer came up out of the courtyard, Ynen covered his ears. What made it seem all the more dreadful was that their cousin Irana was carried out screaming, their cousin Harilla actually fainted, and all the rest, boys and girls alike, were sick as dogs.

'It *must* have been horrible!' Hildy said, quite awed.

After that, neither she nor Ynen went near their Uncle Harchad if they could help it.

The gales dropped, and the earls all went home. Hildy's cousin Irana Harchadsdaughter ran feverishly from window to window trying to get a last glimpse of the Earl of the South Dales. This sentimental behaviour so disgusted Hildy that she said:

'I don't know why you carry on like that. He hasn't even looked at you. And I bet he's twice as cruel as your father is. His eyes are even meaner.'

Irana burst into tears. Hildy laughed and went out for

the first sail of the year in the yacht, *Wind's Road*. But Irana went weeping to her cousin Harilla and told her how beastly Hildy had been.

'She said that, did she?' said Harilla. 'Right. It's time someone taught Lady Superior a lesson. Come with me to Grandfather. I bet he doesn't know she's gone out sailing.'

Hadd did not. He was in a very bad temper anyhow, having quarrelled furiously with Earl Henda. And the coming of the ship from the North had brought home to him just how important it was to have an alliance with the Lord of the Holy Islands. The thought that this alliance was at that very moment in danger of drowning in a squall was almost too much for him. He was so angry that Harilla was almost sorry she had gone to him. She got her face slapped, as if it was her fault. Then Navis was summoned. Hadd raged at him for half an hour. And when Hildy came in, she found herself in the worst trouble of her life. She was utterly forbidden ever to go sailing again, in any kind of boat whatsoever.

For three days after that, even Ynen hardly dared go near Hildy. She stole a fur rug from her aunt and sat wrapped in it, up on the leads of the roof, looking out over the lovely whelming sea, streaked grey, green-blue, and yellow where the sandbanks were, too angry even to cry. It's just the alliance. He doesn't care about *me*, she thought. Then, after two days, she remembered she would be able to sail once she got to the Holy Islands. I wish I could go now, she thought. Away from this horrible cruel place. She spent the rest of the day making a loving drawing of *Wind's Road*. When it was finished, she cut it carefully in half and labelled one half 'Ynen', and the other 'Hildrida'. Then she crossed out 'Hildrida' and wrote 'Ynen' on that half, too. After that, she came down from the leads and handed both halves to Ynen.

'There you are. She's all yours, now.'

Ynen sat holding both halves of the drawing. He was glad, but it seemed a shame. It was the high price Hildy had to pay for being important. Ynen reflected that this autumn he would at last be old enough to take part in the Sea Festival. He swore to himself that, if he died in the attempt, he would catch his grandfather one on the nose with a rattle. Hadd deserved it, if ever anyone did. Then he thought about the Earl of Hannart's sons and hoped Uncle Harchad would be in the procession too. He would catch a whopper.

Down in Holand, they were still talking about the Northmen. As Milda said, it seemed hard to hang them when they had only come in for shelter. Hobin said it was only to be expected. Mitt gradually forgot his mixed feelings. As time went on, he remembered more and more his glimpse of the Northerners shuffling like all prisoners. It came to something, he thought, when the tyranny of Holand could make free men of the North look so abject. In fact, as a free soul himself, he despised the Northmen a little for it. Come autumn, and I'll show them! he thought.

Most people were sorry for the Northmen. Feeling ran high against Hadd all that summer. Then rumours were heard that the North had defeated the South in a great battle, and blocked the last of the passes in the mountains between them. After that even people who were in favour of Hadd began saying it was Hadd's fault. He had let them in for a shameful defeat by hanging twenty innocent men.

'Good,' said Siriol. 'Things are going our way nicely.'

The Free Holanders were planning long and carefully, all through that summer. Among other things, it suddenly dawned on Mitt and Milda that no one must connect Hobin with Mitt, when Mitt threw his bomb. Give

Harchad's spies half a clue, as Mitt said, and Hobin would be hanged. Mitt was confident that he could lie well enough to keep Hobin out of it. 'I've had years of practice,' he said. 'The wonder is that I know how to tell the truth these days. But will Hobin keep himself out of it?' That was the trouble. Hobin seldom bothered to watch the Festival. But he might take it into his head to do so, and if he saw Mitt being arrested he was quite capable of going with Mitt and spoiling everything. 'That's the worst of him being so honest,' Mitt said.

Mitt took this problem to the Free Holanders. They put their heads together. The result was that Ham, who had always liked Hobin, struck up a proper friendship with him. The two of them went for walks together, out in the Flate, all that summer. Ham managed surprisingly cunningly. He got Hobin used to longer and longer walks. By the end of the summer, they were spending all day in the Flate, having supper at an inn, and not getting back to Holand until after nightfall.

'See?' Ham said, with his big slow grin. 'Then on the day of the Festival, we go out to High Mill, twenty odd mile, and we'll be seen. I'll make sure the innkeeper swears to us.'

Then, to Mitt's exasperation, another society of freedom fighters put its oar in. It was called Hands to the North. It tacked notices to the gates of the Palace and the barracks, which promised, in crude writing and even cruder language, to kill Hadd during the Sea Festival. AND AS MANY ER THE REST ER YU AS WE CAN GIT.

'That's torn it!' Mitt said, as soon as he heard the news. Milda broke the eggs again, and a jug of milk for good measure, and she and Mitt both seized a baby apiece and hurried round to see Siriol. 'What shall we do?' said Mitt. 'There'll be spies and soldiers all over now. Who are these Hands to the North anyway?'

'Not any lot I know,' said Siriol. 'This is bad. It could have the Earl stopping the Festival.'

'He'd better not!' said Milda. 'I've trained Mitt for this for years. And the clothes won't fit him if we have to wait another year.'

Siriol thought, in his customary unhurried way. 'If the Palace thinks of staying at home,' he said, 'we'll hear it soon enough on the grapevine. Meanwhile, it wouldn't do no harm to see if we couldn't start a bit of a panic. Go round letting on that it'll be terrible bad luck for Holand to stop the Festival, and that kind of thing.'

So the Free Holanders dropped a word here and another there. Most of them were content simply to hint at dire bad luck. But Mitt felt he could not leave things so much to chance. Whenever Hobin was not by to listen, Mitt would whisper passionately to anyone who happened to be in the workshop, of floods, fires, famines, and plagues. 'And that's just the least of what'll happen if old Hadd's too scared to hold the Festival,' he would conclude, and pull a dreadful face to suggest all the other unspeakable kinds of bad luck. When Milda was out shopping, she said things even more highly coloured.

Four days later, the rumour came back to Mitt when the arms inspectors called on their weekly visit. 'Hear what they're saying?' said one. 'They say if Hadd stops the Festival, the sea rises up and spews out monsters over Holand, and all manner of ignorant nonsense.'

'Yes,' said the other. 'Monsters with heads like horses and horns like bulls. I mean, I know it makes you laugh, Hobin, but you must admit it shows how much happier everyone would be to know there *is* going to be a Festival this year.'

Hobin was still laughing after they had gone. 'Monsters!' he said. 'Don't let me catch you listening to that sort of nonsense, Mitt.'

'No fear!' said Mitt. Secretly, he was awed by the way the rumour had grown.

Next day, Hadd announced that the Festival would be held as usual. Hadd was no coward, and no fool either. The news Harchad's spies brought him showed him well enough how much he was hated in Holand. He knew that to cancel the Festival might be the thing that could spark off a real revolution. So he did not cancel it. But he forbade any of his grandsons to take part in the procession. The procession, this year, was to consist of servants and merchants and their sons—all people who did not count.

The news was a great blow to Ynen. He had looked forward to the Festival for months. He had *counted* on hitting Hadd with a rattle. He had dreamed of himself whirling the rattle round and round under Hadd's great pointed beak, closer and closer, and at last, *bash*. But now . . . It did not console Ynen in the least that he was allowed to come to the feast afterwards. And it was the last straw to learn that his father was to be in the procession. Harl was quite content to stay in the safety of the Palace. Harchad of course would be busy supervising the soldiers and spies posted to keep Hadd safe. But someone in Hadd's family had to carry Libby Beer, and Hadd chose Navis. Navis was his most expendable son. Besides, Hadd did not like Navis much.

'It's not fair!' Ynen said to Hildy out of his disappointment. 'Why is Father allowed in the procession, and not me?'

'Now you know how I feel,' Hildy said unsympathetically. Girls were never allowed in the procession at all.

When this news filtered down through devious ways to the Free Holanders, Siriol was rather pleased than otherwise. 'Less chance of our Mitt being recognized,' he said.

70

The other safety measures were much more disturbing. In the week before the Festival, all boats were ordered to the far side of the harbour. Siriol had to move *Flower of Holand* to a distant mooring, where she was bumped and rubbed by six other boats crammed in round her. He grumbled furiously. He grumbled even more when, for two days before the Festival, no boats were allowed in or out of the harbour, and all were searched by soldiers every few hours. At the same time, Harchad had all the tenements on the waterfront knocked down, and a large rubbly space cleared in front of the harbour. This was more serious. The street where Mitt was supposed to join the procession vanished. They had hastily to choose the next inland. Milda and Mitt were furious. They had lived in one of those tenements.

'The whole lot down, just to keep his nasty old pa safe!' said Mitt. 'Talk about callous tyranny!'

'They should have come down years back,' said Hobin. 'They were nothing but rats and bedbugs. And "callous tyranny" is the kind of talk I'm not having.'

'But those poor people are turned out in the street!' Milda protested.

'Well, it's cleaner there,' said Hobin. He was combing his hair and getting ready for a Guild meeting. 'Anyway, to my certain knowledge, three trades have offered them room in their guildhalls, Gunsmiths included. But there's new houses being built for them, back in the Flate.'

'The Earl's building them houses?' Mitt asked incredulously.

'No,' said Hobin. 'Would the Earl do a thing like that? No. It's one of the sons—Navis, I think.' He put on his good jacket and went away downstairs, as far as Mitt could see, rather annoyed with Navis for stealing the Gunsmiths' thunder.

'He'll come back talking of Waywold,' Mitt said, as

the door slammed. 'You see. Still, it won't matter you going back there after tomorrow.'

'Mitt, I'm nervous!' said Milda. 'All our planning!'

Mitt felt pleasantly excited, no more. 'Don't you trust me or something?' he said. 'Come on. Let's have a look at those clothes.'

Milda laughed excitedly as she fetched the red and yellow costume from its hiding place under her newest carpet. 'I don't think you know the meaning of fear, Mitt! Honest, I don't! Here, now. See if they fit.'

It was a strange and rather ridiculous costume. The breeches, which came halfway down Mitt's thin calves, had one yellow leg and the other red. The jacket was red and yellow in the opposite halves. Mitt was a bit thin for the jacket. But he buttoned it up and added the jaunty cap, which had a double crown like a cock's crest. 'How do I look?'

Milda was delighted. 'Oh, you do look handsome! You look just like a merchant's son!'

Mitt looked in the little mirror, all prepared to agree. He felt very fine. And he had rather a shock. He looked good, it was true. But there were things in his face one never saw in the smooth faces of wealthy boys—lines which made it look old and shrewd. It was the knowing face of the poor city boys who ran about in the streets, fending for themselves. And yet—this was the thing which shocked Mitt most—it was a babyish face, too. Under the lines, there were empty curves, emptier than in any boy's face he had ever seen, and his eyes stared as round and wide as his baby sisters'. Mitt made haste to alter it by putting on his most joky smile. The empty cheeks puckered and the eyes leered long and sly. Mitt flipped the crest of his cap. 'Cock-a-doodle-do!' he said. 'Roll on Festival!' Then he turned away from the mirror and did not look in it again.

72

7

On the day of the Festival, Ham called for Hobin soon after dawn. That's got rid of him! Mitt thought, hearing them clattering away downstairs. To tell the truth, he had not slept as well as usual. But, since this was a holiday, he stayed in bed another good hour. I reckon they'll be questioning me all tonight, he thought. I better get all the rest I can. But when Milda called him, he was very glad to jump up and put his own holiday clothes on, on top of the Festival costume. They were supposed to be spending the day at Siriol's house. So they went there first, Milda, the two babies, and Mitt, very bulky and warm in his double set of clothes. They were not to go to the side street until word came that the procession had already left the Palace.

The procession left the Palace a little before midday. Ynen watched it from the upstairs window of a merchant's painted house. He was crowded round with hearthmen and hearthmen's sons, all of whom had strict instructions to keep Ynen safe. Ynen could hardly see for them. His was the first and worst position anyway. The other boy cousins were all in houses from which they could see the cleared space by the harbour. Ynen could only see it if he craned and, if he craned, someone was sure to take hold of the back of his jacket and pull him respectfully back inside.

Ynen could hardly bear it, even before the first of the procession came past. When at last he heard the *thump, thump, thump* of the horsehair drums, followed by the

73

squealing of scarnels and joined finally by the groaning of cruddles, his frustration was almost boundless. Perhaps he was not very musical. It struck him as the most exciting sound in the world. Then he heard shouting. Then the lovely, lovely din of the rattles. And at last came the first of the procession, ribbons fluttering from silly hats, banging and blowing and scraping as they marched, with a beribboned bull's head bobbing amongst them, and the lucky boys with rattles tearing in and out between their legs. Lucky red and yellow boys.

'Oh why can't all the revolutionaries drop dead!' wailed one of the hearthmen's sons.

Ynen wished they would, too. But for Hands to the North, he would be down there in the stirring din and the bright colours. And here came Grandfather, looking strange and rather silly. Ynen had an excellent view of Hadd's cantankerous old face under a hat loaded with fruit and flowers. On Hadd's shoulders, and trailing behind him, was a magnificent creamy mantle, embroidered with scarlet and cherry-red and gold. Over that was draped a garland of wheat-ears and grapes. Not much of the rest of Hadd was visible, because Old Ammet was in the way. Ynen had very little attention to spare for Old Ammet. All he saw was ears of wheat bristling at head, hands, and feet, cherry ribbons and a girdle of apples. Ynen was chiefly impressed with Hadd's skinny legs, cased in scarlet stockings, strutting underneath Old Ammet. Ynen giggled at the important way those legs walked. He had not realized before how vain his grandfather was, and how much he enjoyed being an earl. At the sight of those red, strutting legs, Ynen longed to seize a rattle and whirl it in his grandfather's face. To his annoyance, the red and yellow boys were on their best behaviour. None of them dared wave a rattle at Hadd. If only they would! Ynen thought, craning, and being pulled back.

Navis came next. Ynen giggled again. His father's feet were in buckled boots, so his legs did not look as ridiculous as Hadd's. But he had ribbons at his knees and fruit in his hat. And juice was coming out of Libby Beer and running into Navis's ribboned sleeves. Flies were following her. Navis was looking hot and bothered—most unusual for him—and obviously wondering if he could get Libby Beer to the harbour still in one piece.

Behind Navis were two merchants who had been pressed into the procession. One wore a hat with ears, the other a hat with horns. They looked right idiots, and they knew they did. All the boys at the window shrieked with laughter. Ynen leant out again and yelled insults, which were drowned by the next batch of cruddle-players. After that, the procession was all music, things on sticks, boys with rattles, until it got smaller and smaller and wound downhill out of sight. Ynen sat back with a sigh. He desperately envied Hildy. She and the girl-cousins, as the most important of Hadd's grandchildren, had seats at the window of a house on the very edge of the cleared space.

Mitt was by now in the side street, with Milda, Siriol, and Dideo, hastily climbing out of his own clothes. In front of them were the backs of the crowd lining the main street. They were solidly Free Holanders and their families. Most of them had been there since dawn to make sure of the position. Mitt could already hear the thumping and skrawking of the procession, very near. As he passed his jacket to Siriol and put the crested cap on his head, a bull's head on a stick went by above people's heads. The noise was deafening.

'Be careful, Mitt,' said Siriol. 'And remember you say, "I've come to meet Flind's niece," to the one that meets the cart at Hoe. If he says, "She's expecting another little one," then it's all right to go with him. Got that?'

'Yes, all in my head,' Mitt said, attending to this no more than he usually did when Siriol talked of such arrangements. The din of the scarnels was making the back of his legs jump.

'Old Ammet's coming!' said someone in the crowd. 'Pass it back.'

'Old Ammet in sight.'

Siriol handed Dideo the lighted taper. Dideo bent over the bundle he was carrying.

'Oh, Mitt, be careful!' Milda said. She was smiling and looking sad, both at once. Mitt looked from her to the sister in her arms, and then down at the other sister, unsteadily standing and holding Milda's hand. They upset him. He could not think of anything to say to them.

He was glad when Dideo passed him a bundle on a strap. It was scarlet to match Mitt's left side, and it had a stiff twist of paper coming out of it, which sent off little puffs of smoke. 'There,' said Dideo, and his face was netted in smiles. 'That's long enough to last to the cleared space.' He patted Mitt's shoulder as he hung the bag on it.

Siriol passed Mitt a rattle and banged his other shoulder. 'Off you go. Good luck.'

Mitt slipped in among the crowd, and they parted to let him through. He was on, after years of waiting, and he could hardly believe it. He came to the soldiers, who stood in a line in front of the crowd. They ought to stop him.

A soldier glanced down and saw the red and yellow suit. 'Sorry, sonny,' he said, and moved to let Mitt by.

Mitt was in the roaring, skirling, streaming procession. For just one second, he was small and sort of blunt, and did not believe he was really there. But he was. And there was Hadd. Mitt had not seen Hadd close to before, but he knew him by Old Ammet in his arms. The bad-tempered old face was exactly what he expected. 'That face,' Mitt told himself, 'is asking to have a rattle under its nose before it gets blown up.' And he was off to do it, whirling from one side of the procession to the other, rattle spinning, crested cap flopping, and keeping a wary eye on the puffing bundle under his arm as he went.

He caught up with Hadd just on the edge of the cleared space. Hildy saw him clearly, from where she sat at the window jammed in among her five cousins. They had soldiers in the room with them, soldiers downstairs, and soldiers lining the new open space by the harbour. They were safe. Nevertheless, the cousins were very nervous and disposed to scream at things. They screamed when the first musicians came between the soldiers and straggled across the open. They screamed at the bull's head.

'Oh, look!' screamed Irana, as Mitt ran in front of Hadd, whirling his rattle neatly under Hadd's irascible nose as he went.

Mitt checked after he had done that. Holand looked so strange with no waterfront buildings and all the shipping cleared to one side of the harbour, that he had another moment when he could hardly believe it was real. But the bundle under his arm fizzed. Sparks puffed out with the smoke. Mitt knew the time had come to get rid of it. He turned and plumped it down at Hadd's scarlet feet. Then he did not know quite what to do next.

Hadd's legs stopped walking. His bad-tempered look did not alter. He simply stopped and stood like a statue, with Old Ammet beneath his chin. Both of them stared at Mitt, and Mitt stared back. And the cousins round Hildy screamed in earnest at the sight of the smoking bundle on the ground. Behind Navis, everyone in the procession began to run into the backs of the people in front, and still Hadd stood, and so did Mitt. Hildy could not think what the boy thought he was doing. It seemed stupid behaviour, even for a revolutionary. Old Ammet seemed to be staring at him, unblinking as a cow over a gate, from under raised wheat-ear eyebrows, as if he shared Hildy's wonder.

Sparks poured out of the bundle. Navis saw that nobody else was going to do anything. He hoisted Libby Beer to his shoulder and dashed forward. This was more what Mitt had expected. He got ready to pretend to run. But, to his astonishment, Navis took no notice of Mitt. Instead, he aimed a great kick at the fizzing bundle. Mitt saw the ribboned leg go out, the buckled boot connect, and the bundle, in an arch of smoke, sail away behind into the open space.

And the fellow hasn't a hair out of place! Mitt thought, rather astonished. He wanted to shout to Navis, 'Hey! I dedicated a lifetime to this lot! And you just wasted it!'

By this time, the merchant with ears on his hat had pulled himself together, too. He made a rather dubious grab for Mitt. Mitt dodged him easily.

This made Mitt think: Might as well give them a run for their money.

He turned to run. As he did so, the explosion came and sent him reeling. The force of it rattled all the windows and sent a gust into Hildy's face. The cousins screamed again. The rest of the procession came jostling out from behind Navis, some of them demanding to know what had happened, some of them after Mitt. Hadd turned and made a sign to one of the captains that Mitt should be taken alive. Since Hildy now knew that this was the worst way to be taken, she shivered a little as she watched the boy running. He ran like a deer, ribbons fluttering, dropping his rattle as he ran, straight towards the soldiers coming out from the edge of the crowd to meet him. Hildy thought that, if it had been her, she would have run to the edge of the harbour and jumped in.

So would Mitt have done, if he had meant to escape.

But he was supposed to be caught. His ears hurt from the explosion. They seemed to be plugged with wool. He saw the soldiers mouthing as they came, but could not hear a word. Mitt dodged and swerved as only someone brought up in the poorer parts of Holand could. Looks more natural, he thought. A huge hand snatched at his face. Mitt ducked under it and twisted sideways. A blurry face mouthed curses. A bevy of big boots clodhoppered at him from all directions. This way and that, went Mitt, that way and this. He leapt a boot, dodged another, missed an enormous stretching arm and tripped over another great boot. A jerk and a sudden coldness on his back told him—where his furred-up ears could not—that his jacket had been grabbed and torn. He was flat on his face and up again in one movement. But he was still not caught. He felt his jacket leave him, jerk, jerk, and he was still sprinting forward. Too good to last, Mitt thought, and he dived, pushing and shoving, among the big bodies of the ordinary people crowded behind the soldiers.

Come on, some of you! Stop me! he thought. But no one succeeded, though Mitt thought some of them tried. Just barely, he could hear their voices now: 'Stop him! Don't let him get away!'

Ah. Ears come to their senses again, Mitt thought. Good. Couldn't see myself lipreading all the questions I'm going to be asked.

He pushed on, very glad he was not deaf. And shortly, the voices round him were saying, quite loudly, 'What's happened then?' and, 'Who are you shoving?'

Mitt, to his extreme astonishment, plunged out from the back of the crowd into a narrow street. Hey! he thought. This won't do. He stopped. He turned round and saw the backs of the people filling the street heaving and bumping about as the soldiers tried to force their way through after him. He cast a longing look up the narrow street. He could really almost get away. They would not run fast in those boots.

Better make it easier for them, Mitt thought, sighing. And he went back into the crowd.

Out in the open space, the procession had re-formed and was straggling towards the water's edge. Hadd behaved as if nothing had happened at all. As soon as Mitt vanished among the soldiers, he went on walking as if the whole thing was not worth thinking about. Hildy could not help admiring him. That was how an earl should behave! Hadd's behaviour was so dominating that Hildy and everybody else were soon watching the procession going up and down the quays, drumming and droning and skirling, as if Mitt had never existed.

Mitt was in the crowd just beneath Hildy's window. He found he was still wearing one red and one yellow sleeve. They were a nuisance, so he took them off and threw them on the ground. He seemed to have lost his cap. He stood there in his threadbare undershirt, hoping the soldiers would recognize him by his two-coloured breeches. But he was surrounded by tall citizens and nobody saw him. Above the noise of the procession, he could hear the boots of the soldiers hammering away up the narrow street.

Right fools, some people are! Mitt thought. Better make myself obvious.

He squirmed his way along the painted wall of the house until he came to its front door. It had six steps up to it, for fear of flooding, as did most houses in Holand. People were crowded on the steps, staring out towards the harbour. Mitt climbed up and squeezed in among them. He was easy enough to see, had anybody been looking his way. But everyone was watching the Festival.

The procession had formed into a line along the jetty, with Hadd and Navis in the centre. The heads on poles

80

were lowered. Garlands were taken off. Everyone waved these downward, pretending to beat the water. In fact, the water was too far below to reach, but the Festival went back to the days when Holand harbour was just a low ring of rocks and none of it had been altered since. The same old words were said:

To tide swimming and water welling, go now and come back sevenfold. Over the sea they went, on the wind's road. Go now and come back sevenfold. For harbour's hold and land's growing, go now and come back sevenfold.

This was repeated three times by everyone in the procession. It was a growling, ragged chorus. Yet, by the third repetition, Hildy's arms were up in goose pimples from sheer awe—she did not know why. Mitt's eyes pricked, as they always did, and he was annoyed at himself for being so impressed by a load of out-of-date nonsense. Then the musicians gave vent to a long groaning chord. Hadd raised Poor Old Ammet above his head, ready to throw him in the harbour.

A little star-sparkle of flame blossomed for a second on one of the ships tied up at the side of the harbour. Hadd jerked, half-turned, and slid quietly to the ground. It looked at first as if he had suddenly decided to lay Poor Old Ammet carefully at Navis's feet. Then came a tiny, distant *crack*.

Nobody understood for a moment. One of Hildy's cousins laughed.

After that there was a long, groaning uproar. Mitt's voice was in it. 'Flaming Ammet! I been *diddled*!' The fat woman beside him was saying, over and over again, 'Oh what bad luck! What terrible bad luck!' Mitt had no idea whether she meant bad luck to Hadd or to Holand. The ladylike girls overhead somewhere were screaming. Mitt leant his head against their painted front door and cursed. All he could think of was that the unknown marksman had cheated him. 'Half my life, and now it's wasted!' he said. 'Wasted. Gone!'

Overhead, the cousins hung on to Hildy and to one another, whimpering and crying. Hildy found herself saying, 'Ye gods, ye gods, ye gods!'

A soldier in the room behind shouted, 'He's in that boat—*Proud Ammet*! Run, you, and we'll get him!'

'They mustn't leave! We're not safe!' screamed Harilla.

They had already left. The door behind Mitt burst open and soldiers pelted out of it. Mitt leapt clear. But he had no chance to make himself obvious. Everyone on the steps was pushed off and toppled in all directions. The fat woman landed almost on top of Mitt and knocked him sprawling. By the time he had picked himself up, and then her, the soldiers had pelted off.

'Shut *up*!' Hildy snapped at Harilla. She was trying to see what was happening on the waterfront. Navis was bending over Hadd, and the rest of the procession was crowding round. Soldiers were running. People from the crowd were surging forward to see. Uncle Harchad, keeping prudently among a crowd, was running, too. Hildy saw her father stand up and point to the boat where the shot had been fired, wave to the soldiers and wave the crowd back. Then he stooped again, and stood up holding Poor Old Ammet. He turned this way and that with him, showing people what he was doing, and then threw him into the harbour with the traditional shout. Then he picked up Libby Beer and slung her after.

Hildy felt a mixture of pride and horrible embarrassment. She could see her father was trying to assure the citizens of Holand that this did not mean unmitigated bad luck. But it was doubtful if anybody noticed. People were surging about. Numbers were leaving. Soldiers were running out to *Proud Ammet* along the curving harbour wall. There were screams and shouts which drowned Navis's voice. Nevertheless, the rest of the procession followed his lead. In a ragged, unconvinced way, garlands began to loop out from the quay and fall on the water. By this time, Uncle Harchad had reached the waterfront. Hildy watched him and Navis kneel down beside her grandfather, with red and yellow garlands sailing around them, until the harbour seemed full of bobbing fruit and wet flowers, and wondered what they were feeling. She could see Hadd was dead, but she seemed to have no feelings about that at all.

8

The fat woman was very grateful to Mitt. She clung to him, and he had to help her to the street beyond the house. 'You're a sweet boy,' she kept saying. 'Come on up to the stalls and I'll buy you something.'

Mitt refused. He had to be where the soldiers were. It was the only thing left for him to do. Half his life's work had fallen to someone else's bullet. Hands to the North, curse them! he thought. He knew he would never get a chance to be revenged on Hadd now. But the other half remained. He had to get caught and get questioned and, with the utmost reluctance, let out that it was Siriol, Ham, and Dideo who set him on to plant the bomb. So, as soon as he had shaken off the fat woman, he went back to the waterfront.

By the time he got there, the other murderer had very thoroughly stolen his thunder. Soldiers were shouting to people to get back and get home, while other soldiers tried to open a path for what was left of the procession, carrying Hadd's body. More soldiers were in and out of the house where the screaming girls were. The place was full of groups of people hurrying purposefully this way and that, in uniform, in Festival dress, or in holiday best. The result was utter confusion. The only thing which did not seem to be happening, Mitt thought bitterly, was the revolution the Free Holanders had confidently expected once Hadd was dead.

Mitt shrugged. For lack of any better plan, he did as he used to do three years back, and joined a hurrying group of total strangers. With them, he was swept right across the waterfront to the other side of the harbour. And when we're there, I bet we hurry all the way back again, he thought.

He was right. An officer stopped them near the harbour wall. 'Only authorized persons past this spot.'

Mitt's group obediently turned away. 'Alham must have gone up Fishmarket then,' someone said, in a worried, busy voice, and they all set off again in the opposite direction.

Mitt lagged and let them hurry away. He could see the masts of the smaller boats from here, sawing the sky as heavy soldiers jumped from one to another, hunting the murderer. Even the masts of the big ships were swaying sedately, so many were the soldiers searching them. A group of seamen who had been on the ships were being herded and prodded roughly along the harbour wall. They'll catch *him* all right, Mitt thought resentfully.

A new group of people surged up beside him. These were clearly important. They were officers in braid, well-nourished men in good cloth, with, in their midst, a tall thin man with a pale jagged profile. The man's clothes had a wonderful sober richness. Mitt saw the sleek glint of velvet, and fur, and the flicker of jewels, worn where they did not show, because the man was too used to having them to bother with their value. Mitt knew that pale, jutting face, though he had never, to his knowledge, seen the fellow before. It had the same bad-tempered lines as Hadd's. The nose was the one he had whirled his rattle under. The rest of the features were like the ones he had seen advancing on him behind Libby Beer to kick the bomb away. This could only be Harchad.

Proper flinty flake off the old block, he is, Mitt thought, looking up at him with interest. Wearing six farms and ten years' fishing on his back, and *he* don't care!

85

'Oh, stop bleating, man!' Harchad snapped at the man with the most braid. 'Those seamen are to be questioned till we get something. I don't care if you kill them all. And I want the brat who threw the bomb, too. He was obviously an accomplice. I want him brought to *me*, when you find him.'

Mitt's stomach, for the first time in his life, gave a cold little jolt. He lowered his eyes from Harchad's face and gently backed away. Wonder how he'd look if he knew I was right beside him, he thought. Accomplice, was I? Oh flaming Ammet! I think everything's gone wrong. He tiptoed hurriedly sideways to join the nearest group of hurrying citizens.

The man in braid shouted. 'There he is now! That's him!'

'Who?'

'The brat who threw that bomb.'

Mitt had the merest glimpse of them all staring at him. Harchad's face jutted out of the rest in a way that dried Mitt's mouth, tongue and all, and almost wrung a scream out of him. It was as horrible as his nightmares about Canden. He turned and ran, mindlessly. His only idea was to make his legs go faster than their fastest. He had to get away from the gathering shouts behind him. He had to escape from that face. He shot across the waterfront, not knowing whether he hit people or avoided them as he ran. He dived into the nearest road and ran there for all he was worth. It filled with banging feet behind him. Mitt ran harder still, turned a corner and ran, and ran again, and went on running. The only thing in his mind was the shouting and ringing feet behind him, and he did not stop running until they had grown faint and died away.

When his breath came back, he wandered wearily round a corner into the next street. He was deeply ashamed of himself. What had got into him? What had made him, the free soul, fearless Mitt, who had never turned a hair during all the errands he had run for the Free Holanders—what had possessed him—to panic at the mere sight of Harchad and run away? Mitt could not understand it. What had made everything go so wrong?

'Here, love. Have hold of this and cheer up.'

Mitt looked up to find himself in an airy respectable street, quite some way above the waterfront. It was full of handsomely painted houses. Mitt dimly remembered the one just up the hill from him, with the double gable and the two stiff figures painted on it. The street was full of quiet, cheerful people in respectable holiday clothes, who were buying things at the stalls which lined the street. It did not seem as if a whisper of the events at the harbour had reached this far. All was peace, and sober enjoyment.

The person who had spoken to Mitt was a woman behind one of the stalls. She was leaning forward across rows of little Ammets and Libbies, holding a toffee-apple out towards Mitt. She smiled when he looked, and waggled the apple invitingly on its stick. 'Here. Take this for luck. Your face is as long as Flate Dyke, my love.'

Mitt did his best to grin. Running had filled his mouth with thick, bitter juice. He did not want a toffee-apple. But he could see the woman meant to be kind. 'Oh, no thanks, lady. I just lost a lifetime's work, see, and I'm off my food a bit.'

'Well then, you need an appetizer,' said the woman, and she tried to push the toffee-apple into Mitt's hand.

Mitt found he really could not bear the thought of sticky toffee and sour apple, and he backed away. 'No thanks, lady. Honest. Much obliged.'

'Please yourself,' she said. 'But I've got to give you *something* now I've started, or it's bad luck for both of us. Here.' She picked up one of the little images of Libby Beer from the line on the front of the stall and held her out to Mitt. 'You can have her, then. I'm just clearing up to go anyway.' Mitt did not know if the woman really wanted luck, or if she was simply trying to cheer him up, but he took the little image and tried to grin again. 'And don't try eating her. She's made of wax,' said the woman. 'The year's luck to you.'

'Luck to you, ship and shore,' Mitt said politely, just as he should. He wandered on down the street, clutching the knobby little figure and wondering what to do with it. Perhaps I could make Harchad a present of her, he thought.

He was three stalls lower down, when boots hammered on the flagway behind him. Six soldiers with an officer at their head swung round the corner the way Mitt had come and halted by the woman's stall. 'Hey, you. Anyone. Seen a boy in Festival breeches, no jacket, very skinny?'

The sober respectable hum in the street died away completely. Nobody moved. Mitt froze, bending over the stall beside him, pretending to look at little Ammets. He tried to will himself to make a dash down the street and bring the soldiers after him. But there was no question of that, somehow. He could only wait for the woman who had given him Libby Beer to give him away.

'Yes, indeed I have seen him, sir,' she said. 'Just this minute. I offered him a toffee-apple and he went away down the street.'

The soldiers nodded and came on down the street.

Mitt stood with a bright imitation Libby Beer in one hand, and the other stretched out to touch the plaited corn of an Ammet, and still could not move. He did not blame the woman. Other people had seen her talking to Mitt, and she dared not deny it. In the old days it used to make him amused and rather scornful, the way even respectable people like these went in dread of Harchad's soldiers. It made him think he must be the only free soul in Holand. But now he did not seem to be a free soul any longer. He dared not move. He had to stand there till the soldiers saw him.

The boots clomped by. Mitt could see and feel everyone's eyes moving between him and the green uniforms. But nobody said a word. The boots clomped on to the end of the street and faded out of hearing. There was sighing and shifting all round. Someone behind Mitt, who must have blocked the soldiers' view of him, said, 'Go on, lad. Run while the going's good.' Mitt did not see who said it, but he ran.

Isn't that Holand people all over! he thought as he ran back round the corner and plunged downhill towards the harbour again. Where they could be, they were kind. But you could never count on it. Yesterday, this kindness had amused him. Now there did not seem to be anything left to laugh at. Tears trickled across Mitt's cheeks as he ran, as he thought of all those years of planning gone to waste.

I wonder if there's something wrong deep inside of me, he thought. It don't surprise me. He tried to wipe the tears off his face and found he was brushing it with something knobbly. He looked, and there was the little Libby Beer, made of wax cherries and rose-hips and miniature apples, glistening with his tears. 'Goh!' said Mitt and stuffed her angrily in his scarlet pocket. Crying did no good. Next time he met any soldiers, there would be no mistake. He was going to get caught.

He came down into the old town, through a street of peeling houses breathing the smell of the poor quarters out through their open front doors—the smell of too many people, dirt, damp plaster, and cheap food. All the children from the houses were playing in the road. There was hopscotch nearest, marbles a little way on, and then two of the running, shouting kind of games. And through

89

the shrill yells, Mitt sensed more soldiers coming. The rhythm of their boots was in the very air.

Mitt did not decide what to do. He moved without thinking, round the hopscotch to the game of marbles, and dropped down to squat in the ring of smaller boys. It was a trick he had often played three years back. Unless the boys were doing something very secret, they usually did not mind. But, as he hurriedly wiped the tears off his face with his wrist, Mitt was amazed at himself. Here, he thought, what am I doing?

The rhythm of boots beat in the dirty pavement under him and a green block of soldiers swept round the corner. When they saw the children, the clump-clump of their boots slackened and became a slow puttering. They had broken step and were coming slowly down the street, looking very carefully indeed.

The yelling and the games stopped. The children stood in awkward rows, staring. The small boys round Mitt were not really playing marbles any more. They were waiting for the soldiers to pass. And Mitt crouched with them, in such terror that he could hardly see or feel. He had not known it was possible to be so frightened. He knew he stuck out like a sore thumb among these children. He was half as big again as any of them. His red leg blazed and his yellow leg shone. And he could not trust little kids like these not to give him away, either by accident, or on purpose, for spoiling their games. At any moment, a shrill voice might say, 'That's the one you want, mister.'

As the soldiers puttered towards him, Mitt no longer had any doubt what he was doing. He was trying not to be caught. And, as wave after wave of pure fear swept over him, he knew he was going to go on trying. By the time the soldiers were level with him, his terror was worse than the worst pain he had ever known. Mitt crouched down over his blazing legs, squeezing himself into himself to look as small as possible, and forced himself to put out a hand, take a marble, and roll it casually into the middle of the ring. He had to fight his terror every inch in order to move at all. He thought he could have rolled Siriol's boat across the pavement more easily. The effort made him weak.

As soon as the marble left his hand, he was sure he had done the wrong thing. The boy next to him shot him a nasty look. The puttering boots went slower, as if the movement had attracted their attention. Mitt almost lost his senses, he was so terrified. Time swam forward, sickeningly slow and blurred.

The boots puttered down past the hopscotch, stopped, and started again, in step this time. Clump-clump-clump, they went, away into faintness.

'Buzz off,' said the boy. 'You spoilt my go.'

Mitt stumbled to his feet. He felt dizzy, and as cramped as if he had spent a winter night fishing. He had to limp down the street. None of the games started again. The children watched Mitt as they had watched the soldiers. Bad, that was bad. They would tell of him to someone. Mitt hoped they would not tell too soon, because he felt far too tired to run. He felt like curling up in the nearest doorway and crying himself to sleep.

Get a hold of yourself! he thought angrily. You're on the run, that's all. People go on the run all the time in this place. I don't know how it keeps happening, but it's like I can't help myself from running. What's gone wrong with me? This was a question Mitt simply could not answer. He only knew that he had got up this morning, intending, as he had intended for the last four years, to finish Hadd and the Free Holanders at one stroke. And now he had failed to finish Hadd, his one idea seemed not to be caught.

Oh, now, wait a minute! Mitt stopped and pretended to loiter in a yard doorway. There were still the Free Holanders. If he was too scared to get himself caught, he could easily just go to Siriol's house, or Dideo's. Where Mitt went now, Harchad's spies would swiftly follow. It was just as good a way of getting the Free Holanders caught. But the reason Mitt stopped, leaning on the doorpost and gaping at nothing, was that he was not even tempted. 'Not even tempted!' he repeated to himself. And it was true. It was nothing dramatic. Mitt could not tell himself he would rather die than go to Siriol's house—he knew he would do anything rather than die—but he was still not going there. Or to Dideo. 'What do you think they are, then? Friends?' Mitt asked himself derisively.

It seemed as if they were. He remembered the smile on Dideo's netted face, when Mitt brought him the first little packet of saltpetre, and Siriol glowering at him over a rope's end, but never hitting him more than just that once. And I reckon he ought to have done, Mitt thought. He ought to have knocked me through a Mittshaped hole in the side of *Flower of Holand*, over and over. He found himself smiling a little. Siriol always understood his jokes, and Ham scarcely ever did. Then there was Alda, puffing arris at everyone, and Lydda going to marry that sailor off *Lovely Libby*. I got to know them too well, Mitt thought.

It did no good to stand there, smiling and staring. Mitt walked on. He supposed his best plan was to use the escape arrangements Siriol had so carefully made for him.

'No!' Mitt exclaimed. It was not that he did not want to use them. He did. He would have given his ears to. But he could not remember a thing about them. Thinking he would not need to escape, he had attended to Siriol's plans probably even less than he had listened to Hobin telling him about guns. He had a vague idea there was a cart somewhere, and a password. But that was absolutely all he knew. Of all the fools!

But what was he to *do*? He could not spend the rest of his life sneaking round the streets of Holand. If he looked for all the carts he could find, he would certainly be caught. The soldiers would think of that. He dared not go home. That would get Hobin and Milda arrested too. The only thing he dared do was take to the Flate, like so many freedom fighters before him. But he knew a bit about that. You got hunted down there. And it was a miserable life, unless you were lucky enough to have a gun and could shoot marsh-birds for food. Mitt had no gun. He knew where guns were, though: locked up in Hobin's workshop. And he dared not go near there. Oh, it went round in circles. *Why* hadn't he attended to Siriol? Mitt knew why, really. He had simply not thought of anything beyond the moment when he was to plant that bomb. 'I must be flaming insane!' Mitt said to himself. '*Do* something, can't you!'

He wanted to go home, that was what he wanted to do. And he dared not.

Or dared he? Hobin was out for the day. Milda was at Siriol's with the babies. If Mitt went there, spies would follow. But spies would probably go there anyway, because Hobin had gunpowder. Suppose Mitt were to go there, take gun and ammunition, and make it look like a burglary? It would have to look like a burglary anyway, because he would have to break locks, and the seals of the inspectors, to get anything. Hobin could not be blamed for being burgled. It would be a way of keeping suspicion from him. In fact, the more Mitt thought about it, the more it seemed his duty to go and burgle Hobin. Then do what? Go out in the Flate and try to get North, Mitt supposed.

It made a considerable difference to have a purpose again. Mitt felt far less tired. Flate Street was quite near.

Mitt purposely doubled the distance to it. He wanted to be seen in as many places as possible, to confuse the spies. When he finally arrived behind the high greasy wall which cut the light off the back of the workshop, Mitt was fairly confident that any spy trying to trace him would not arrive until tomorrow. He thought two days was more likely. But he said tomorrow, because it never paid to underestimate Harchad's spies.

The wall made one side of an alley, with another sightless wall opposite. Mitt stood facing it, breathing deeply. He had to reckon on being seen going over the top of the wall. If he allowed time for whoever saw him to fetch help and break down the front door of the workshop—or fetch soldiers to do it—there should just be time to take what he wanted and then break the place up a bit. But it was only a very short time. Mitt knew it might be a close thing. He wished his knees would not tremble and his heart knock so. He was not *used* to being frightened like this.

9

'And I missed *everything*!' was Ynen's disgusted comment, when at last Hildy arrived back at the Palace and he managed to find her.

The Palace was all doubts and hushed voices and indecision. Only one thing was certain: Hadd was dead and Harl was now Earl of Holand. But when you had said that, you had said everything. Nobody knew if there was an uprising, or whether to take off their Festival clothes, or what would happen about the feast which had been prepared. Harl did nothing but sit in his room. He had not given one order. Harchad came and went and gave orders perpetually, but nothing seemed to come of them.

'Well, in that case there can't be an uprising,' Hildy said rather snappishly, when Ynen told her what it had been like. 'We didn't see anyone but soldiers all the way back.' She felt as if she wanted to be alone, but Ynen looked so lost that she stayed with him. They wandered stairs and corridors together, among people who had as little idea as they had what to do.

Ynen told Hildy some of the rumours about the murderer. He had been caught; he had not been found. He was a discontented seaman; he was a dangerous revolutionary and an agent for the North. He was a superb marksman; he was a fool who had fired a lucky shot; he had used a new secret weapon from the North. He had poisoned himself; he had jumped into the harbour and escaped. No one knew what the truth was. 'Now tell me what it was *like*, by the harbour,' Ynen said.

'I don't know,' Hildy said, quite honestly. 'Anyway, you know what it's like when Harilla has hysterics.' But she did try to describe what had happened. It was not Ynen's fault he had missed it.

'Did Father really do all that?' Ynen asked. 'I didn't know he could move fast enough.' He added wistfully, 'I *wish* I could have seen that boy twirl a rattle under Grandfather's nose.'

'It wasn't as funny as you think,' said Hildy. 'It—it was queer. He didn't run away. I suppose he's caught by now.' Then she found she really did need to be alone and went to her room. But Ynen came with her and she had not the heart to tell him to go away. He sat curled up on the window-seat, while Hildy sat cross-legged in the middle of her big square bed.

Here Hildy tried for the hundredth time to sort out how she felt. It was a very shocking thing that her grandfather had been murdered. That she knew. And it was a shocking time to kill him. Everybody said it meant terrible bad luck. Hildy found she was still far more embarrassed than proud at the way her father had tried to save the day. It was the way nobody had noticed that made her so uncomfortable. But about the actual murder, she simply felt awed and respectful—and subdued all over, so that she moved gently and quietly and wanted to be alone. She could not manage to feel strongly about it. And this was odd, because she knew that somewhere, about something, she felt very strongly indeed. She was raging with feelings, but she did not know what *about*. It reminded her of the way she had felt when her father had told her she was engaged to Lithar.

Here Hildy sprang up. 'Wait,' she said to Ynen, when he sprang up, too. Ynen sat down with a sigh, and Hildy sped to her father's rooms.

96

She knocked at the heavy door. There was no answer. Hildy, a little hesitantly, turned the handle and went in. There was no one in the first room. She went on to the second.

Navis was sitting by the window, still in his Festival clothes. Perhaps he was trying to sort out how he felt, too. At any rate, he was not reading the book he had in his hand. He was staring out into the Flate.

Hildy saw at a glance that he had gone back to being cold, idle, and proud. There was little chance of anybody making him do anything which was not absolutely necessary. Hildy ground her teeth with fury. How could he rise to the occasion at the waterfront and then sink from it like this? And if he was still mourning about her mother, Hildy had no sympathy for him whatsoever. He had been like this far too *long*!

'Father,' she said.

Navis jumped slightly. 'Did I forget to lock my door?'

'I'll go away in a minute,' said Hildy. 'Are you sorry Grandfather's dead?'

'Er,' said her father. 'He was an old man.'

Hildy thought angrily that *that* was no way to speak. She wondered whether to flatter him by saying she thought he had behaved extremely well by the harbour. But it was beside the subject, it was not true, and she did not think it would rouse Navis anyway. 'I came to ask you,' she said, champing at the words because she was so angry, 'if I need to marry Lithar now.'

'What's that got to do with the situation?' Navis asked.

'Grandfather arranged it,' Hildy said, trying to be patient. 'But I don't want to marry him. So will you cancel it, please.'

Navis looked at his book as if he would rather attend to that than Hildy. 'I think you'll find the alliance is prized quite as much now.'

'What does that mean? *Can't* you cancel it?' Hildy demanded.

'I doubt it,' said her father.

'Don't you *care*?' said Hildy.

'I fancy I do,' Navis admitted. 'But with things in this state of upheaval—'

Hildy lost her grip on her temper. 'Ye gods! Nobody cares in this place! You're the worst of the lot! You just sit there, after all that happens, and you don't even care that nobody even knows if there's going to be a feast or not!'

'Don't they?' Navis asked, rather surprised. 'Really, Hildy, there *is* nothing to do at the moment but sit. I'm very sorry—'

'You're *not* sorry!' raved Hildy. 'But I'll make you sorry! You just wait!' She turned to storm out of the rooms.

Navis called after her. 'Hildy!' She turned round to find him looking oddly anxious. 'Hildy, will you make sure you and Ynen stay where I can find you?'

'Why?' Hildy said haughtily.

'I may need you in a hurry.'

This was such an unlikely thing that Hildy simply made a scornful noise and crashed out of her father's rooms, slamming each door behind her as hard as she could. She was so angry, and so determined to make Navis sorry, that she reached the gallery outside her Uncle Harl's rooms on a surge of blind fury and had almost no idea how she got there. She was fetched back to her senses by running into her cousins Harilla and Irana. They were hurrying the other way. Harilla's face was still streaked with red from her recent hysterics. Irana's was red all over.

'It's no good,' Irana said. 'If you're going where I think you're going. They're both pigs.'

Harilla gasped, 'I wish I was dead!' and burst into tears. Irana led her away.

98

Hildy wondered what was the matter with them this time. When she saw that there were guards outside her uncle's rooms, she supposed that meant Harl had refused to see them. She marched up to the guards, prepared for battle. But they stood aside, most respectfully, and one opened the door for her. Hildy marched on into the antechamber, rather puzzled. The servants there bowed. She heard her Uncle Harl's voice from the room beyond.

'I tell you I owe the fellow a favour! He killed old Haddock, didn't he? Let him get away.'

'Don't be an ass, Harl!' snapped Uncle Harchad's voice.

'With my blessing,' added Harl.

'Look, Harl, if we don't catch him—' Harchad broke off irritably as Hildy came in.

Harl looked at her and let out a great guffaw. He was sitting in great comfort, with his shoes off and his feet on a chair. A table under his beefy elbow was crowded with wine-bottles. He seemed very happy. He was grinning and sweating with happiness all over his big bluff face. Harchad, on the other hand, was sitting tensely on the edge of his chair, nervily twiddling a full glass of wine. His face was paler than usual.

'Ha! Ha!' bellowed Harl. 'Now it's Hildrida. That makes the full set of them. We haven't any more, have we, Harchad? Daughters and nieces and things?'

'No,' said Harchad. He did not seem to find it funny. 'If you please, Hildrida. We are trying to talk business. Say what you have to say quickly, and then go.'

Hildy stared at them. She had never paid much attention to her Uncle Harl before. He had always been a lazy, sober, silent man—and so ordinary. Nothing he said or did was ever remarkable. But now Uncle Harl was drunk, drunker even than the soldiers got on their nights off. And he was not drowning his sorrow either. He was celebrating. And Uncle Harchad was no more sorry about Grandfather than Harl was. But he was frightened: scared stiff in case he got shot next.

Harl pointed a drunken finger at Hildy. 'Don't say it. We know. All the rest said it.' He put on a high squeaky voice. *'Please, Uncle, will you break off my betrothal, please?* Who's she betrothed to?' he asked Harchad.

'Lithar,' said Harchad. 'Holy Islands. And the answer's *No*, Hildrida. We need all the allies we can get.'

'So it's no good asking,' said Harl. He wriggled his stockinged toes at Hildy, and produced strange cracking sounds.

At this, Hildy's anger blazed up again. 'You're quite wrong,' she said haughtily. 'I wasn't going to ask. I was going to tell you. I am *not* marrying Lithar, or anyone else you try to choose for me. I'm quite determined about it, and you can't make me.'

Her two uncles looked at one another. 'She's quite determined and we can't make her,' said Harl. 'This one had to be different. Her father's Navis.'

'I'm afraid you'll find you're mistaken, Hildrida,' said Harchad. 'We *can* make you. And we will.'

'I shall refuse,' said Hildy. 'Utterly. There's nothing you can do.'

'She'll refuse utterly,' said Harl.

'She will not,' said Harchad.

'She can if she wants,' said Harl. 'She'll be married by proxy anyway. Can't expect Lithar to come all this way. You refuse, my dear girl,' he said to Hildy. 'Refuse all you want, if it makes you happy. It won't bother us.' He wriggled his toes at Hildy again, and once more they cracked. Harl was impressed. 'Hear that, Harchad? That noise was my toes. Wonder why they do that.'

Hildy clenched her teeth in order not to scream at him. 'Lithar might bother if I refuse.'

Harl bawled with laughter. A small smile flitted on Harchad's face. 'Well, it'll be you he takes it out on, won't it?' said Harl. 'That doesn't worry me!' He lay back in his chair and grinned at the idea.

'All right,' said Hildy. 'Don't say I didn't warn you.' She swung round and swept out, with her back very straight and her chin up, willing herself not to let the tears in her eyes fall until she was past the attendants, and then the soldiers. Then she ran. She ran to find Ynen. He was the only person in the Palace who was kind.

She could not find him. She dried her tears on her sleeve and searched grimly, high and low, right down to the kitchens. The cooks there were cursing. Hildy discovered that Navis had bestirred himself sufficiently to cancel the feast. She was angrier than ever. To think that out of what she had said to him, this was the one thing he had attended to! She wanted to bite something, and tear things up. She stormed to her own room, wondering if a sheet or a curtain would be best to tear.

Ynen was there, still curled up on her window-seat. By this time he was feeling very doleful. Hildy was a little ashamed to think she had clean forgotten telling him to wait.

'Hildy,' he said plaintively, before he noticed her state of mind. 'Why is it all so miserable?'

'Can't you *think* why?' Hildy snapped. She seized the coverlet on her bed, a good handful in each hand, and wrenched. It gave way with the most satisfactory ripping noise.

Ynen's eyes widened. He wished he had not spoken. Now he knew he would have to say something else, or Hildy would turn on him for sitting there like a dumb idiot. 'Yes,' he said. 'It's because nobody's even pretending to be sorry Grandfather's dead.'

'How right you are!' Hildy snarled. Carefully, almost with enjoyment, she tore a long strip off the coverlet.

Ynen watched her anxiously and kept talking. 'People are more sorry about the Festival being messed up. They go on about bad luck. And the awful thing,' he said hurriedly, as Hildy began on another strip, 'is that I don't care about Grandfather either. I just feel sort of shocked. It makes me think I'm wicked.'

Hildy finished the second strip. Then, fists up and elbows out, she began on a third. 'Wicked! What a stupid way to talk! Grandfather was a horrible old man, and you *know* he was! If people didn't do exactly what he wanted, he had them killed, or tried them for treason if they were lords.' She dragged the third strip down to the selvage and wrenched to tear that. She began on a fourth. 'The only people who dared argue with him were other earls, and he quarrelled with them all the time. Why should you be sorry? Even so,' she said, rending the fourth strip loose, 'I felt sick when I heard Uncle Harl calling him old Haddock.'

Ynen judged that Hildy's temper was cooling. He risked laughing. 'Everyone called him that!'

'I wish I'd known,' said Hildy. 'I'd have said it too.'

This encouraged Ynen to believe she was almost calm again. 'Hildy,' he said, 'that was rather a good coverlet.'

It had been a good one. It was blue and gold, and worked in a pattern of roses. The sewing women down in Holand had taken a good month to embroider it. Hildy's four furious strips had left it a square of ragged, puckered cloth about four feet long. 'I don't care,' said Hildy. Her rage flared up again. She seized the puckered square and tore it and tore it. 'I hate good things!' she raged. 'They give us good coverlets, and golden clocks, and beautiful boats, and they don't do it because they like us or care about us—all they think of is whether we'll come in useful for their plans!'

'Nobody thinks I'm useful at all,' Ynen said. That was the reason for his misery, but he had been ashamed to say it before.

Hildy glared round at him, and he shrank. 'I could murder them for thinking that!' she raved. 'Why do you *have* to be useful? You're nice. You're the only nice person in this whole horrible Palace!' Ynen went pink. He was very flattered, but he would like to have been told he was useful, too. And he wished Hildy would realize that she was quite as alarming raging *for* him as she was raging *at* him. 'I intend to teach them a lesson,' Hildy proclaimed.

'They probably won't notice,' Ynen said. 'I wish we could go and live somewhere else. Somebody told me Father preferred living in the country. Do you think if I asked him—?'

Hildy interrupted him with a squawk of angry laughter. 'Go and ask one of the statues in the throne room! They'll pay more attention.'

Ynen knew she was right. But now he had talked about going away from the Palace, he knew it was the one thing he really wanted to do. 'Hildy, couldn't we go out for the rest of the day? I hate the Palace like this. Couldn't we go sailing—oh, I forgot. You're not allowed to any more, are you?'

'Don't be a fool! The place is full of revolutionaries. They won't let us go out,' said Hildy. But she could see from the window behind Ynen that it was perfect weather for sailing. 'Won't all the sailors have a holiday today?'

Ynen sighed. 'Yes. I wouldn't have a crew.' Still, it had been a good idea. 'Suppose we rode out to High Mill, then?'

But Hildy stood looking from the window to the ruins of her coverlet. There was going to be trouble about that. It was a silly thing to get into trouble about on its own. She ought to do something worse. She was aching to do something really terrible, and show everybody. She remembered Navis had asked them to stay where he could find them. That decided her. 'Let's go sailing, Ynen,' she said. 'And let's give them a fright. Let's knot the coverlet and hang it out of the window, and make them think we've run away.' Ynen looked at her dubiously. 'I can crew,' said Hildy. 'You can be captain, because it's your boat.'

'You don't mind getting into awful trouble?' said Ynen.

'I do not,' said Hildy.

Ynen jumped up, so full of pleasure and mischief that he looked like a different boy. 'Come on then! We'll need warm clothes, and we'd better pinch some food too. We'll have to sneak out past the kitchens anyway.'

Hildy laughed at the change in him as she snatched up two strips of coverlet and knotted them together. She pulled the knot tight. There was an ominous ripping noise. 'It wouldn't bear a sparrow, this stuff,' she said.

'It's only got to look used,' Ynen pointed out. 'Pull it as tight as you can without tearing it.' He helped her make the knots and then to tie the fraying strip to the window-frame and let it down outside. It did not reach very far. 'It'll do,' Ynen said, hopefully. 'We could have jumped down on to the library roof.'

Hildy leant out beside him. Their rope dangled a pitiful sixteen feet. The library dome was twenty feet or more below that. 'They'll wonder how we didn't break our necks,' she said. 'Go and get warm clothes. I'll come to your room when I've changed.'

Ynen raced off, hardly the same boy who had sat miserably on Hildy's window-seat half the afternoon. Hildy, as she changed into a short woollen dress, seaboots, socks, and a pea-jacket, told herself she was doing right. Ynen was so happy. She still felt wonderfully rebellious, but she was also just a little scared. There were people in Holand with bombs and guns. She had seen them.

'They won't know who we are,' she told her reflection in the mirror. 'And I'm sick of being important.' She took her hair down and did it in pigtails, to look as ordinary as possible, and collected dust from all the corners where she could find it and rubbed it on her face. Then she threw her good clothes to the back of a cupboard and set off for Ynen's room.

Her cousins Harilla and Irana were coming along the passage. Hildy dodged behind a grand china vase. She heard them go into her room. Harilla was saying: 'Well, Hildy, did they let you break off your betrothal? You needn't think—Oh!'

Hildy dodged out from the vase and ran, as quietly as she could in seaboots. 'Quick!' she told Ynen. 'Harilla found the coverlet.'

'It would be her, wouldn't it?' said Ynen.

They could tell the alarm was up as they crept down towards the kitchens. There was a great deal of noise and running about. But everyone seemed to believe that Hildy and Ynen would be found in the direction of the library. It was easy to avoid the people running there from the kitchens, and, once they reached the kitchens, there were very few people left there. They heard someone whistling, and dishes clattering, but the sounds echoed with emptiness. Ynen risked opening the door of a pantry.

'Look at that!' he said. The pantry was full, from floor to ceiling, with pies—glazed pies, golden pies, puffy pies, tarts, flans, pasties, and pies with flowers and birds on them. 'Pass us a couple of those sacks,' said Ynen. 'Let's make it look as if we took enough for a week.'

They pulled the pantry door to behind them and, in the half dark, seized what pies came first to hand and stuffed the sacks with them. While they were doing it, footsteps hurried outside, backwards and forwards. They waited for whoever it was to go away, and took the opportunity to eat a pasty each.

'Seems quiet now,' Hildy whispered.

They wiped gravy and crumbs off their mouths and tiptoed out. The kitchen gate was just beyond. The footsteps had been Uncle Harchad's. He had done them a favour. The soldiers who should have been on guard at the gate were standing stiffly just inside the kitchen door up the passage, listening to Harchad, along with the scullions left in the kitchen.

'And you're absolutely sure neither of them have gone past?' they heard Harchad saying.

'Quite sure, sir.'

'If you see them, I want them brought to me, understand? Not to Earl Harl,' said Uncle Harchad.

Nobody saw or heard Ynen and Hildy tiptoe to the gate, open the small postern carved in the big door, and slip out of it with their sacks.

10

Mitt took a last deep breath, hurled himself across the alley, and ran up the wall. If you are light and strong and determined, you can get a long way up a wall like this. Mitt's feet scrambled, his breath sawed, and his fingers caught and slipped in the greasy bricks overhead. His right hand managed to clench in a crumbly crack. He threw the other arm over the top of the wall. Then, with a rasping slide and a slither, he was over and down, in his own back yard, terrified at the noise he had made.

It was queer. It looked like a strange back yard already. Mitt had not remembered it so small and grimy, nor the target on the wall so pitted, or the mangle so rusty. As he stole over the slippery earth, he could hardly believe that, just as usual, he would be able to slide up the workshop window and unlatch the back door. Yet, just as usual, he put his arm in and the cold latch clicked upwards under his fingers. He pulled open the door, *creeeak*, and slipped round it into the grimy gloomy workshop.

Remember to break that window, Mitt thought. Noisy. Pity. Do it last. He crept across the room and picked up a crowbar. He looked at the rack of finished guns—locked, with the seal of Holand dangling from the lock—and the chests of powder—each kind separate, and locked, with the seal of Holand dangling there too. He wished Hobin was not so careful. He was going to have to break everything, mix his own powder, make his own cartridges.

There was a soft, purposeful movement behind him. Mitt's heart hammered and his tongue suddenly grew too fat for his mouth. He whirled round, with his hand wet on the crowbar. Hobin was just latching the door which led upstairs to the house.

'That you, Hobin?' Mitt said weakly. Cold despair set in. Everything was going wrong. Hobin should have been out at High Mill, but he was here instead, and wearing his good clothes, as if he had never been out for a walk at all.

Hobin nodded. 'I was hoping you'd be along. You've got some sense left, I see.' He walked deliberately across the workshop, even more solid and grave than usual. Mitt could not help backing away, even though he knew he would be cut off from the back door. And he was. Hobin stationed himself by the back window, and Mitt knew he was doing it on purpose.

'But you went out,' said Mitt. 'With Ham.'

'And I came back,' said Hobin. 'Without him.'

'And—' Mitt pointed jerkily upwards with the crowbar. 'My mother. She in?'

Hobin shook his head. 'At Siriol's, isn't she? We'd best keep her out of this. Mitt, what kind of a fool do you think I am to get taken in by someone like Ham? And what did you think you were aiming to do?'

Mitt swallowed. 'I—I came for a gun. I was going to make it like robbers broke in. Honest, Hobin, I wasn't meaning to get you into trouble.'

'No, I mean out there on the waterfront,' said Hobin.

'Oh,' said Mitt.

'You do take me for a fool, don't you?' said Hobin. 'I can tell my gunpowder to a grain. I knew it was you taking it, but I never thought it was you who was going to use it. Who was the one that shot the Earl? Another of your precious fishermen?'

'I don't know. Hands to the North, I suppose. Hobin,' said Mitt, 'let me have a gun. Then I'll go away and never bother you again. Please. Everything went wrong.'

'I saw it go wrong,' said Hobin. 'I was right by you when you chucked your fizz-bang. And it was lucky for them, after that Navis kicked it away, that none of them caught you. Then there was nothing I could do but hope you'd have the sense not to trust those fishermen to get you away. Because you're in really bad trouble, Mitt. And it's not funny. Not this time.'

'I know!' said Mitt. 'I know! There'll be spies here by tomorrow asking for me.'

'Tomorrow!' said Hobin. 'You must be joking! They'll be here by sundown. I give them till then to notice it was one of my guns shot the Earl.'

'One of yours? How can you tell?' Mitt wished Hobin would come away from the back door. He felt trapped.

'It had to be one of mine to throw straight over that distance,' said Hobin. 'And it fired first time. Now do you see why I keep well in with the arms inspectors? Or was that what you were counting on?'

'No I was not,' Mitt said wretchedly. 'Why do you think I set Ham on you? What did you do with Ham anyway?'

'Nothing, only gave him the slip,' said Hobin. 'Knowing the fool he is, he's still walking round in the Flate looking for me. No, I didn't see you thinking that way, but I couldn't help being riled over Ham. I could see through Ham easier than through that window.' Hobin pointed to the grimy glass and came away from the back door at last. Mitt eyed the distance and was wondering whether to dash for it, when Hobin said, 'What did you aim to do when you'd pinched a gun?'

Mitt heard keys jingle. He looked round to see Hobin unlocking the rack of guns. He could hardly believe it. He knew the risk Hobin was running. 'Go out on the Flate,' he said. 'See here. I don't want you in trouble. Make it look as if I stole it.'

Hobin looked at him over his shoulder, almost as if he was amused. 'You keep taking me for a fool, Mitt. I'm not giving you one of these. If a man can make one gun, he can make two, can't he?' The whole rack of guns swung out from the wall. Hobin took two loose bricks out of the wall where it had been, and reached into the space they left. While he was fumbling inside it, he said, 'I wish you'd tell me what made you start on this freedom fighting nonsense, Mitt. Was it your father, or what?'

'I suppose it was,' Mitt admitted. It seemed like confessing to one spot when you had measles, but it was the best he could do. Like an admission of failure, he laid the crowbar gently down.

'I thought that was it.' Hobin wriggled the bricks back into place and swung the rack back to its usual position. He turned round carefully carrying a strange, fat little gun. 'And I hoped you'd grow up, Mitt,' he said. 'You've got your own life to live.' Gently, he spun the strange fat barrel of the gun round. Mitt had never seen a gun like it before. 'Have you ever thought,' Hobin asked, 'what kind of a man leaves you and Milda on your own like that?'

This was such an untoward question that Mitt was quite unable to answer it. 'What kind of a gun is that?' he said.

'The one I had in my pocket while you were planting your banger,' said Hobin. 'In case of trouble. I kept it loaded for you. But I can only let you have the six shots in it, so go easy on them. I can't cheat the inspectors much more than you can.'

'*Six* shots?' said Mitt. 'How do you do for priming?'

'You don't. Ever thought what I did with those percussion caps I set you making?' Hobin said. 'They're in

110

here, see, on the end of the cartridges, and the hammer fires them off. There's a barrel for each shot. You spin the next one up after you've fired. It doesn't throw far, or I wouldn't let you have it. This is to get you out of trouble, not get you in it, see. If it wasn't for Milda and the girls, I'd have kept you with me and sworn myself blue in the face you were with me all along, like I used to for Canden. But there's them to consider, too. There you are.'

He put the gun in Mitt's hands. Like all Hobin's guns, it was beautifully balanced. Mitt hardly felt the weight of the chubby six-holed barrel at all. 'What did you make this for?'

'Experiment,' said Hobin. 'And because one of these days there's going to be a real uprising, here in the South. The earls can't hold people down for ever. So I've made ready. I hoped you'd be patient, and be ready, too. But there. You'll find your pea-jacket on the stairs, and my belt to carry the gun in.'

Mitt went to the stair-door. There, sure enough, were his old pea-jacket and the belt. 'You—you had this all ready,' he said awkwardly.

'What did you expect?' said Hobin. 'Sometimes I think I'd make a better freedom fighter than any of you. I put a bit of thought into it. And I'll give you some advice too. Don't go out in the Flate.'

Mitt stopped in the middle of fastening Hobin's belt round himself. 'Eh?'

'Eh?' said Hobin. 'You're all the same. Do what the other man did. You've got a brain, Mitt. Use it. They'll expect you out in the Flate. You'll be caught by tomorrow lunchtime if you go that way. What you want to do is go up along the coast and see if you can't get a boat at Hoe or Little Flate. Or it's worth looking at the West Pool.'

'Over those mucky dykes?' said Mitt.

'That won't kill you, and it's nearest. But I don't know

what guard they set over their boats there. See how you go. And if you get anywhere in Canderack or Waywold where there's a gunsmith, go to him and tell him I sent you. They'll all know me. Come on,' said Hobin. 'I'll give you a lift up over the wall.'

Mitt pushed the gun into the belt and put on his jacket. 'But what are you going to tell them when they come— these spies?'

'Nail up this window for a start,' said Hobin. 'Then you may have tried to break in, but you didn't manage it. I'll be very grieved and disappointed in you, Mitt. You'll never darken my door again.'

Though Hobin smiled slightly as he said that, Mitt knew that he was not likely to see Hobin again. As he went across the yard with him, Mitt felt unexpectedly wretched about it. He had never treated Hobin right, never even thought of him in the right way. He wanted to apologize to Hobin. But there seemed no time to say anything. Hobin had his hands joined ready for Mitt to tread in. Mitt sighed and put his foot on them.

'Happy birthday,' Hobin whispered. 'Luck ship and shore.'

There had been so much else on Mitt's mind that he had clean forgotten it was his birthday. He wanted to thank Hobin for remembering. But Hobin heaved. Mitt went upwards. He had only time for a hasty grin down at Hobin, before he was on top of the wall and slithering over the other side.

No one seemed to have seen him. Mitt set out into the depressed corner of Holand between the causeway to the West Pool and the dunes. It was not far. Flate Street was some way west to start with. And Mitt saw Hobin had been right to tell him to go this way. He only saw one party of soldiers, and these he hid from in a doorway, fingering

112

the fat little gun as they passed and thinking: Better not come too near. Hobin gave me a birthday present you won't like.

The soldiers passed without seeing him. Mitt went on. The town petered out into marsh, and shacks made of pieces of boat. There was no one about at all. Mitt, the seagulls and the rubbish thrown into the pink marsh-plants had it all to themselves. Mitt was glad of his coat. There was a fresh wind ripping over the dunes on his left, from the sea which brimmed to the horizon above the dunes and looked higher than the land. Ahead was a bright green stretch, where a network of brackish dykes broke through the dunes. Mitt would have to cross those in order to get to the sea wall of the West Pool. He was still not too keen on the idea. But beyond that black line of wall, there were masts—several hundred pleasure boats, large and small, awaiting Mitt's pleasure.

Good old Hobin! Mitt thought, making squelching strides through the pink marsh.

Then he came to the dykes. They were grey-green muddy ditches, just too wide to jump, threading the squashy green turf in front of the wall as intricately as the patterns Milda used to embroider on hangings for the Palace. Once they had been simply sea-marsh. Now they were where the Palace sewers came out. As the tide was going out, they were running sluggishly, with scummy bubblings and a foot of grey mud above the waterline.

'Yuk!' said Mitt, and looked rather desperately towards the causeway, wondering whether he dared go that way instead. There were people on it. He could see them moving between the trees. Once again that awful, unusual fear seized him. He was afraid to move at all. I better wait for dark, he thought.

But the people, whoever they were, continued flickering slowly to and fro between the trees. Mitt, with his hands shaking, tore up an old stake and prodded the nearest ditch with it. The nasty water was only knee deep.

I'll have a go, thought Mitt. He slithered down into the sour, salty mud. 'Oh yuk! Shershplottle-shloosh! What filthy filth!' said Mitt. He waded through and climbed out. 'Careful of that gun, now,' he warned himself. A couple of yards on was another ditch. 'Second sewer,' said Mitt, sliding in with a shudder. 'And now,' as he climbed out, 'here comes another.'

He was struggling out of that ditch, when there were shouts from the causeway. Figures ran between the trees and leapt gingerly down on the green morass—green figures, darker than the marsh. Harchad had thought of the West Pool too. Mitt went down, through and up out of that next dyke quicker than the rats through the garbage on the waterfront. He was through the next two before the running soldiers reached their first. As he plunged down yet another slimy bank, he saw them stop there, about a hundred yards away.

Take them a while to bring themselves to go in, he thought. The wall of the Pool was about a hundred yards away, too. Mitt knew he would never get there. It was hopeless. He doubled over and ran along the ditch, splashing and squelching, keeping one hand over his coat and the gun. 'Keep it dry. You might get one or two with it,' he said to himself. The ditch bent, and joined another one. When Mitt looked up, the wall of the Pool was quite a bit nearer. There was a buttress he might climb up. But he would have to come out of this ditch to get to it. Mitt rolled out, and dived across the moist green turf.

Something went *pheeew* past his head and thudded *smick* into the bank of the dyke beyond.

Mitt found himself up and running. He was so frightened that he felt as if he had got some dreadful disease. His legs hurt, his breathing hurt, and he felt giddy. Bullets were going *pheeew-smick* all round him now. He thought he was like a chicken, running about with its neck wrung. He was sure he was dead.

Hey! thought Mitt. He was on the edge of another dyke. *Pheeew-smick.* He threw up both arms, spun round, and fell. While he was falling, he had time to hoik Hobin's belt round him, so the gun was at his back, out of harm's way. He fell on his face on the cold, salty turf, and let himself slide over sideways into the bubbling slime in the dyke. He hardly noticed the smell.

There was one more shout from the distance, then business-like silence.

Good, thought Mitt, and began to claw his way along below the bank on hands and knees.

'There are a lot of people,' Ynen said uneasily, when he and Hildy were halfway along the causeway. 'Soldiers, I think. By the Pool gate.'

They stopped, confounded, and humped their sacks of pies to the side of the road, where the trees hid them.

'It must be the uprising,' said Hildy. 'Do you think they'd let us past if I offered them a gold piece? I've got one.'

'I don't know. There are an awful lot of them.'

They loitered forward, under the trees. It was hard to know what to do. The soldiers might not stop them. On the other hand, Uncle Harchad had told the guards by the kitchen to bring them to him. He could have sent the same message to these soldiers.

'And it would be the most terrible waste, if they sent us back *now*,' said Hildy.

Before they were near enough to see or be seen clearly, they saw the figures at the end of the road flicker to the side of it, one after another, and disappear through the trees. It looked as if they had jumped off the causeway.

115

'Don't they want us to see them?' Hildy said, and stopped, thinking of bombs and revolutionaries.

'Oh, come on!' said Ynen, and began to run. 'Quick! While they're away.'

Hildy caught him up and they ran hard, with the pies butting at their shoulders and the trees flicking past on either side. There was a salvo of little blunt bangs down below the road. Between the flicking trees, they saw puffs of smoke and a flash or so. It sent both Hildy and Ynen over to the other side of the road, where they ran still, but more slowly. Neither of them wanted to run straight into a battle.

But the firing stopped after a round or so. Ynen panted to Hildy to hurry, to get to the gate before the soldiers came back. But no soldiers appeared. They reached the big pitch-painted gates before they saw them. There were about twenty soldiers, all down in the marsh to the left, jumping and slithering among the smelly dykes there. They were peering into each one they came to, and shouting to one another to cover the next one. Some had poles and were prodding the mud.

'They're looking for someone,' Ynen said, greatly relieved. 'I bet it's the murderer.'

'I suppose they shot him,' Hildy agreed. 'Ynen, how lucky! They've left the gates open. They must have been searching the Pool.' It did not really occur to them that someone's misfortune had caused their good luck.

Mitt slithered up that buttress. Like a horrible great slug, I am, he thought. He rolled on to the top of the wall. Left a slimy trail like one, too, he thought, looking at the wide smear of grey-green mud behind him. Below, the soldiers were prodding at ditches, convinced he was dead. Mitt rolled off the wall and thumped on to the jetty beyond before any of them chanced to look up and find reason to revise their opinion. He lay propped on his elbows, panting, clammy and almost tired out, and wondered which of these many little boats he had better get into. He knew it would have to be one he could manage easily alone. For that reason he rejected the beauty moored about ten yards down. 'Too big, my lovely,' he told her. 'One of them Siriol used to spit at, too.'

He looked round the rest. Some were big, some tubby, some the merest cockleshells. They all gleamed with splendid paint. Mitt thought he was weighing each one up as he looked at it, but, in fact, all he was doing was comparing them with that blue beauty ten yards away and finding them trash in comparison. He did not have time to make himself decide reasonably. A soldier down in the marsh yelled. Mitt bolted on hands and knees like a monkey. He was rolling across the blue beauty's cabin roof before he had time to think. She had a steering-well—purest pleasure-boat stuff, Mitt thought, dropping down into it. At least it hid him from the soldiers.

But not for long. Before Mitt had believed it possible, footsteps were pattering on the jetty outside. He tore open the double cabin doors and dived inside. If he had not been in such a hurry, he would have stopped then, and stared. He never could have imagined a ship's inside could be so beautiful—blue blankets and blue plush, a charcoal cooking stove, white paint and gold, and everything carved and ornamented and cleaned until it was more like a floating palace than a boat.

Ah, I always said the best wasn't good enough for me! Mitt thought, tiptoeing in a trail of green slime to the far end of the cabin. The boat's name was embroidered on all the blankets. Mitt could not resist pausing to spell out the name all this luxury went under. *Wind's Road*, he read. Very suitable. Suits me fine.

The next second, *Wind's Road* dipped and swung under people's feet. 'Isn't she beautiful!' Ynen said, dumping his sack on a locker. Mitt fumbled open a gilded cupboard, sweating with panic, and found himself confronting a bucket with a gilded seat. The bucket seemed to have roses painted all over it.

Flaming Ammet! thought Mitt. There really *is* nothing but the best on this ship! He shot the polished brass bolt to the cupboard with slimy, shaking fingers, and leant against the gilded wall, listening to feet scampering and shrill haughty voices calling overhead.

Part 3

Wind's Road

11

'Help me get the mainsail up, and then stand by to untie her,' Ynen said. 'Oh, look at this! She's all over mud! I knew those blessed sailors used her for lobsters when my back was turned!'

'I'll wash it down when we're sailing,' Hildy said. 'But do let's get going before those soldiers come. Most of the mud's only on the sail-cover.' She jumped on the cabin roof and helped Ynen unlace the cover.

Ynen unlaced busily beside her. He was not often angry, but he was now. Someone had been on *Wind's Road*, the apple of his eye, the one lovely thing that was truly his own, and made a mess of her in his absence. He could not forgive them. 'Honestly!' he said. 'Green smelly mud! You trust people, and they go and take advantage of you.'

'Father said you can't blame people for that,' said Hildy. 'I'll fold from my end, and be *quick*! He said the poor see the rich as their natural prey.'

'Just the kind of thing he would say!' Ynen said irritably. 'Fold it, don't just scrunch it! Mind you, he was probably right. I'll ask for a guard in future.'

'Some soldiers have just come through the gates,' said Hildy, causing Mitt to stand stiffly in his cupboard with his hands clenched. He had no idea who these arrogant fugitives could be, or why they were in such a hurry, but he knew they could not be in too much of a hurry for him.

'Cast off the moorings and push her off, then,' Ynen called, 'while I get the sail up. Make sure you don't push us out of the deep channel, though.'

121

Yes, and hurry up about it, for Old Ammet's sake! Mitt thought.

In a flurry of thumping, Hildy untied the mooring ropes and threw them on the planking, ready to be coiled later. Then she heaved on the jetty with all her might. Mitt gathered from the shifting and dipping what was happening. He heard the rhythmic *rattle, rattle*, as Ynen sent the mainsail up, hand over hand, and then a further pounding of feet combined with a stiff tilting, as Ynen bounded to the bows to get the foresails up, and Hildy plunged to the tiller and turned *Wind's Road* to catch the wind. After that came a slow *ripple, ripple*. *Wind's Road* got gently under way and slid along the channel towards the open sea.

They won't find us so easy to stop now, Mitt thought. Whoever these rich youngsters were, they could handle a boat all right. He supposed it was lucky they could. But he was still scared stiff. He could not see them getting away with it.

Hildy and Ynen anxiously watched the harbour wall glide by, and wished it would glide faster. Four or five soldiers were now running along the jetty behind, stumbling among ropes and shouting.

'What are they saying?' Ynen wondered.

Hildy gave a nervous giggle. '*Stop*, I think.'

'What am I supposed to do? Pull on the reins?' Ynen said, and laughed, too.

Soldiers appeared on the harbour wall, struggling up from the marsh behind, most of them muddy and all in a great hurry. No sooner did they see *Wind's Road* sliding proudly past and beginning to lean a little in the sea wind, than they became quite frantic. They shouted to one another and yelled at Hildy and Ynen to come back. One or two raised their guns.

'They're awfully close,' Hildy said.

'I know, but I daren't leave the channel,' said Ynen. The soldiers seemed so angry that he thought he had better pacify them. He jumped up on to the seat of the steering-well, with his foot on the tiller, and waved. 'It's all right,' he shouted cheerfully. 'We're only going out for a sail.'

A soldier sighted along a gun at him. Ynen over-balanced out of sheer astonishment and pitched down into the well, kicking the tiller as he went. As *Wind's Road* veered, the shot fizzed slantwise across where Ynen's head had been, only just missing the lovely whiteness of her mainsail.

'Ye gods!' said Hildy, and plunged for the tiller. Wind was hard in the sail, and she could feel the deep keel dragging in the mud of the Pool. Another shot zinged across behind Hildy's head.

Ynen rolled over as if he had been stung and stared anxiously up at the sail. 'Filthy swine! If he's holed my canvas, I'll have his guts for garters!'

Hildy dragged the tiller across. *Wind's Road*, her sail now properly filled, gathered majestic speed and foamed past the end of the wall. If the soldiers fired any more shots, they were lost in the sudden buffet of waves and the singing of the fresh wind. 'They can't possibly stop us now,' said Hildy. 'But, Ynen, they fired at us! What *did* they think they were doing?'

'They must all be filthy revolutionaries,' Ynen said. He was still very shaken. 'I'll make sure they're all hanged when we get back.'

'I think it must have been a mistake,' Hildy said, almost equally shaken.

Mistake all right, Mitt thought, shaking all over. They thought one of you was me. Now you had a taste of the way the rest of us feel. Don't like it, do you? What did I have to go and choose this boat for? I can't do a thing right today, can I? If only I'd got on any of the other ones, I

123

could have sat tight and let the soldiers think these two was me.

'It must have been a mistake,' Ynen agreed, recovering. 'I was just furious in case they'd spoilt the boat. We can sort it out when we get back.'

'We might not be able to,' said Hildy. 'Don't forget we'll be in awful trouble when we get back.'

'Oh, don't let's think of that now,' said Ynen. 'Hand over the tiller. I want to stand well out to miss the shoals.'

It was beyond Mitt to imagine what these two thought they were doing. First they ran from the soldiers as fast as he had. Now they talked about going back. The one thing Mitt was certain of, was that he was going to change that idea for them. He wriggled the bolt quietly back and came out of his gilded cupboard. There, he suddenly felt tired out. He stood listening to the sea frilling briskly past the hull and the creak and rattle of ropes. Feet batted the roof as Hildy began coiling ropes and resetting the foresails. Then came the clank and slosh of a bucket being dipped overboard. Rubbing and trickling sounds told Mitt that someone was washing off the mud he had brought aboard.

That's right, he thought. Bustle about. Siriol taught me to keep my boats particular. Ah, I feel like a wet wash-leather! And, since it was obvious that neither of his companions was intending to come into the cabin, Mitt flopped onto the port bunk for a rest. He could wait a bit to change their plans. The cabin, as small places do, quickly got up a fug. The mud on Mitt, the blankets, and the floor dried in big green flakes. Mitt drowsed.

When Hildy had washed the deck, she joined Ynen in the well. 'I love the way the wind blows in your face and makes your eyes all cool,' she said.

'It's my favourite feeling,' Ynen said.

124

Mitt hoped they would not go on like this. He did not want to hear their silly private thoughts. He was glad when Hildy said, 'The land's a long way off already.'

'The tide's running out,' Ynen explained. 'We'll be past the shoals in a minute. Then we'll turn north.'

'I like the south best,' Hildy objected.

'So do I. But the wind's wrong. We'd be close-hauled and I wouldn't dare tie the mainsheet when we had supper.'

'But there's a current to the north, isn't there? If we get into that, we'll never get back before dark, not close-hauled,' Hildy pointed out.

'I wasn't going that far,' said Ynen. 'I want to be back in daylight because of the shoals. I thought we'd go north till slack water, and then have supper, and then come back when the tide turned.'

'Supper at slack water sounds a nice idea,' Hildy admitted. 'And you are captain.'

Mitt thought supper at any time was a nice idea. And you'll share it three ways, he thought. Two for me and one for you. Then we'll see about who's captain, and carry on up North. He bestirred himself enough to fetch out Hobin's gun and see how it had fared in the dykes. To his relief, it was dry. He laid it by his head, within easy reach, and dozed again. *Wind's Road* rose and fell. The wind creaked in her sails. The water splatted past. Ynen and Hildy did not talk much. They were too happy. Time and the land slid away.

The next thing Mitt knew, *Wind's Road*'s motion was a more sluggish one. Hildy was saying angrily, 'Why did you tell me you knew, if you didn't?'

Ynen answered patiently, in the over-firm way people use when they are trying to convince themselves as much as the other person, 'I do know. That must be Hoe Point over there, and I'm sure Little Flate is in the dip beyond it.

All I said was that we'd come a bit further than I expected.'

Mitt blinked at the gilt and white portholes and was surprised to see it was still daylight, if they had come that far. *Wind's Road*, even allowing for the tide which helped her, was a fine fast boat. Unless it was tomorrow, of course. So much had happened to Mitt today that he felt as if it had gone on for a fortnight, even before he boarded this boat.

'Are you saying you think we've got into that current?' Hildy asked sharply. 'Because, if so, we'd better turn straight round now.'

'No, no. It's only slack water,' Ynen assured her anxiously. 'I can tell it's slack water by the way she's sailing.'

Mitt thought about the new motion of *Wind's Road*. It felt much more as if she were in a current to him, which suited him perfectly. In which case they were not where that flaming amateur at the tiller thought they were.

'Where does the current begin?' Hildy demanded.

'That's the trouble,' Ynen admitted. 'It may be Hoe Point, or it may not be till Little Flate. I'm not sure.'

Mitt cast his eyes to the elegant ceiling. The current began off Hoe Point, and Hoe Point came after Little Flate. I thought everyone knew that, he thought. Anyway, what's the fuss about? You can go right out to sea and get out of it again.

But *Wind's Road* was simply a pleasure boat. Ynen had never been out of sight of land in her. And he had always had sailors with him before, who knew the coast. 'I think perhaps you'd better fetch me the chart,' he said to Hildy. 'It's in the rack over the port bunk.'

'I think I'd better, too,' said Hildy, and she set off.

Woops! thought Mitt, as he heard her coming. The time had come for him to act. He snatched up Hobin's gun and cocked it as he scrambled off the bunk. Then he grabbed open the door and whirled out through it, just as Hildy was trying to come in.

They collided heavily. Hildy was slightly taller than Mitt and weighed a good deal more. But Mitt was moving twice as fast. Hildy crashed over backwards with a shriek. Mitt was thrown against the cabin. The gun went off with a bark and a jerk, and all but kicked itself out of Mitt's hand. It was like being hit over the wrist with a hammer. The shot, in a spatter of splinters, ploughed across the deck and into the sea. The well filled with sharp-smelling smoke.

'Ye gods!' wailed Hildy. She thought her back was broken.

Mitt choked for breath against the cabin door and peered resentfully through the smoke at the gun. He thought Hobin might have warned him that it kicked like that. Then, as the smoke cleared, he saw Ynen in front of him, hanging on to the tiller and the rope from the mainsail, very white in the face, and staring at the long splintered groove in *Wind's Road*'s beautiful planking. A right ninny, Mitt thought. Cares more about his boat being damaged than he does about his brother—sister, I mean. Hildy was painfully up on one elbow, glaring at Mitt. Mitt looked at both of them with the utmost contempt. They both had such a smooth look, with their skin well-filled and their hair thick and dark and healthy. He could see neither had gone hungry in their lives. What aroused his dislike most—though he did not realize it—was that Hildy and Ynen both inherited their looks from their father. Mitt looked at Ynen and saw a gentle version of Hadd's nose, and at Hildy and saw the narrow pale face of both Navis and Harchad; and though he did not recognize either, he detested them both on sight. And, since his opinion of females was low anyway, he encountered Hildy's glare and thought: She makes me sick—worse than her brother!

It was not surprising that they felt much the same about Mitt. They stared at Mitt's young-old face, and his lank, dull-coloured hair. They saw his bony hand was gripping a gun that looked like a collector's piece, that his pea-jacket was ragged, and that green mud was peeling from his long skinny legs. They knew he must be riff-raff from the waterfront. They suspected he was a thief, too. They thought he was disgusting.

'Well, we know what the soldiers were after. And where all the mud came from,' said Hildy.

'Are you badly hurt?' Ynen asked her. He felt very helpless. He dared not let go of the tiller to help Hildy, nor did he dare turn straight round and head back to Holand, much as he wanted to, for fear this disgusting stowaway loosed off with his gun again.

'No. I'm all right,' said Hildy, and struggled to her feet. 'He missed me, of course.'

'I was not aiming to hit you,' Mitt said, with great scorn. 'You ran into me like a whole herd of cows. You want to look out. This is a hasty kind of gun.'

'I like that!' said Hildy.

'If it's that hasty, why don't you put it away?' Ynen suggested.

Mitt ignored him. He looked up at the sail and the streaming flag at the masthead. It was a fair wind for the North, all right. The land was low blue hummocks to his right. It took Mitt only one glance to spot Hoe Point nearly a mile astern. The hump Ynen had taken for Hoe Point was Canderack Head. Mitt was impressed. It was still an hour off sundown too. He could not help grinning.

'Well, well,' he said. 'A good fast boat you got here. All set for the North, aren't we?'

Ynen's face went rather whiter as he grasped what the

stowaway might be planning. 'We're not going to take you North,' he said. 'If that's what's in your mind.'

'Not got much choice, have you?' said Mitt. He pretended to rub the gun on his sleeve. He did not really rub it, because he was very much afraid it would go off again. 'I've got this gun, haven't I?'

'You can shoot me if you want,' said Ynen. 'But I'm not taking you North.' He wondered if it would hurt very much, and thought that it probably would. He could only hope he would die quickly.

'Ynen, don't be an idiot!' said Hildy.

'He thinks I wouldn't dare,' said Mitt. 'Well, I would. Because I happen to be a desperate man.' That sounded good. And it had the advantage of being true. Mitt began to enjoy himself. 'If you won't take me North,' he said, 'I wouldn't kill you. I'd just put a bullet in your leg. Maybe both legs.' He was pleased to see Hildy glaring at him. 'Then in her,' he said. 'And then it would be rather a pleasure to knock this boat about a bit—scrape off the pretty paint, carve silly pictures in the decking, and so on.'

As Mitt had hoped it would, this threat truly upset Ynen. 'You dare touch my boat, you guttersnipe!'

'He doesn't know any better,' said Hildy.

'I thought that would worry you,' Mitt said, in high glee. 'All you've got to do to stop me is carry on as you are. Just keep sailing north.'

Ynen and Hildy exchanged a miserable look. They seemed to have gone from perfect happiness to a nightmare in a matter of seconds. Hildy wondered what had possessed her to lead Ynen into this. She had known there were revolutionaries at large. They should have stayed in the Palace. Ynen was thinking mostly of that current, and how he could persuade the boy that *Wind's Road* simply could not take him all the way North.

'Look here,' Ynen said, trying to sound fair and reasonable. 'We can't go North. We have to be back in Holand tonight or people will worry. What do you say to our landing you somewhere on the way back? How about—' Ynen looked over at the land and could not help feeling extremely uneasy about the shape of it. 'Hoe Point?' he said doubtfully.

Mitt gave what he hoped was an evil laugh. 'Go on! You couldn't get back to Holand tonight even if you went this second! You're in a nice fast northerly current, and in this wind you'll be lucky if you make it back by morning. Hoe Point is where that current starts, and that's Hoe Point back there, you flaming amateur! Look at your chart, if you don't believe me.' He saw he had demoralized them. Ynen's face was warm pink, and he was staring at Hildy as if the end of the world had come. Mitt was so pleased, that he added, 'I was sailing out of Holand before you were born.' That was a mistake. Hildy gave him a jeering look. Mitt scowled at her. 'Just sail North and don't give me any trouble,' he said. 'And you won't have any trouble from me. I can't say fairer than that, can I?'

Hildy sighed, to cover up her thoughts. Unpleasant as this boy was, he did bluster rather. Judging by Ynen's face, he was right about the current, but that did not mean he had thought of everything. 'I suppose we'd better humour him, Ynen,' she said. She stared hard at Ynen, slowly shutting her eyes and opening them, to show him that the boy would have to sleep sometime.

Mitt knew that, too. Even a sweet boat like *Wind's Road* would take three or four days to reach North Dalemark waters. No one could stay awake that long. Mitt was tired to death already. He felt his only course was to keep these children thoroughly intimidated by being as rough and dangerous and brutal as he could. He seemed to have

130

made a fairly good start. So, while Ynen was nodding gravely at Hildy to show her he understood, Mitt roared out, 'Right then. Now that's settled, go and get out your eatables. I'm starving. Hurry up!'

Hildy gave him a poisonous look. But it was fully supper-time, and she was hungry herself. She got up and dragged one of the sacks of pies out of the locker. Ynen took a careful breath, hoping it was not his last, and said, 'I'd rather you didn't speak to my sister like that.'

'What's she done to deserve any better?' Mitt said nastily. 'You watch it.' He was annoyed to see the two of them exchanging a look which was anything but intimidated. 'Come on. What's in that sack?'

He was relieved to see it was pies. He had been wondering how he could eat and still keep hold of Hobin's gun. He was afraid that if he let go of it for a moment, he would find himself being pushed overboard. But he could eat a pie with one hand.

The pies were scarcely as tempting as they had been. Gravy had run and juice had leaked, and then mingled and soaked back into other pastry. But Mitt was not in a state to care. He had not properly eaten anything since breakfast. He intended to go on with the intimidation by eating with great gobbling noises and huge slurpings, but as soon as he had a pie in his hand he forgot everything but how hungry he was. He only thought of eating. He was hardly able to attend to the splendid, unusual tastes, he was so frantic for food. He ate five steak pies, a pheasant patty, six oyster puffs, a chicken flan, four cheese-cakes and nine fruit tarts. He thought, as he drew at last to a gentle halt, that his gluttony had served to intimidate the children almost as well as making noises. They were staring, looking thoroughly chastened. Mitt managed, with no effort at all, to produce a monstrous belch, to make sure they knew exactly how rough and foul he was.

131

In fact, Ynen and Hildy were simply awed. They had not known it was possible to be so hungry.

That explains those thin legs, Hildy thought, looking at them. The sun was melting down into the sea, in a buttery haze. By its strong yellow light, Hildy saw that most of the mud had flaked off the boy's legs, showing him to be wearing odd old-fashioned breeches, with one leg red and the other yellow. The sight gave Hildy such a jolt that she burst out, 'I know who you are! You threw that bomb Father kicked away!'

12

Mitt looked from Hildy to Ynen. He saw the likeness now. His huge meal had left him slow and almost unbearably sleepy. His first thought was that it was funny. Hadd ruined him. Navis spoiled all his plans. And now these were Navis's children who were willy-nilly rescuing him. He chuckled. 'Now that's what I call justice,' he said. 'Navis is your pa then?'

Hildy stuck her chin up and did her best to overawe Mitt. 'Yes,' she said haughtily. 'And I'll have you know that I am betrothed to Lithar, Lord of the Holy Islands.'

'Oh, shut up,' Ynen said uncomfortably. 'You sound just like the cousins.'

Hildy had been imitating her cousin Irana boasting of her betrothal. She was annoyed with Ynen for noticing. She turned her back on him and looked hopefully at Mitt, hoping she had upset him by it at least.

Mitt laughed. 'Betrothed!' People got betrothed at Lydda's age, when they were eighteen and grown up. Hildy was only a little girl in pigtails. 'Bit young for that, aren't you?' Then the implications struck him. He was quite as alarmed as Hildy could have hoped, but he kept on laughing. He dared not let them see he was upset. This girl was important all right. He remembered Milda telling him about Lithar. That made certain that ships would pursue them from Holand, and more ships would be out to meet them from the Holy Islands. Mitt knew he was going to have to make them take this boat right out into the ocean. It was going to take days, and even then he might be caught. Just to think of it made him feel tired. 'Well, it's your business,' he said. 'Doesn't worry me.' He stood up. 'I'm off for a visit to that silly bucket in the cupboard. The one with roses on. No tricks while I'm gone now.'

Ynen's face was pink in the yellow light. 'They aren't roses. They're poppies,' he said.

'Roses,' said Mitt. 'And with a golden rim too. Amazing the way your kind has to have things pretty!' He went into the cabin.

Ynen shouted after him, 'Your kind built this boat!' Then, as soon as Mitt was at the end of the cabin, he whispered to Hildy, 'What are we going to *do*?'

Now Mitt had laughed at Hildy for being betrothed, she was determined to get the better of him. 'I've got an idea,' she whispered, 'to make him go to sleep.'

'Then we'll turn round,' Ynen agreed. 'What idea?'

'What are you whispering about?' Mitt yelled.

They dared not whisper any more. Ynen looked at the long splintered groove in *Wind's Road*'s planking and shivered. It was getting hard to see now. The sun had swum down below the horizon, leaving a yellow sky spread with straight black clouds. The sea was a melting, lighter yellow, as if the light had soaked into it. Hildy's face was dark. 'We're saying we ought to have a light at the masthead,' he called. 'It's the law.'

'Haven't you noticed?' Mitt bawled. 'I got nothing to do with the law.'

'Unlike you, we were brought up to be lawful,' Hildy called. 'Can I light the lamp in the cabin at least?'

Mitt came out of the cupboard and fumbled his way through the cabin. It was certainly getting dark. He felt sour and grim, and he ached all over. The red and yellow breeches would not do up properly after his great meal. He came out of the cabin and flopped down on the lockers. 'Please yourself,' he said. He was horribly weary.

134

Hildy smiled slightly and went into the cabin, where she was some time fiddling about before the lamp came on, as yellow as the sky outside. Then she moved on to the fat little water barrel, which was clamped to a special shelf above the stove. She undid the clamps and shook it. The barrel was completely full, so full that it did not even slosh. It took all Hildy's strength to shake it convincingly, but she had been prepared for that, because it was always kept full. No one dared let Hadd's family go thirsty.

'Oh, dear!' Hildy said. She was surprised how convincing she sounded. 'There's no water in this at all! I'm horribly thirsty, too.' This was true, but she thought she could bear it in a good cause.

As soon as she said this, Mitt realized that one of the many things wrong with him was an appalling thirst. It was all those highly spiced pies he had eaten. The thought of going without water for all the time it took to get North nearly made him burst into tears. Ynen was almost equally dismayed. His mouth suddenly seemed quite dry, and he had a moment when he would have liked to report those negligent sailors to Uncle Harchad. He licked his sand-papery lips and said, 'They sometimes keep wine in the lockers over the starboard bunk. Have a look, Hildy, for Old Ammet's sake!'

Hildy turned round to hide a triumphant smile and fetched the two bottles she had already found there. One was a half-full bottle of wine. The other was a square bottle of arris. It had been full before Hildy had poured a generous dollop of it into the wine. One way or another, she thought she had done for this wretched boy.

'Which will you have?' she said, showing Mitt the bottles in the twilight.

Mitt knew the rough, foul drink was arris. But he hated it too much. 'I'll have the wine,' he said, and he snatched the bottle from Hildy, feeling he could make up on

135

roughness and foulness that way, and took a long, guggling swig from it before Hildy could get him a cup from the cabin. He intended to drink the lot. But it tasted rather unpleasant. He passed Hildy back the bottle, a good deal less than a quarter full.

Hildy distastefully wiped the neck of the bottle and shared the rest into two cups for herself and Ynen. They sipped it and settled down to wait, while twilight grew into night.

Shortly, Ynen began to feel cheerful and Hildy slightly dizzy. As for Mitt, the wine, on top of his weariness, on top of his huge meal, had the inevitable effect. The low black humps of land kept spreading under his eyes like inkblots. The stars came out and looked fuzzy. His head kept dropping forward. At length, he stood up unsteadily.

'Going to have a lie down,' he said. 'No stunny fuff, now. Got ears in the back of my head.' He staggered off into the cabin, while Hildy and Ynen each stuffed a fist into their mouths in order not to scream with laughter, and flopped heavily down on the port bunk.

Hildy nudged Ynen meaningly and sat down with her back against the lockers, where she could see into the cabin. They waited for Mitt to fall asleep. But, with the best will in the world to do so, Mitt could not go to sleep. The movements of *Wind's Road* and the movements the wine had set up in his head seemed to be in direct conflict. Sometimes he was convinced the boat had got into a whirlpool. Sometimes he was sure his legs were high above his head. He sat up several times to see what was going on. And each time the elegant gilded cabin was exactly as it should be, gently rising and falling, and the lamp swinging. At length, he realized the queer things only happened when he had his eyes shut. So he kept them open.

The result was a set of horrible, half-waking dreams.

136

Mitt stared at Harchad's face in a gilded porthole, paralysed with terror. He ran endlessly from soldiers. He struggled through innumerable dykes. Several times he was shot in the stomach. Once he threw his bomb in front of Hadd, and Poor Old Ammet bent down, put out his straw arms and threw the bomb in Mitt's face. 'You're in really bad trouble,' he said, and he sounded just like Hobin. Then he fell to pieces like Canden. Mitt sat up with a yell of horror. After this, when he lay down again, things got a little quieter, until it was Libby Beer's turn. She ran at Mitt, with her fruity eyes wobbling on stalks, and kicked the bomb at him. 'I brought you up to do this, Mitt,' she said reproachfully. Then the bomb exploded, and Mitt started up with a scream.

Hildy and Ynen wished he would stop yelling and go to sleep. They wanted to turn round and sail home. The yells perturbed them. The boy must be disgustingly sinful. And the sounds made them think of the things they had heard about Uncle Harchad, and that terrible day the Northmen had been hanged. Meanwhile, true night came on and Ynen became frankly terrified. By this time, he had been at the tiller longer than he had ever been in his life. He had never sailed at night before. He was cold and cramped and tired, and scared of shoals he could not see. What he could see scared him even more. It was not dark the way it was in a closed room. The sea was there, faintly, all round, heaving and swelling limitlessly. The sky was a huge empty bowl, dark blue, covered with a littering of stars, and the land was only a feeling, far away to the right. The sail noises, and the swish and fizz of waves passing, only seemed to show how small and lonely *Wind's Road* was. Ynen suddenly became aware of fathoms and fathoms of empty water underneath them, too. He was hanging all alone in the middle of nowhere. Ynen clenched his teeth and kept the Northern Cross grimly over *Wind's Road*'s bowsprit, and it was all he could do not to yell out the way the boy in the cabin kept doing.

It was midnight before Hildy dared signal that Mitt was asleep. In fact, he had been asleep all along, but so restlessly that Hildy had not realized. She pulled the cabin door quietly shut and shot the elegant little bolt home.

'Thank goodness! You go to the foresails,' Ynen whispered.

Hildy crept forward, round the starboard side, to avoid any noise near Mitt. Ynen could see her clearly against the pallor of the sails. As soon as she was ready, he put the tiller over hard. *Wind's Road* surged round. Her sails ran out to the end of their ropes and swung back. The wind seemed suddenly twice as strong. Ynen kept his foot against the tiller and hauled in the mainsail frantically. Hildy collected the clapping foresails and dragged them the other way. *Wind's Road* stood still, head on to the wind, and seemed to flap and tremble in every part. Then she was round, tipped over much further, and apparently rushing through the water, but actually making very little way against the current. Ynen hauled in the mainsail as close as he could, in order not to waste time tacking, and they were now headed back to Holand. Hildy came back to the well, and they both sagged with relief.

Holand meant safety and bed and warm rooms. They had got the better of that dreadful boy. That was their first thought. Then they both remembered the trouble they would be in once they were back. That could not be helped, but they did wish the thought of the trouble did not go along with an empty, forsaken feeling. It was no good pretending Navis would defend them from the uncles. On the other hand, Uncle Harchad might forgive them a great deal if they brought him the boy who had thrown the bomb.

Hildy and Ynen peered at one another's faces, trying

to see what the other thought about that. The boy was a criminal. He had tried to murder their grandfather. Perhaps he was a friend of the man who had actually done so. But, all the same, he was a human being, much the same age as they were, and having bad dreams in the cabin. They both thought of Uncle Harchad kicking the Earl of Hannart's son, and the Earl's son cringing. It was easy enough to replace the Earl's son with a picture of that skinny, cocksure boy, and quite as unpleasant.

'We could put him off at Hoe Point, couldn't we?' Ynen whispered, and relieved Hildy's mind considerably.

Mitt, as he slept, was encountering Poor Old Ammet and Libby Beer at once. They rushed at him, one from either side. The world spun about and went wrong somehow. When Mitt opened his eyes, he knew the world was still wrong. It was going with a blunt, blundering, bucking motion, and tipping the wrong way. Those early years with Siriol had put some things deep in Mitt's brain. Funny, he thought. Close-hauled against a current. *Flaming Ammet!* He snatched up Hobin's gun and burst out of the cabin. He did not even notice the door had been bolted.

Outside, he had only to feel the wind on his face to know he was right. The children's smitten faces in the lamplight confirmed it. So did the Northern Cross low down behind them.

'Turn her back round!' he yelled. 'You sneaking idle rich, you! You think you can do just as you like, don't you! Go on, turn her back round!'

At this, despite the waving gun, Hildy lost her temper. He spoilt her entire scheme, and then he shouted insults. 'Don't you talk to me about doing just as we want!' She was so angry that she stood up and yelled in Mitt's face. 'You sneak aboard our ship, and order us about like dirt, and eat our food, and make us go where *you* want to go,

139

and then you have the nerve to say *we* always do what we want! You're worse than—than Grandfather! He was honest about it at least!'

'*Honest!*' bawled Mitt. 'Haddock honest! Don't make me laugh. He was robbing all Holand for years!'

'So you try to murder him, and order us about like dirt on top of that!' Hildy screamed.

'You *are* dirt, that's why!' Mitt thundered, waving the gun. 'Turn this boat back round!' Ynen clutched the tiller and feared for Hildy's life. In fact, neither he nor Mitt noticed that Mitt had not even remembered to cock the gun. He had not spun the empty barrel on either.

Hildy did not know and did not care. 'If we're dirt, I shudder to think what your family is!' she roared.

'Oh, shut up!' Mitt pointed the gun at Ynen. 'Turn this boat round, I said!'

For the second time that night, Ynen thought he was about to be shot. It gave him a cool kind of resignation. 'You did try to murder our grandfather,' he said. 'Give me one good reason why we should do anything to help you.'

Mitt noticed he was pointing the gun at Ynen and realized that Ynen did not regard the gun as a good reason. It sobered him rather. He felt considerable respect for this smooth-faced, hawk-nosed little boy, though, as for his sister—! 'Well then,' he said, 'your precious grandfather bust up my family. Is that a reason?'

'How did he do that?' Ynen asked, shivering with cold and weariness. Hildy added angrily, 'Whatever he did, *we* didn't do anything to you!'

'I'll tell you,' said Mitt. He rested his arm on the cabin roof and began to talk, jerkily and angrily at first, and then more reasonably, as he realized neither of them were trying to interrupt. He told them how he had been born at Dyke End, and how the rent had been doubled, and how this had forced his father to work in Holand and then forced them out of the farm. He told them how his father had never found proper work and so joined the Free Holanders, and how he had been betrayed over the warehouse—though he did not mention names—and disappeared, leaving Milda and himself to manage alone. He described how they had lived after that, and he could not help thinking as he talked that this was a funny kind of way to tell your life-story, with *Wind's Road* bucking through the water in the dark, and the half-lit faces of Hadd's grandchildren staring up at him as he talked. He told them about Hobin. 'And if it hadn't been for him,' he said, 'we'd have been turned out into the street when they knocked the houses down to make the Festival safe.'

'They didn't just turn them out, did they?' Hildy said. 'I thought—'

'Father had houses built for them,' said Ynen. 'But I don't think anyone else was going to bother. All the same,' he said to Mitt, 'you and your mother weren't there then. You were all right. You still haven't given me a reason.'

'Isn't that a reason?' Mitt demanded. 'There was Hobin never daring to put a foot wrong for fear of the arms inspectors, and us near on as hard up as ever because Hadd would put the rents up all the time. But never the price of guns—not he! We had to pay through the nose to support those soldiers, so that they could make us scared to stir hand or foot. You don't understand—can't you think how it feels when everyone you know is scared sick, all the time? You couldn't trust people. They'd turn round and tell on you, any time, even if it weren't you done it, because they didn't want to get marched off in the night themselves. That's not how people should be.'

'It isn't,' Hildy agreed.

'I grant you that,' said Ynen. 'But you're talking about

141

everything. You haven't told me one thing Grandfather did to *you*. I still don't see why we should help you. But I've heard things about Uncle Harchad. I don't mind landing you at Hoe Point, so you'll have a chance to get away.'

Yes, Mitt thought, in full view of all the ships coming out to look for them. Very safe. Talking to this boy was like bashing down a weak little plant that kept springing up again in your face. 'You might as well take me back to Holand and be done,' he said. 'If I'm not caught landing, I'll be caught in the Flate straight after.'

'Well, you did throw a bomb,' said Ynen. 'And I can't see why you did. There must have been lots of people in Holand far worse off than you. Why did *you* do it?'

That was a home question. Twenty-four hours earlier, Mitt could have given all sorts of answers. He could have told them at least that it was to be revenged on Siriol, Dideo, and Ham. But he had gone out of his way *not* to be revenged. And he had run and run and run. He did not know what he thought he had been doing. He was reduced to answering with another question. 'Could *you* have seen things so wrong and not think you ought to do something about it?'

This in its turn was a home question to Ynen and Hildy. They had indeed seen things wrong. All Ynen had done was wish he could whirl a rattle in Hadd's face. All Hildy had done was tear a bedspread and make empty threats. Then they had gone out sailing—a piece of defiance which had thrown them in the way of this boy. And he had not only told them more things that were wrong, but he had demanded that they help him. With the result that they were now sailing back to Holand to deliver him to Uncle Harchad.

'Ynen—' said Hildy.

'I know,' said Ynen. 'All right. We'd better take you North. Hildy, could you go to the foresails again?'

142

Mitt was rather taken aback. He knew he had not given Ynen a reason. He felt dishonest, and shamed. What would happen to these two in the North? He thought of the Northmen shuffling through Holand to be tried and hanged. 'See here,' he said. 'All you got to do is land me near Kinghaven or whatsits—Aberath—and I'll do nicely. Or you might try Tulfa. Then you go back to the Holy Islands. You'd be all right there if she's betrothed to Lithar—What's your name, by the way?'

'Hildrida,' said Hildy. 'Hildy for short. And this is Ynen. What's yours?'

'Mitt,' said Mitt.

'Oh not another Alhammitt!' said Hildy. 'That must make at least twenty I know!'

'Common as dirt,' agreed Mitt.

Ynen had been thinking over what Mitt had suggested. Tired as he was, he began smiling. 'Let's go to the Holy Islands, Hildy. I'd love to see them.'

Hildy just could not see herself sailing up to the Holy Islands and announcing she was Lithar's future wife. The idea made her stomach squirm. But she looked at Ynen and decided he was too tired to be argued with.

Mitt could see how tired Ynen was too. He remembered how he used to feel on a long stint aboard *Flower of Holand*. 'How about you getting some rest, now we seem to know where we're going?' he said. 'I can sail her for you. Can she?'

'Naturally I can,' Hildy said haughtily.

So it was settled that they divide the rest of the night into three watches. Ynen reluctantly took his numb hand off the tiller and watched Mitt settle into his place. He felt very dubious as he stumbled off to the cabin. But he supposed that if Mitt could tell in his sleep when they turned the other way, he must be able to handle *Wind's Road*. As Ynen lay down, he heard Hildy walking uncertainly forward over the roof, half blind from the light of the cabin. He saw Mitt's bony hand pushing the tiller firmly over. Once more *Wind's Road* surged round. Her sails ran out, clapped and filled. Ropes rattled as Mitt and Hildy reset them. And shortly Ynen felt the tug and surge of *Wind's Road* riding properly northward, and he knew Mitt could indeed manage her. He fell asleep, to the creak of ropes and the hurrying of dark water.

13

The night seemed extraordinarily long. Mitt stayed at the tiller for as much of it as he could. He wanted to get a good start Northwards. It felt good to be handling a boat again, particularly a responsive racing boat like *Wind's Road*. But with the good feeling went long, mindless boredom. There was nothing to do but watch the slowly wheeling stars and listen to the whelming of the huge sea. Mitt did make several honest efforts to decide just what he thought he had been doing back in Holand. But every time he started to think, he came to, some time later, to find he had been thinking of nothing at all. At length, the stars began taking little jumps through the sky. Mitt did not know if he had been asleep while they moved or not, but he saw he had had enough. He hitched up the tiller and woke Hildy.

Hildy was so sleepy that she took her watch almost unconscious. It seemed a very long time. Then Hildy found herself doubled painfully over the tiller in a paler world. The sea was dark and glossy. A white wave fizzing past had woken her. Hildy hobbled off like an old woman and woke Ynen.

Ynen, much more refreshed by six hours' sleep than Hildy felt he had any right to be, went gaily out into whitening dawn. The bank of mist where the land was seemed too near. Ynen corrected their course and tightened ropes, and sang while the sun came melting red and yellow out of the mist. Now it was settled, and they were going North, it felt like the best holiday Ynen had ever had. When Mitt came out a while after, *Wind's Road* was sailing briskly in a brisk wind, under a streaky grey sky. The land was a chalky smudge, and the vigorous grey waves were galloping North too, dividing into two lines of white round *Wind's Road*'s eager bows. Hildy crawled out later still, groaning. It was so early.

They got the pies out. They were staler, soggier, and much less appetizing. 'I reckon,' Mitt said, 'that they'll be old enemies by the time we make Kinghaven—if they last till then.'

'They ought to. We've got two sacksful,' said Ynen, and could not help laughing at the look on Mitt's face.

'Then it's only water that's the worry,' said Mitt.

'Well actually, the water-barrel's full up,' Hildy confessed.

For a moment, Mitt could hardly credit that he had been so taken in. Then, to Hildy's relief, he shouted with laughter. 'I bet you were mad when I didn't have the arris!' he said. 'Us rough fellows are supposed to love that, aren't we?'

Hildy bent her head, embarrassed. She was even more embarrassed when Mitt tasted the water and remarked that it was some of the sweetest-tasting water he had ever drunk. She and Ynen were both shuddering at its musty wooden taste.

Ye gods! What must the water be like down in Holand! Hildy thought. She was so uncomfortable that she jumped up and fled across the cabin roof, babbling that she thought the foresails needed looking at.

'Want a hand?' Mitt called.

Hildy did not know what to say, and did not answer. Mitt was just getting up to help her, when Ynen said, in great surprise, 'I say! What on earth are those doing here?'

Mitt looked. To his astonishment, a number of half submerged apples were bobbing in the waves beside the boat. He watched them apparently climb up a wave, then get left behind by it, the way floating things do. There were dozens of them—bright red and yellow water-sodden apples, all round *Wind's Road*. And there were what looked like wisps of grass as well, and some almost water-logged flowers.

'Oh, I know!' said Ynen. 'Those must be the garlands from the Festival. I suppose the tide brought them out into the current.'

'No good to eat, are they?' Mitt wondered.

There was a scream of excitement from Hildy. She was pointing, jabbing her finger seawards, at something floating ahead. For a nasty second, Mitt and Ynen both thought it was a drowned person. There was sodden flaxen hair and an outflung hand. Then it rolled, and seemed simply a mat of white reeds.

'Can't you see!' screamed Hildy. 'It's Poor Old Ammet!'

Wind's Road veered and shivered in the excitement of that moment. Ynen almost let go of the tiller. Mitt ran from side to side. Whatever the differences between them, they were all three Holanders, and they knew this was the lucky chance of a lifetime.

'We'll miss him, we'll miss him! Hurry up, Mitt!' Hildy screamed. 'Bring me the boat-hook!'

Mitt plunged round on Ynen and seized the tiller from him. 'You go. I'll bring her round for you.'

Ynen knew the manoeuvre was probably beyond him. He let go of the tiller almost before Mitt had it and shot up along the deck, snatching up the mop and the boat-hook as he went. He thrust the mop at Hildy, and the two of them, waving their implements, balanced jubilantly on the pointed prow. As Mitt took *Wind's Road* racing past Old Ammet and then round again towards the wind, he was very much afraid either or both of them would join Old Ammet in the water. But they clung on. Mitt let the

147

mainsail out with a long rattle, to take the speed off *Wind's Road*, and she ploughed on, *bash-bash-bash*, with waves smacking at her bows and spraying Hildy and Ynen thoroughly. When they were a few yards off the floating straw figure, Mitt turned *Wind's Road* right into the wind, and she stood almost still, shaking and flapping. Hildy and Ynen both threw themselves on their faces and lunged at Poor Old Ammet.

Their efforts were agony to Mitt. They knew nothing about how to get things out of the sea, those two. Hildy prodded. Ynen was hanging right under the bowsprit like a monkey, wasting Mitt's accurate work by pushing Old Ammet further and further away. It was so clear that they were going to lose him, that Mitt hitched the tiller up and set off to help. *Wind's Road* promptly jigged round sideways to the waves, where the strong wind threatened to fill her sails again. Mitt saw that she could capsize that way, and hurried back to the tiller.

'Flaming mind of your own, you have!' he told *Wind's Road*. 'Sail me or I'll drown the lot of you—that's you!'

That jigging gave Ynen the extra foot he needed. He managed to get a grip on Old Ammet with the boat-hook. Hildy planted the mop on him to steady him, and together they tossed Poor Old Ammet aboard like the stook of corn he was.

Mitt marvelled that he could have taken that intricate mass of plaited corn for a drowned man. Old Ammet still had arms, legs, and a tufted head, but he was now more the shape of a starfish than a person. Most of his fine red ribbons were gone, and his face was cockeyed and blurred. He was a Poor Old Ammet indeed. All the same, they were delighted to see him. They all shouted, 'Welcome aboard, Old Ammet, sir!' which they all knew was what you said. Mitt turned *Wind's Road* joyfully back on her way again, while Hildy and Ynen first did an unsteady dance of triumph on the cabin roof, and then set about fixing Old Ammet to the prow like a figurehead—which was the other thing you were supposed to do.

Poor Old Ammet was limp and waterlogged. It was no easy matter to make him into a figurehead. Ynen fetched rolls of twine and rope. Mitt called advice. Hildy ransacked the cabin for things which might support that weight of wet wheat. Mitt called so much advice that Hildy snapped, 'Oh shut up! We all know you get Old Ammet out of the sea every year!'

There was really no answer to that. Mitt shut up, bitterly annoyed, and soothed himself by muttering, 'Flaming females! They're all the same. It goes right through.' He watched, haughtily, Old Ammet being threaded on a besom, a gilded picture-rail, and two wooden spoons, and then being lashed to half the door of the gilded cupboard that concealed that rose-covered bucket. Then he was tied very firmly across the bowsprit, where he lifted and fell proudly to the movements of the boat. Mitt knew he could not have done it better himself. So he said knowledgeably, 'He'll stiffen up. He's full of salt. Mind you, he may niff a bit.' Then he gave way to honest pride. 'Looks good, doesn't he?'

Ynen and Hildy thoroughly agreed. 'But,' Hildy said, 'why doesn't anyone ever find Libby Beer?' She lay down to peer under the mainsail, as if she expected to find Libby Beer just in the offing, in the other half of the grey, leaping sea.

'She's all grapes and squashy berries,' said Ynen. 'She must get waterlogged in no time. It would be a miracle if we had her, too.'

Mitt laughed and slapped the knobby pocket of his red and yellow breeches. 'I clean forgot to this moment! Miracle it is. Here. Look.' He dragged the little wax model of Libby Beer out of his pocket. Like Poor Old Ammet, she was rather the worse for wear. The wax berries were flattened, with cloth-marks imprinted on them, and the ribbons were muddy strings. But she could hardly have delighted Ynen and Hildy more had she been new and gay and gleaming.

'Oh, beautiful!' said Ynen. 'We must be the luckiest boat in the world. May I lash her to the stern?'

'Carry on,' said Mitt.

'She's lovely!' said Hildy, fingering Libby Beer while Ynen unrolled more twine. 'I've always wanted one of these, but they won't let us buy things at the stalls. Those little tiny rose-hips. How did you get her?'

'While I was on the run,' said Mitt. 'Lady at a stall gave her me for luck.'

'You mean she knew you were running away?' Hildy asked, reluctantly giving Libby Beer to Ynen to be tied behind the tiller.

'No,' said Mitt. He fixed his eyes on the gently heaving horizon and wished this silly female would understand what Holand was like for the likes of him. 'She found out I was on the run just after, when the soldiers came asking. She give me Libby Beer to cheer me up—I had a face as long as Flate Dyke, see, not knowing where to go or what I dared do. Then when the soldiers asked, she had to say she seen me. She didn't dare not tell. That's how people are. It's different for you.'

Ynen considered this while he tied careful knots round the wax figure. 'We're on the run, too, now—in a way. Why is it different? If a fisherman sees *Wind's Road*, he'll tell. And I don't feel miserable about it.'

Mitt knew Ynen had missed the point. He thought of Milda, Hobin and the babies, of all the waterfront people who used to laugh at him selling fish, all the dozens of people he would never see again, and he was almost exasperated enough with Ynen to push him from the stern where he was crouching, into the sea. 'But you've not put yourself outside the law, have you?'

'Yes we have, in another way,' Hildy said. She thought Ynen had missed the point, too, and the only way to cover it up seemed to be to let Mitt know that they had their difficulties as well. She told him about their pretended escape with the bedspread and their real escape with the pies. Mitt tried not to grin. It was all a game to them.

It did not seem to Ynen that he had missed any point. He looked admiringly at the little Libby Beer, already shiny with spray, and proudly over at Old Ammet, lifting and falling at the bowsprit, while he thought over all he now knew about Mitt. It did not add up properly. He wanted to know why. 'Look here,' he said. 'You must have known you'd be on the run, and what it would be like, once you'd thrown the bomb. Didn't you make *any* plans to get away?'

'Were you standing there waiting to be blown up?' Hildy asked, thinking this would explain Mitt's odd behaviour on the waterfront.

Mitt eyed the heaving horizon. He supposed he might as well tell them, if they could tell him about their silly escape with their pies. There was something odd about Hildy's story, though—something not quite right. Mitt felt that as strongly as Ynen evidently felt it about his. 'They made plans—the Free Holanders,' he explained, 'but it wasn't in me to listen, because I was planning to get myself taken. I was aiming to kill Hadd, and when they caught me, I was going to tell them the Free Holanders set me on, to pay them out for informing on my father. It was them that informed on him. I've been planning that half my life. You might say my mother brought me up to do it. And your pa goes and spoils it in half a second. That's what had me standing there—the waste!'

There was silence from Ynen and Hildy. Mitt did not

wonder he had shocked them. He took his eyes off the horizon and caught them exchanging a look that was not shocked, but deeply puzzled.

'And so it *was* a waste!' he told them aggressively. 'Three years I saved gunpowder. Five years me and my mother planned it. And your pa kicks the bomb instead of grabbing me. Then I run straight at those fool soldiers, and they lose me. What was I supposed to do after that? Walk in the Palace gates and say, "Here I am"?'

'It's not that,' said Ynen. 'You keep saying everyone informs because they're frightened—and I believe you—but why do you blame the Free Holanders for informing and not the woman who gave you Libby Beer?'

'She wasn't a friend of mine, was she?' Mitt said gruffly.

There was a further silence, puzzled and uncomfortable, filled only with the sound of *Wind's Road*'s ropes pulling in a wind that seemed to be slackening. Hildy and Ynen looked at one another. They were both thinking of the Earl of Hannart's son and wondering how to say what they thought.

'I don't understand about mothers,' Hildy said cautiously. 'Not having one myself. But—' She stopped and looked helplessly at Ynen.

'You do know,' Ynen blurted out, 'your mother does know, does she, the kind of things that happen when people get arrested for your kind of thing? Do you know about my Uncle Harchad?'

Harchad's face, and the terrible fear that had gripped Mitt when he saw it, seemed to have mixed in Mitt's mind now with his nightmare of Canden shuffling to the door. Under his thick jacket, his skin rose in gooseflesh. But he was not going to let Hildy and Ynen know how he felt. 'I've heard things about Harchad,' he conceded.

Hildy shivered openly. 'I saw. One thing.'

152

'That's why we said we'd take you North,' said Ynen.

'Thanks,' said Mitt, and he stared woodenly at the horizon. He was not sure quite what was the matter with him. He felt sick and cold. He shook Canden and Harchad out of his mind, but he still felt as if a load of worry had fallen on him, making his head ache and drawing his face into a strange shape. Ynen and Hildy stared, because Mitt's face seemed all old, with scarcely any young left in it. 'See here,' Mitt said, after a minute, 'I feel wore out again. Mind if I go for a lie down?'

Hildy took the tiller without a word. Mitt plunged into the cabin, on to his favourite port bunk, and fell heavily asleep. 'Ynen, what did you have to go and say all that for?' Hildy whispered, wholly unfairly.

'Because I didn't understand,' said Ynen. 'I still don't. Why has he gone to sleep like that?'

'I think it's because you—we—upset him more than he wanted to think about,' Hildy answered. 'He's in an awful muddle. It must be lack of education.'

'He's muddled me, too,' Ynen said crossly. 'I don't know whether to be sorry for him or not.'

The slackening wind brought a drizzle of rain. Ynen and Hildy found a tarpaulin and wrapped it round their heads and shoulders. The rain increased, and the wind strengthened slowly, until the sea was so choppy that Hildy found it hard to steer and hold the sailrope too. The sail was yellow-grey and heavy with rain.

'Miserable!' she said. Water dripped off the end of her nose and chin.

'I wonder if we ought to take in a reef,' Ynen said.

Just before midday, the choppiness woke Mitt. Wind's changed, he thought. Coming more off the land.

He stumbled muzzily out into the well to find a real downpour. Rain was battering down into the well and

153

swirling along the planking, going *putter, putter* on the tarpaulin over Hildy and Ynen's heads, and making a myriad pockmarks in the yellow-grey waves alongside. Mitt was not sure he liked the angry tooth-shape of all those pockmarked waves.

'I've been wondering if I ought to reef—just in case,' Ynen said to him.

Mitt looked at him, frowning sleepily against the cold water in his face. Beyond Ynen, the little figure of Libby Beer was shiny as new with rain water. Beyond her, dim behind veil upon veil of silver rain, was what looked like a mountain walking up the sky from the land, monstrous, black, and impending.

'What do you think about reefing?' Ynen asked.

Mitt stared at that mountain of black weather, aghast. Last time he had seen anything like it, Siriol had made for Little Flate as fast as *Flower of Holand* could move, and they had hardly got there in time. This was twice as near. There was no chance of making land. Those two had been sitting with their backs to it, but all the same! 'Flaming Ammet!' said Mitt.

'Well, I thought I'd reef,' Ynen said uncertainly.

'What am I doing standing here letting you ask?' Mitt said frantically. 'You should have woke me an hour ago. Three reefs we'll need, and let's be quick, for Old Ammet's sake! I bet this boat handles real rough.'

Ynen was astounded. *'Three?'* Hildy was so surprised that she lost her hold on the wet tiller. *Wind's Road* tipped about and the boom swung over their heads. Mitt caught it, braced himself against the weight of wind and sopping sail, and tied it down with such haste that Ynen began to see he was in earnest. He slipped out from under the tarpaulin and scrambled on to the cabin roof in the hammering rain, to the ropes that lowered the mainsail. When he saw the weather the tarpaulin had been hiding from him, he did not feel quite so surprised at Mitt's command. Ynen had never been out in any weather so black himself, but he knew when the sky looked like that, you saw all the shipping making for Holand as fast as it could sail. He let the huge triangle of the sail down a foot or so. Mitt began tying the resulting fold down against the boom by the little strings that dangled from the canvas, and tying as if for dear life. 'We have got a storm sail,' Ynen called.

Mitt shook his head, knowing how long it would take two boys to get in this mass of great wet sail and bend on another. 'We'd be caught with our pants down. Maybe we are anyway. She rides awful high. Get tying. Quick!'

They tied cold wet reef-knots until their fingers ached. Hildy stood on the seat, with her foot on the tiller and laced away at the sail over her head. Mitt and Ynen crawled up and down the cabin roof, tying knots there. They did it again with a second fold, and then all over again with a third. By this time, *Wind's Road*'s sail was an absurd little triangle, with the long bare mast towering above it. The rain was coming in gusting clouds now. They could see nothing much beyond a grey circle about thirty feet across. But, inside that circle, the waves were yellow-green, heaving high and pointed. The bare mast swept back and forth. The deck was up and down, sickeningly steep both ways.

'Don't untie that boom till we got the foresails in,' Mitt shouted at Hildy. Somehow the weather was much louder, though it was hard to tell what was making the noise. Mitt and Ynen hauled and grappled at the clapping sails in the bows, slithering on the wet planks round Old Ammet. One moment they were skywards, soaring into lashing rain. The next, Old Ammet was plunging, like a man on a toboggan, down and down a freckled tawny-grey waveside.

Ynen swallowed giddily. 'Is it going to be bad?' he yelled.

Mitt did not try to deceive him. 'Real shocker!' he bawled back. But he thought it was just as well that he did not have breath to spare to explain to Ynen that these autumn storms sometimes went on for days. Mitt knew they would be drowned long before the day was out. Now he was fully awake, he knew, with nasty vividness, that *Wind's Road* would capsize. He could feel it in the movement of her. She was only a rich man's pleasure boat after all. And, as Old Ammet launched himself furiously down another freckled hill of water, Mitt was as terrified as he had been when he crouched among the marble-playing boys in Holand. He was blind with panic. It was as if he had run away from himself and left the inside of his head empty. Mitt knew this would not do. It was no use thinking Ynen could manage by himself. He had to run after himself, inside his head, and bring himself back with one arm twisted up his back, before he was able to pick up an armful of soaking sail and stagger with it to the hatch. He thought, as he pushed and kicked it down and clapped the cover on and banged the bolt home, that there really was nothing left of the old fearless Mitt any more. He had never been in charge of a boat before. He wanted to whimper, because Siriol was not there.

He and Ynen crawled back across the see-sawing cabin roof. Hildy, seeing them coming, obeyed instructions and started to untie the lashings round the boom. She knew they had been idiots, she and Ynen, sitting under that tarpaulin and letting the storm creep up on them. She had been trying to behave with smart efficiency ever since. She did not want people like Mitt thinking her a fool. But she had no notion how fierce the wind was now. She loosened the main knot.

The wind tore it all out of her hands. The sail slammed round sideways, jerking *Wind's Road* broadside on to the next huge wave. The boom mowed across the cabin roof and caught the side of Ynen's head with a *thuck*. It knocked him clean out. He was carried helplessly with it towards the side.

14

Hildy screamed. Mitt flung himself after Ynen and just managed to catch him round the ankle with both hands. Water thundered down over them, hard and heavy, and fell away, sucking and rilling, pulling Ynen against Mitt's straining arms and dragging both of them down the tilted cabin roof. Mitt had no idea how they survived, any more than Hildy. Hildy knew *Wind's Road* had gone like a bullet, slantwise through the top of that wave. But how she came to have the fighting tiller in one hand and the sailrope in the other she did not know.

'Ye gods! I'm sorry!' she screamed at Mitt, when she saw him, drenched and horrified, sliding down from the cabin roof and heaving Ynen after him.

'Don't dare do that again!' Mitt screamed back. *Wind's Road* was plunging downhill now, and he made use of it to slide Ynen into the cabin. Ynen was alive, to his great relief, stirring and muttering miserably. Mitt did not dare linger with him. He wedged him hurriedly in place with blankets. 'Don't move!' he bawled, though the cabin was almost quiet. 'You took a knock there.' *Wind's Road*, trembling sickeningly, mounted upwards again. Mitt threw himself downhill into the well and wrestled the tiller out of Hildy's weak hand. The storm was too loud even for screaming now.

Mitt found he had arrived just in time. The huge autumn storm roared and howled and bashed around them. *Wind's Road* was half sideways in the trough between two heaving walls of water, caught in the backwash of the last wave. Worse still, while she wallowed there, half the thundering gale was blocked by the water. The sail was coming smashing across and threatening to capsize her. Mitt, as he worked at the sluggish tiller, shrieked and made gestures at Hildy to pull the rope in and hold the sail. It seemed a lifetime before she understood and the rope came yelling over its blocks into her hands. She still had a silly puzzled look on her face, but Mitt had no time to attend. He could only thank Old Ammet he was stronger since he was last in a boat. *Wind's Road* was the hardest thing he had ever had to handle. She would *not* come about. They were creeping crabwise up a great slope of water, up and up, until they were hanging, almost over on one side, just beneath the raving crest of the wave. *Wind's Road* had suicidal urges. Mitt felt her going over, and heaved on the flaccid tiller.

The full force of the storm hit them as he did so. Mitt and Hildy both screamed. Their voices burst out of their throats without their being able to help it. The wind hit with a roar and a crash. The sailrope yelled out from between Hildy's fingers, nearly dislocating both her shoulders. Great lumps of water loomed and fell, smashing across the bows, banging down on the cabin, thundering over Hildy and Mitt, until they were as bruised as they were wet, and went fizzing and boiling away behind.

The man in the bows with the flying fair hair understood their danger and leant into the wave, dragging at *Wind's Road*'s forward rigging. *Wind's Road* did not want to come, but Mitt thought the man dragged her round by main force. He saw him clearly for a moment, with his hair as white as the snarling spray, gesturing aside the horses that were trying to overwhelm *Wind's Road*. Then *Wind's Road* lashed herself over the edge and down another watery hillside, and Mitt had all his work cut out to hold her straight. Beside him, Hildy, to his relief, was trying to help the sailrope as it came rattling in again when *Wind's Road* plunged.

Mitt could not hold her straight. *Wind's Road* went down into that valley of water and wallowed sideways, with every intention of never coming up. But the man was there against the foam-laced surface of sliding black water, wrenching *Wind's Road* straight for him. Mitt wanted to thank him, but by that time *Wind's Road* was on her sickening way upwards again to lay herself sideways to the next wavetop.

And so it went on. Mitt thought they went from sudden death to sudden death so often that they lost count of how long. The world was a lathering uproar, and *Wind's Road* hit and buffeted until she jerked all over. Mitt and Hildy were bashed by water until they hardly felt it. Water fizzed into the cabin and swirled round Ynen. The tarpaulin floated round the well, mashed up and neglected, and got in the way, but neither Hildy nor Mitt had time to get rid of it. Hildy's attention was all for the rope, either yelling out or rattling in, and Mitt's for battle with the tiller, *Wind's Road*'s yawing death-urges, and the gestures of the fairhaired man when the wind hit with a clap and a shout.

He and Hildy got quite used to seeing him, up there in the bows, either grey with storming rain or whiter against the black side of a wave. They were glad to see him there. But the horses bothered them both. They were beautiful grey horses galloping, arching their necks under flying manes, dashing up the slopes of waves, frolicking and rearing on the crests. Mitt and Hildy never had time to look at them properly, but they saw them all the time out of the corners of their eyes. They knew they were imagining things. Sailors told stories of horses playing round doomed ships, frolicking at the death of mortals.

Mitt and Hildy would much rather not have seen them. They kept their eyes ahead on the next danger coming. But there were still horses galloping on both sides of the boat, though ahead there was nothing but fizzing foam and shuddering waves, and occasionally the man with the flying light hair.

He's doing us no harm, that's for sure! Mitt thought.

In the cabin, Ynen got to his elbows and put a hand to the big tender lump on the side of his face. He could have sworn somebody had shaken him and told him to get up. But he was all alone, lying among sopping blankets. 'Ugh!' he said. He could feel *Wind's Road* yawing and staggering, and he wondered what was causing this awful sluggish movement.

The cabin door slammed open against the stove, and a wave of dirty water rushed down on Ynen, soaking him to the bone. He stared uphill at two pairs of slithering feet and more water bashing across them. Ye gods! he thought. The water we must be shipping! He scrambled up while he was thinking it and climbed uphill into the well.

The first thing that met his eyes was the lovely head of a thoroughbred grey horse, flying past among the rain and spray. It was gone at once, as if it was galloping faster than *Wind's Road* could sail. Ynen was hit by the rain and gasped. It was lashing down. He could hardly see the withered and wind-whipped figures of Mitt and Hildy, let alone the woman kneeling on the stern behind them. It was as much as Ynen could do to make out that this woman had long red-gold hair, flapping and swirling in the wind. He saw she was giving Hildy a hand with the rope—or he thought she was, until he realized she was pushing at the tiller as Mitt braced his feet and shoved it. The rain made Ynen very confused. But he realized the woman was pointing at the locker where the pump was.

161

'Yes, of course,' Ynen said to her. He was still dazed, but he clipped the lid of the locker up, moved the tarpaulin off the scuppers and began to pump.

The storm raved on for another hour or more. Ynen pumped away, without a hope of emptying the boat, but perhaps doing just enough to prevent *Wind's Road* swamping. Sometimes he wished, in the fretful way one does in dreams, that the lady in the stern would help him, too, though he knew she had enough to do with Mitt and Hildy. Sometimes he thought the man up in front might come back and give him a hand. He knew this was an ungrateful thought. The man had stopped *Wind's Road* turning over several times, and he was keeping off the horses too. But Ynen's arms ached so.

At length, the roaring and thundering grew less. *Wind's Road*, from sliding up and down, went to heaving and lurching, and from that to a staggering *slap-slap-slap*, with only the odd spout of water coming aboard. They sailed through a brown light. The rain hissed down and seemed to flatten the tossing sea further. Then the rain stopped. Ynen, pumping and pumping, felt far too hot.

'We did it!' Hildy said. 'It's over.' As she said it, Ynen heard the squelching that meant the bilge was nearly dry. He straightened his back thankfully.

There was a blinding sun right in front of the bows, low on the edge of the sea. The storm clouds were above the sun in a heavy black line, getting smaller and smaller. It was hot. *Wind's Road* had steam rising from her decking and salt crystals forming like frost on her. The small triangle of sail sagged. There was a mess of tangled ropes everywhere, and *Wind's Road* was riding with a surge and swing unlike any Ynen or Hildy had ever experienced. Mitt knew it for the surge and swing of deep ocean. He looked back, across the little salt-coated figure of Libby Beer, away and away over empty sea. There was no land.

Weak and trembly though they all were, they burst out talking and laughing, in over-loud hoarse voices, telling one another what each had thought the worst bit was. Ynen said it was when he saw the boom on its way to hit him. Hildy said it was the horses.

'No,' said Mitt. 'It was that first time she tried to capsize, just before we saw the man.'

'I thought that, until the horses kept being there,' said Hildy. 'And I tried to tell myself I was just imagining them because I was so scared and tired. But I knew they were there.'

'I saw one quite close to, just before Libby Beer told me to pump,' Ynen said. 'Didn't they go fast!'

'Hey, look,' said Mitt. 'We haven't all run mad, have we?'

'Of course not,' said Ynen. 'Libby Beer was sitting behind you, helping you sail her, and Old Ammet was standing in the bows stopping her sinking and keeping the horses off. I saw both of them.'

Hildy looked anxiously at the big purple bruise on the side of Ynen's face, and then at the tiny, salt-coated figure of Libby Beer on the stern. 'I didn't get a chance to turn round, but isn't she rather small?'

'Old Ammet got carried away in that first big wave, for sure,' Mitt said, and hoisted himself weakly on the cabin roof to see.

He could see a bundle of whitish straw, gently rising and falling in the bows. He crawled forward, hardly able to believe it. Old Ammet was still there, contrary to all reason, every plaited wheat-stalk of him, miraculously in one piece. There were strips of seaweed wrapped about him and tangled in his wheaten hair, as if he had got his lost ribbons back, changed by the sea to green and brown. But round his neck, broken and sodden, was draped a garland made of wheat, burst grapes, and drooping flowers.

'Come and look at this!' Mitt yelled.

They left *Wind's Road* to sail herself and stood in a row with their clothes steaming, looking down at Old Ammet and his garland from the Festival. 'I think we ought to thank him, and Libby Beer,' said Hildy.

Mitt was very self-conscious at the idea, but he made himself growl 'Thank you, sir,' with Hildy and Ynen, and then turn round and say 'Thank you, lady,' to Libby Beer. After all, he had seen Old Ammet with his own eyes.

Then Hildy started to shiver violently. Mitt knew what was needed. He waded through the soaked blankets on the cabin floor and fetched the bottle of arris. He made Hildy and Ynen have a good swig, and then took one himself. They stood about in the well going *'Um-pwaugh!'* and making awful faces.

'Shocking taste, isn't it?' said Mitt. 'Wait a moment, though. There comes a sort of *boing* inside, and then it warms the insides of your ears.'

The *boing* came. It made them feel so much better that they got out the pies and fell on them ravenously. Their hands shook as they ate, and their fingers were white, wrinkly and blistered, even Mitt's, which had got a little soft-skinned in Hobin's workshop.

'I can't sail all through the night,' Hildy said wearily.

'We've got a sea-anchor,' said Ynen, and looked at Mitt to see what he thought.

Mitt was dog-tired too. But he knew autumn storms could come one on top of the other. He did not know what to do.

'I know,' said Hildy, and she crawled forward to the mast. Mitt, with Ynen nodding and yawning beside him, stared at the soles of her feet and heard her say, 'Please, Old Ammet, can you look after the boat tonight? But if there's another storm, could you wake Mitt up and tell him, please.'

'That's right! Pick on me!' Mitt called. 'Tireless Mitt, they call me. Think I don't wear out or something?' He turned to the figure of Libby Beer. 'Excuse me, lady. She wants you to wake me if there's trouble. She thinks I'm made of the same stuff as what you are. So, if I'm needed, and you have to give me a nudge, do you mind waking her up too? She can sit and feed me nips of arris.'

The cabin was crowded and close that night. Nobody needed blankets, so they hung them in the well to dry. They all slept like logs, even Hildy, who had the small forward bunk which had been designed for her when she was nine. If Old Ammet or Libby Beer had tried to call Mitt in the night, he did not hear them. But all seemed well in the morning. The sea was flat and the sun made a liquid yellow path to the gently drifting *Wind's Road*.

'I think I hate pies,' said Hildy.

'You want to try mixing about a bit,' Mitt told her. 'You know—cherry flan and steak. Makes a change.'

'You're cheating,' said Ynen. 'Those were squashed together anyway. Try oyster and apple, Hildy. It's—well, it's different.'

After this decidedly strange breakfast, they cleaned up *Wind's Road*, and got very hot doing it. The heat told them all that they could not yet be very far North. None of them had the slightest idea where they were. As there was no land in sight, no chart Ynen could produce was any use to them. The only thing they were sure of was that they had been blown out into deep ocean, probably more west than north.

'I'll steer north and east,' Ynen said. 'When we sight land, I'll keep it just on the horizon, until we see somewhere we can recognize. Tulfa Island should be easy to find. And we know that belongs to the North. Let's get the sails up.'

Shortly, with sails set again, in a light wind, *Wind's*

Road was sailing on. Mitt sat lazily just above Old Ammet, listening to the water running past her sides and admiring the way her bows cut the sea sweetly asunder. In fair conditions, *Wind's Road* was a beauty, he thought. He could hardly believe she had been doing her damnedest to drown them all yesterday.

'There's something to port over there,' Ynen called. 'Can you see what it is?'

Mitt looked too far, then too near, and finally saw a small dark thing lolloping on the swell, about quarter of a mile away. 'Could be a boat,' he called.

'That's what I thought,' Ynen called back, and pushed the tiller over, with a fine *ruckle-ruckle* of water from *Wind's Road*'s elegant bows.

'Hey! What are you doing?' Mitt called, jumping up.

'Going to look. If it's a boat, it will have been in the storm,' Ynen said and, for the first time for over a day, he gave Mitt a frankly unfriendly look. Hildy, beside him, gave Mitt the same look.

Mitt felt hurt, and irritated. 'You don't have to look at me like that! I don't want to get seen and caught, do I?'

'If there's anybody in it, they can't possible hurt you,' said Ynen. 'But I have to make sure. It's the law of the sea.'

'Or weren't you brought up to keep to any law?' said Hildy.

Mitt felt Hildy need not have said that. He knew the rule as well as she did. 'Don't talk so stupid!' he said. 'Can't neither of you get it in your heads this isn't a pleasure trip?' Then, as Hildy went white and drew in her breath to make a powerful answer, Mitt added, 'But please yourself—please yourselves. Don't mind me. I'm only the passenger.' He could see the thing was a boat now, but only a small one. It looked to be just a ship's cockboat, torn loose in the storm. No danger there, Mitt thought.

But when *Wind's Road* had leant nearer, in a pleasant riffling of water, they saw the boat was larger than that, about a third the size of *Wind's Road* herself. There was a mast in it, still flying tag-ends of rope and some fluttering pieces of sail. There was no sign of life in it.

'It *was* in the storm,' Hildy said, rather hushed.

'I'll go alongside,' said Ynen.

Mitt stood up to offer to do that for him. Ynen pretended not to see. *Wind's Road* was his. Mitt sat down dourly by the mast. So Ynen did not trust him not to sail straight past then? Very well. Mitt grinned as Ynen went about too soon and hit the smaller boat a fair old wallop. Ynen winced at the damage to *Wind's Road*'s paint. The smaller boat simply bobbed about. It was salty, battered, and draped with seaweed. It had to be hard to sink, Mitt thought, to have survived the storm. It was empty, except for a tangle of tarpaulin in the bottom. Ynen had scraped *Wind's Road* for nothing, by the look of it.

Hildy read the name painted on the stern of the derelict. '*Sevenfold II*.'

'Funny!' said Mitt, coming to look. 'That's a big merchant ship out of Holand. She was tied up in harbour there the day of the Festival. What's her boat doing here with a sail in it?'

'She must have sailed out later and got caught in the storm,' Ynen suggested. 'I suppose her crew took to the— Oh, dear!'

The tangle of tarpaulin heaved and humped. A wet and unkempt head was thrust out, as if its owner was shakily on his hands and knees. A hoarse and wretched voice said, 'Take us aboard, for pity's sake!'

No one had expected this. Hildy and Ynen were quite as dismayed as Mitt. In fact, it was Mitt who first pulled himself together and said, 'Up you come, then. How many are you?'

167

'Just me, guvnor,' said the man, and seemed to fall flat on his face again.

Mitt exchanged a resigned and dubious look with Ynen and swung himself down into the bobbing derelict. The worst of it was, it could be someone who knew him. He heaved back the tarry canvas. Underneath were several inches of water and, lying sprawled in it, a soaking, unshaven man in sailor's clothes. He was a square, powerful sort of fellow—the kind of man you could trust to survive a storm, Mitt thought, taking the man under the arms and trying to heave him upwards. He was no one Mitt knew. But, when Mitt had wrestled the fellow to his knees, he thought the man had a faintly familiar look. He must have seen him around on the waterfront. One thing was certain about him. The man was a good deal better nourished than most people in Holand. Mitt simply could not lift him.

They only got him aboard *Wind's Road* because the man seemed to come to his senses enough to help a little. Mitt boosted. Hildy leant over and dragged. The man, groaning and feebly scrambling, pulled himself over the side into the well and collapsed again. It took them some time to pull and push him into the cabin and get him on to a bunk. Meanwhile, Ynen left *Sevenfold II*'s boat to bob by itself and sailed on.

'Would you like a drink of water?' Hildy asked, thinking the man must be parched with thirst.

The answer was a growl, in which the only words they caught were 'little lady' and 'arris'.

'Give him a nip of it,' Mitt said. 'Bring him round.'

Hildy fetched the bottle and put it to the man's pale, waterlogged lips. He took such a long drink that she was alarmed. When at length she managed to drag the bottle away, the man made a feeble pounce after it. 'Arragh!' Hildy backed away quickly. He seemed like an angry wild

168

beast. But he became calmer almost at once and mumbled something else with 'little lady' in it. 'S'some sleep,' they heard him say.

'That's right. You drop off. Do you good,' Mitt said heartily. He took Hobin's gun off the rack above the bunk, where he had left it, and put it in his belt, just to be on the safe side.

Hildy, in much the same spirit, put the arris bottle in a locker and shot the bolt. She looked back as they left the cabin and saw that the man's eyes were wide open. He could have been watching. But he could also have been half unconscious. 'Do you think he's all right?' she whispered.

'You do get rough types,' Ynen said, very much wishing he had left *Sevenfold II* to drift.

'He'll survive,' said Mitt, 'if that's what you were asking. Must be made of iron to be still alive. Let's hope he'll be more agreeable when he's had some sleep.'

'So do I,' said Hildy. The man's eyes were still wide open, staring from a broad pale face covered with long black stubble.

15

For the rest of that day, the new passenger slept, with his face turned to the wall. Everyone felt this was the best thing he could do. They left him alone, and almost forgot he was there.

Ynen stayed at the tiller. It was his way of claiming *Wind's Road* back after the storm. He did not exactly resent Mitt taking charge then, but *Wind's Road* was *his*. She was the loveliest and the luckiest boat out of Holand, and Ynen loved her passionately. This left Hildy and Mitt nothing much to do but lounge on the cabin roof. Hildy understood Ynen perfectly. Mitt was amused, though he had to admit that if he had had the luck to own *Wind's Road*, he might well have been just the same. And a bit more careful of my paint, he thought.

Wind's Road clipped her way elegantly north-east. No land came in sight. While they watched for land, they fell to talking, mostly about Holand. Mitt irritated Hildy, because he would seem to think that life in the Palace was one of perfect bliss. So she told him what it was really like. It was beyond her to describe properly the emptiness and the lonely neglected feeling she and Ynen had lived with, but she could tell Mitt how Hadd was as much of a tyrant in his own home as he was in his earldom.

'Everybody was so—so obedient that they'd no characters,' she said. 'The aunts were just fine ladies. And those cousins! All Yes, Grandfather and No, Grandfather and pretty dresses, and despising people who didn't feel like being obedient.'

'The boys were worse,' Ynen said feelingly. 'They had such a good opinion of themselves under the obedience.'

'Like the uncles,' said Hildy. 'I don't think Uncle Harl ever did anything but crawl to Grandfather while he was alive, and go around looking smug and being boring. But when Grandfather got shot, Uncle Harl got drunk to celebrate. It made me feel awful. And I will say this for Father—he wasn't like that.'

'Then what was—*is* he like?' Ynen asked resentfully. 'You got more sense out of a fish on a slab!'

'Except fish don't make jokes at your expense,' Hildy added.

'Ah, now I've had quite a bit of dealings with fish, on slabs and off,' Mitt said. 'Sad look, they often have. And speaking as an authority, as you might say, I get to feel quite sorry for your pa, hearing you talk. Happy family, weren't you?'

'*Sorry* for him!' said Hildy.

'I know. That's a fine thing, coming from me, isn't it?' said Mitt. 'But, as far as I can see, he's not let do anything, except maybe play soldiers or go out for a shoot now and again. All he's let do is sit about in the happy family and take orders, and, since he's not booked to be Earl or anything, he'll be doing that till he dies. Not much of a life, is it? On a slab, you might say, until he's under one.'

Hildy and Ynen sat digesting this unusual view of their father for some time. Even then, all Ynen could think of to say was, 'Well, I don't know,' which he said very dubiously indeed. They seemed so perplexed that Mitt tried to cheer them up by telling them stories from the time he used to fish with Siriol, and how he used to sell the fish. He amused Hildy and Ynen mightily. Hildy nearly rolled overboard laughing, and Ynen doubled up over the tiller. But this led to another difficult moment. Ynen

171

straightened up, tenderly shifted *Wind's Road* a point or so, and asked:

'Is Siriol a Free Holander? He seems to have been very kind to you.'

'Yes.' Mitt went to pick at a blister the storm had raised on the cabin paint. He caught Ynen's eye and stopped, trying to grin. The puzzled serious look he was growing to dread was settling on Ynen's face. 'All right. He was one of them that informed,' Mitt said. 'Only don't start asking things again! I tell you straight I don't know *how* I feel about him. So he was good to me. So I didn't want to go near him after the bomb, for fear I brought the soldiers on him. That's all I know.'

Ynen's mouth opened to ask another question. Hildy saw Mitt's face had gone elderly. She nudged Ynen and hastily got out the pies. The survivor from *Sevenfold II* was still asleep, so Hildy left a rather withered steak pie between his face and the cabin wall. When she came out into the well again, Mitt was still elderly, and she could tell from Ynen's face that he was going to ask more questions any minute.

Hildy began to talk brightly about the Holy Islands. She was not sure why she did, except that it was clear to her that Mitt's feelings were in a most painful muddle, and she knew a little how that felt. Perhaps the Holy Islands was not a good choice of subject. Hildy's feelings about them and about Lithar were in as bad a muddle as Mitt's about the Free Holanders. Because of this, and because she was so anxious to keep off Mitt's feelings, Hildy began to boast. All through the long afternoon, while *Wind's Road* ruckled her way gently through small blue waves, Hildy sat on the cabin roof and boasted about Lithar's famous fleet, and the beauty and the strangeness of the Holy Islands. She told Mitt about the magic Bull, the mysterious piping, and the old man of the sea and his horses. She told him the Holy Islands were the most favoured place in Dalemark. Before long, she began to feel that she was indeed extremely lucky to be going there, and she told Mitt all over again about the fame and beauty of the Holy Islands, in even more glowing terms.

On the third repetition, Mitt felt he had had enough.

'All right,' he said. 'You were so lucky to be betrothed, you ran away the first opportunity. So stop swanking.'

'Yes, do stop, Hildy,' said Ynen, who was as bored as Mitt.

Hildy was furious. 'Why should I?'

Ynen looked at her whitening face and did not answer. Mitt could see Hildy was angry too, but he did not see that was any reason for holding his tongue. 'Because you said three times,' he said, 'that you're going to be Holy Hildrida. You're going to ride about on a bull, blowing a little whistle and hopping from island to island granting everyone wishes. Now tell us how poor old Lithar feels about it. Pretty sick, I shouldn't wonder.'

Hildy stood up on the cabin, so blazing white that Ynen winced. How dared Mitt make fun of her! She had only been trying to help him, too! And he repaid her like the street-boy he was. She was so angry that she wondered whether to jump down on him where he sat in the well and hurt him as much as she could. Mitt grinned up at her, not in the least dismayed. Hildy realized he was probably stronger than she was. 'You,' she said, 'are just a horrible little murderer, and don't you forget it!' She turned on her seaboot and stalked to the bows of the boat.

Mitt saw he had gone too far. He was sorry at first. Then, as Hildy continued to sit, white and blazing, looking out over Old Ammet, he became resentful. 'Give me the tiller,' he said to Ynen. 'You need a rest anyway. And go and tell that sister of yours to jump in.'

Ynen took Hildy a pie instead. She refused to speak to him. He took a pie to the man from *Sevenfold II*. The man had not eaten the first pie. Ynen was just going away, when the man roused a little. When Ynen asked if he wanted a pie, he growled. The only word Ynen heard was 'guvnor'. He leant over, rather nervously, and asked the man his name. The man growled to call him Al, guvnor. Then he reached out and snatched the pie Ynen was just taking away again. Ynen retreated to the well, feeling he was the only good tempered person aboard.

'He's horribly hard to get on with,' he said to Mitt.

'He's a right brute,' Mitt agreed. 'Mind you, he may be better tomorrow.'

They settled the watches for the night, with Ynen having to run back and forwards between Mitt and Hildy, because Hildy would not speak to Mitt. Mitt took the dawn watch. He wanted to be on hand in case they reached land then.

But by morning there was still no sign of land. The wind was brisker and the day promised to be clear. Mitt leant against the side of the well, with his foot up on the seat, humming a tune and feeling fresher and calmer than he had felt for years. He wondered what he would do when he reached the North. Go back to fishing, he supposed, or get work on a farm. But he was sure there were a hundred other things, as yet unthought of, which he could do quite as well.

He was so cheerful and confident that he was really hurt when Hildy came out of the cabin and pushed past him without a word. 'What am I supposed to have done—bar teased you a bit?' he demanded.

'And why should I put up with that?' said Hildy. 'It's not your place to criticize me.'

174

'Oh, go and get me a nice long drink of arris!' Mitt said disgustedly.

Hildy was looking at him, uncertain whether to laugh or fly at his throat, when *Wind's Road* vibrated to a string of swearwords. Hildy had never heard the like. Even Mitt had seldom heard so many at once. Al stuck his head out of the cabin and gave Mitt a bloodshot look.

'Isn't there a razor in this godforsaken tub?'

'There may be,' said Hildy. 'The sailors often leave things. I'll look.'

'I didn't mean you, little lady. I meant him,' said Al. 'Let him look.'

'I'm steering,' said Mitt. 'And I don't know where to look.'

Al gave him another bloodshot look. 'Then she'd better do it,' he said, and went inside again. Hildy followed him, and found a razor. Mitt stood outside, scowling, hearing things like, 'It'll be none the worse for a bit of sharpening, little lady,' and the sound of Hildy stropping the razor. 'This is all the soap you have, is it? Thank you, little lady, much obliged, but a man needs a bit of hot water to shave with.' That meant Hildy had to get the charcoal stove alight, draw water, set it to boil, and work away at the stove bellows. Mitt watched her working away with a set, cross look on her face, while Al sat at his ease on the bunk, and wished they had left that boat to rot.

When Ynen came out, he was wishing the same, though all he said was, 'No land yet?'

All Mitt said was, 'No. I reckon that storm blew us a good long way out.' But he could see Ynen knew how he felt.

Al emerged from the cabin at last, rubbing his smooth chin and looking satisfied. He climbed on the cabin roof and stretched. He was square and stocky.

His face, now they could see it properly, was square too, and unremarkable except for some bitter creases round the mouth and a general look of being well pleased with itself. His clothes, in spite of being faded and creased by the sea, were better than Mitt had realized, and he had a well-nourished look that made Mitt think he must have been Mate or perhaps Bosun on *Sevenfold II*.

'What are you staring at?' Al demanded. Hildy was looking at him resentfully. Ynen was puzzled, because he had a feeling he had seen Al before somewhere. Al laughed, and looked round *Wind's Road*. 'Lucky ship, eh?' he said, nodding from Old Ammet to the little Libby Beer. Then he nodded at Mitt. 'Hand that tiller over, and let's have something to eat.'

'I'll do it,' Ynen said, opening the locker where the second sack of pies still lay untouched.

'Don't you, guvnor,' said Al. 'Let him.'

'It's still Mitt's watch,' said Ynen.

'Yes, but it's his station,' said Al. 'It's not your place to cook.'

'Nobody's cooking,' said Mitt. 'And what do you take me for?'

Al shrugged his wide shoulders. 'Servant. Bodyguard, by the look of that gun you got there.'

Mitt looked down in annoyance, wishing he had buttoned his coat over Hobin's gun. 'I'm no servant,' he said.

'Don't tell me!' Al said, laughing loudly. 'I suppose you come aboard and held the guvnor and the little lady up at gunpoint!'

Mitt could not look at anyone. Hildy seized the sack out of Ynen's hands and dumped it on the cabin roof. 'Help yourself,' she said. 'That's what everybody else is doing on this boat.'

'Thank you kindly, little lady,' said Al. 'After you. After the guvnor.' He would not touch a pie until Hildy and Ynen had each taken one. Then he took one himself, remarking that Mitt could eat when he came off duty. Ynen promptly passed Mitt his own pie and took another. But Al was clearly not a man to pick up hints. He waved a piece of oyster patty at Ynen and asked with his mouth full, 'And where, may one ask, is this boat bound, guvnor?'

They munched in uneasy silence. They all realized that they had forgotten to invent a story to tell him. 'Kinghaven,' Ynen said at last, in a haughty way he hoped would shut Al up.

Al ducked his head respectfully. 'Sorry I spoke. Sorry I spoke, guvnor. Never wish to offend the gently born. Friends in the North, have you? Not many Holanders could say the same. I mean, I know you'll pardon me for mentioning it, but I can see this boat's from Holand by the images back and front. Not a deep water boat, either, is she? Pleasure vessel, more like.'

Hildy drew herself up, as her aunts did when they were displeased. 'Yours was hardly even that, was it?'

Al shut his eyes and muttered things. 'Oh, it was horrible! Filthy little tub. Never been so seasick in my life!' That surprised them, in a sailor, but Al's other remarks had so alarmed them that they all tried to look sympathetic. Al grinned. 'I lay down in the bottom and let it all happen. Only thing I knew how to do. That was after I lost my gun. Damned wave took it off me. I regret that gun. It was as good as the one you got there.' Mitt found Al's eyes open again, staring at Hobin's gun in his belt. 'Mind if I have a look?' said Al.

'Sorry,' said Mitt. 'It's got sentimental value. I never let anyone else touch it.'

'Fair enough,' said Al, to Mitt's considerable relief.

Mitt finished his pie, handed the tiller to Hildy and retired to the cabin, sick of Al already, and hoping heartily that it would not prove far now to Kinghaven. They must all make sure to give Al the slip there. Mitt did not trust Al. He disliked his elaborate deference to Hildy and Ynen, his plain intention of not doing a hand's turn, and, above all, his smug and prying manner.

Above him, Mitt could hear Al asking if they had anything to eat but pies. He added discontentedly that it seemed rather a rich diet. Yes, let's have you seasick again, Mitt thought, and went up the cabin to the rosy bucket.

When he came out, Al's voice was in the well, saying, 'Oh, no offence, little lady. It's not my place to question the provisions. I just thought you could get that lazy boy to catch a few fish now and then. His kind get above themselves if they're let stay idle.'

'You can fish if you want,' Ynen said. 'We don't want you idle either.'

'That's right, guvnor,' Al agreed heartily. 'I'll go and set him to it, shall I?'

There was a frustrated silence in the well. Al bent down and entered the cabin. Mitt braced himself against the remaining half of the cupboard door, ready to whisk past Al and out on deck. Al would soon find Mitt was nobody's servant. Al advanced. Mitt waited his moment and shot forward. But, instead of sliding by under Al's elbow, Mitt found himself hurtling into Al's solid body and grunting with the impact. He was seized in a punishingly strong grip. Al laughed in his ear. 'No, you don't!'

Nothing like this had happened to Mitt for years. He was as humiliated as he was angry. He struggled hard. They bashed against the cupboard, a bunk, and the cupboard again. 'Let go of me!' panted Mitt, as they bounced against the gilded door.

Al, by this time, had both Mitt's hands helpless under one brawny arm. 'Right you are,' he said. He plucked the gun out of Mitt's belt and let go of Mitt the same instant. Mitt was flung against the bunk again.

'How dare you!' said Hildy.

'Give that back, please,' said Ynen.

Both of them had come into the cabin too, which explained why *Wind's Road* was tipping about so, Mitt realized, as he was rolled on to the floor.

Al raised the gun. 'You see to the boat, guvnor,' he said, and walked towards the cabin door. Ynen, Hildy, and Mitt too, backed out in front of him in a dismayed cluster, treading on one another along the tipping floor. Ynen seized the tiller and set *Wind's Road* to rights again, while the other two crammed themselves beside him, as far as they could get from Al in the cabin doorway.

'That's right,' said Al. 'Now this is much more comfortable. I didn't feel safe with this gun where it was. Went off once already, didn't it?' he said, pointing to the splintered groove beside the well. He turned the gun over admiringly. 'Where did you pinch this?' he asked Mitt. 'This is one of Hobin's—one of his specials.'

Mitt set his face sullenly. He was not going to discuss Hobin with Al.

'Well, it's in good hands now,' Al remarked. 'Five shots in it. Got any more?'

'No,' said Mitt.

In rippling, rope-creaking silence, Al swung himself up to sit facing them on the cabin roof, with his legs dangling and the gun laid across one knee. Mitt watched his square smug face and was almost shamed enough to cry. He knew he was having a very vivid experience of exactly how Ynen and Hildy felt when he first came out of the cabin himself, and it made him feel sick. It seemed hard on Ynen and Hildy to be having it again.

179

'Now let's make sure we understand one another,' Al said comfortably. 'I've been having a good deal of trouble lately, and it's made me nervous. I don't want any more, understand—guvnor? Little lady? You?'

'The name's Mitt,' said Mitt. 'What trouble?'

'I'll tell you,' said Al, 'so you won't get any wrong ideas about me. I'm a marksman. Best shot in the South— so do remember I don't want more trouble, won't you? That's why I'd rather be on the right end of this gun— nothing personal. As for the trouble, I had the good fortune to be employed by a noble gentleman in Holand— well, let's call him Harl, shall we?—to take one of my best shots at a certain Earl—let's call him Hadd, not to beat about the bush—'

Hildy's eyes and Ynen's slid sideways to one another. *Wind's Road* veered. Mitt had to nudge Ynen before he realized. Mitt felt nearly as bad himself, and the nature of the badness dragged his face elderly again.

'And I did,' Al said earnestly. 'It was as sweet a shot as you ever saw, and dropped Hadd like a stone. But then the trouble started, because I had to get away, hadn't I? Naturally, Harl had promised me I'd be safe, but I knew better than to trust that kind of promise. Noble gentlemen who make these arrangements always prefer you to be dead, too. You can't blame Harl. I'd have done the same myself. So I made a little outlay of my own, on some soldiers, not to search a certain ship's boat where I was. But there were so many soldiers, and they got so eager, that I had to knock a couple into the water and then cast that filthy tub loose. And I got shot at, and rowed after, and if I hadn't happened to catch the tide, I wouldn't be here now. So I don't want more trouble this time. You don't blame me, do you, little lady?'

'I can't honestly say,' said Hildy, 'that I don't.'

Al blinked a little at this, and scratched his tousled head. He smiled incredulously at Ynen. 'She's a sharp one, your sister. She is your sister, isn't she? Lucky I never mind what people say.' He moved Hobin's gun round on his knee until it pointed to Mitt. 'You. Find some tackle and catch us a fish for lunch.'

'If you don't mind what people say—no,' said Mitt.

Al snapped back the trigger so that Hobin's gun was ready to fire. 'You can say what you like as long as you do it,' he said, and the look he gave Mitt made it quite clear he intended to shoot him.

'There may be some tackle in one of those lockers,' Ynen told Mitt, in the slow serious way people only use when they are truly frightened.

16

For the rest of the day, Mitt sat fishing. Neither venison, oyster, nor pheasant tempted any fish to bite. Mitt sullenly watched the line trailing a little pucker in the sea and hated Al more every hour. It was no comfort to see Ynen and Hildy hated him too, for Al had divided them from Mitt in every possible way.

Al liked talking. He lounged on the cabin roof, between Mitt and the well where Ynen and Hildy were, laying down the law about this, telling them the truth about that, and always treating Hildy and Ynen with great deference and Mitt with none at all. He told them the North was nothing like as free as it was cracked up to be, that a diet of pies would give them scurvy, and that Waywold was a better place to live than Holand. Then he came round to Poor Old Ammet and Libby Beer.

'Funny superstition, having a couple of dummies in your boat,' he said, waving from the straw figure to the wax one. 'It's not as if you Holanders believed in them. When I was in Waywold, they had a saying there that Holanders kept gods they didn't own to. And that's true. I bet you didn't know they were gods one time.'

'They're all right now,' Mitt said.

'And we know they're something special,' said Ynen.

'Surely you do, guvnor. No offence. But I've been in the Holy Islands all this year past, and I know a bit more than you do. They call those two things gods there. That's how the islands got their name, see. But—this is a funny thing—they don't call them anything there. You ask what are the names of these two dummies, and people just look at you. Oh, they're funny people—half crazed with godfearing, if you ask me—and all the gods are is two dummies.'

'I think you might let Mitt stop fishing now,' said Hildy.

'Little lady,' said Al, 'you've a kind heart, and he can stop when he's caught a fish. You hear that?' he said to Mitt. 'She's a nice girl—considerate. All her kind are like that. They can afford to be nice, and frank, open and generous too. They've got the means behind them, see, where your kind and mine can't afford it. It's a high-priced luxury, being nice is.'

Mitt humped his shoulders bitterly. He was sure Al was right. Al could not have chosen any better way of describing the way Ynen and Hildy had treated him all along. It hit the nail on the head.

Ynen said to Hildy, as Al talked on, 'Who *is* he? I've seen him before somewhere.'

Hildy knew Ynen had a far better memory for faces than she had. 'I don't care who he is,' she said. 'I'm going to push him in the sea.' She meant it.

But Al was too old a hand to let any of them have a chance to harm him. Having divided them from one another, he talked until he had bored them into numbness. Then he demanded food. Then he talked until nightfall, and still no land was in sight. By now, they all thought of land as the thing which would rescue them from Al.

'Well,' said Al, as soon as supper was over, 'I think I'll be turning in.'

They made an effort to suggest he took a watch during the night.

'Who me?' said Al. 'I don't know the first thing about this game. I'm a landsman.'

183

'You had a sail up in that boat,' Ynen said. 'And you're a Holander. I've seen you. Holanders aren't landsmen.'

'I never denied it, guvnor. But that was all years back, before your time. Good night, then.' And, since none of them could stop him, Al went into the cabin and fell asleep with the gun hidden under his body where nobody could get it.

While Mitt was dourly stowing the fishing-tackle back in the locker, Hildy looked vengefully into the cabin. 'He's just like the cousins, Ynen, only I hate him more.'

'I hate him harder every time he calls me guvnor,' said Ynen.

'He's bound to,' Mitt said, kicking the locker to vent some of his feelings. 'He's respectful of you.' It was on the tip of his tongue to ask them if he had been as bad as Al, but he had not the heart to. He knew he had been. Instead, he found himself arranging the night's watches, in a constrained and businesslike way, and taking the dawn watch himself again. Mitt felt in his bones it would be dawn when they sighted land.

In fact the numb hatred they all felt for Al was very different from the way Ynen and Hildy had felt about Mitt. Ynen pondered about this while he steered *Wind's Road* into darkness. Mitt had scared them horribly at first. But Ynen had never felt unequal to him, the way he felt with Al. As soon as Mitt had started to argue, Ynen had stopped being scared. There were things they had in common with Mitt; but with Al there was nothing. You could not trust him nor argue with him. Ynen hoped the wind would be fresh tomorrow, because, if it was, and if Al stayed on the cabin roof, he was fairly sure he could bring himself to give the tiller a quick shove and sweep Al off the roof with *Wind's Road*'s boom.

Hildy spent her watch thinking wretchedly of Uncle Harl. Ye gods! It was as if she, or Ynen, had paid Al to shoot Navis. Hildy felt so sickened that she was truly thankful Mitt had forced them to sail North, out of that horrible situation. Only now they had Al on board. Hildy knew they were going to need all their cunning, and Mitt's too, to escape from Al once they did reach land. And she had quarrelled with Mitt. Of all the stupid things to lose her temper over! After what Al had said, Mitt was not going to believe in anything friendly Hildy said. Hildy hated Al for the way he had treated Mitt. It was like Uncle Harchad and the Earl of Hannart's son, except that Al had used words instead of kicks.

She tried to show Mitt she was friendly by being very pleasant when she woke him up for his watch. Mitt hardly spoke to her. He pretended to be very sleepy, and stumbled past her into the well, mumbling. When he took the tiller and set Wind's Road heeling away into the faintly silvering sea, he was too perplexed and miserable to notice what he was doing. The awful similarity between himself and Al was all he could think of. 'He did it for money, and I did it for a cause—that's all the difference I can see,' he said to himself. 'But what cause?'

He felt a sharp nudge on his back. He looked up to find Wind's Road yawing about in a white sea, against a white sky. The wind had dropped and changed. It was quite a bit colder. Mitt set Wind's Road to rights, buttoned his coat, and turned to have a good look at Libby Beer. She was a tiny, dark figure, too far away to have nudged him. Yet she had.

'See here, lady,' Mitt said to her, in his misery, 'can I talk to you? Will you answer?' The little dark knobby shape did not move or make any sign. 'What I want to know,' said Mitt, 'is: am I going to end up worse than that Al, if I started so young?' Libby Beer gave no sign of having heard. 'All right,' said Mitt. 'I promise to leave murdering alone in future. Will you help me now?' There was silence, except for the fitful rilling of water. 'I can't

185

seem to think things in my head, without talking them,'
Mitt explained. 'I went through life thinking I was on the
right side—one of the good ones, you know—and now I
can see I'm as bad as Al. So I got it all to think about
again. I want to know what I thought I was doing, there in
Holand.' There was still no sign from Libby Beer. She sat
at the end of the tiller among her twine lashing, and the
faded colours began to come back to her because the sun
was rising. Mitt did not dare talk any more, in case
someone in the cabin heard him. He stared round the
welling yellow waves. There was still no land in sight.

No land came in sight all that day. The wind sank to a
light, fitful breeze, in which they all buttoned their coats
and shivered. It was so much colder that they were sure
they must be in Northern waters. That was their one
comfort. The pies were smelling strange, the water was
low, and got lower still when Al refused to shave in sea-
water—and there was Al.

Al announced he was bored. 'You must have brought
a pack of cards or some dice with you,' he told Mitt,
evidently thinking he was the most likely one.

Since Libby Beer had nudged him in the dawn, Mitt felt
just a little more equal to Al. 'Me?' he said. 'People in
my station can't afford games.'

Al roamed about grumbling for a while. Then he
suddenly went below and came up with the bottle of arris.
'This'll have to do, then,' he said. 'Should just be enough.
Mind you, little lady, I'm not grumbling, but you should
be sure your bottles are full before you sail.'

He settled himself on the cabin roof and got drunk.
They could all see Hobin's gun stuck in his belt, but Al's
hand was never far off it, and he patted it lovingly from
time to time. Al sang a little. Ynen looked yearningly at
the sail. But the wind was so light that he knew the boom

would only give Al a gentle bump if he did swing it over. He sighed, and handed the tiller over to Hildy, hoping she would have better luck.

When Al had drunk half the arris, he began to talk again. They all closed their ears. It was easy to do. They were all half asleep after their night watches. For an hour, not one of them heard a word Al said. Then he began to laugh uproariously and shout at them.

'I tell you, I've been around all right! And my advice to you is *two games at once*! Rich against rich—they pay better—but rich against poor, if you can't have that. I'll tell you—I'll tell you—*Come here and look, the lot of you!*'

Hildy was steering, but Ynen and Mitt did not dare disobey. Reluctantly, they went towards the cabin roof, where Al was fumbling and pawing at his jacket and staring at them with angry, unfocused eyes. As they reached him, he managed to turn the top of his jacket inside out, to show the drab strip of tape in the lining. Fixed to the tape was a tiny round piece of gold with a wheatsheaf crest on it.

'There. Know what that is?'

'Yes,' said Ynen. 'You're one of Harchad's spies.'

Al slapped himself with triumph. 'Right!' he said. 'Right, right, right! Been Harchad's man for seven years now. So you see what I done?' he asked shrewdly, and became earnest and confiding before either of them could answer. 'Rich against rich is the best way. Harl pays me to shoot old Haddock. Harchad gives me a bounty to shoot old Haddock. Offers of safety from both. Al's all right whatever happens, see.'

'Just what we'd have expected of you, Al,' said Mitt.

Ynen was quite unable to stay near Al any longer. He backed away beside Hildy, and was glad when she took a chilly hand off the tiller and squeezed his arm so hard that it hurt.

Al seemed quite content to concentrate on Mitt. He laughed and waved one finger under Mitt's nose. 'You take my advice and go in for the double game. Do what I done. You can't beat the earls, so you join them. Find freedom fighters, join them with the Earl's blessing. Then bust them up. I done that all over South Dalemark. Harchad pays—wants information. Earls pay. Lovely life.'

Mitt felt his face being pulled elderly as he listened. There seemed no end to the similarities between Al and himself. He turned away from Al's wagging finger and saw that Hildy and Ynen were as hard hit as he was. Their heads were hanging at wretched doll-like angles, and their faces were blurry. Mitt would have liked to say something—something rude to Al at least—to cheer them up. But he was in such blazing misery himself that he thought: Being nice is a high-price luxury. Why should *I* bother? He jumped up on to the decking and scrambled towards *Wind's Road*'s bows.

'Hardest bunch of freedom fighters are in Waywold,' said Al. 'Where are you going?'

'To talk to Poor Old Ammet,' said Mitt. 'He's better listening. He keeps quiet.'

'But the cushiest job,' said Al, as if Mitt had not spoken, 'was in the Holy Islands. They don't know the meaning of freedom fighting there—only I'm not telling Harchad that. I'm on to a real good thing there.' He laughed. 'They think the world of me. And all because of my name. Did you know my name was Alhammitt? But I'm not telling that in Holand. I'd have half Holand coming and trying to set themselves up in style there.'

'Oh, shut up!' Hildy whispered.

But Al talked on, until there was very little arris left in the bottle. Then he sang the *Ballad of Fili Ray*. It was about a man who was hanged.

'At least he knows what he deserves!' Ynen said. 'Hildy, I know where I saw him before. He was in the Palace last week. The first time I saw him, he was with Uncle Harchad. The other time was out at the back, where Father was having those new houses built. Al came out and talked to Father there, I'm afraid.'

Hildy knew, by the dead, sick feeling inside her, that she had feared this all along. 'You—you think Father paid him to shoot Grandfather, too?' If Navis had been expecting someone to shoot Hadd, it would explain his unusual presence of mind.

'I don't know,' Ynen whispered wretchedly. 'He kicked Mitt's bomb away.'

'But that could have been because it wasn't part of the plan,' said Hildy, and they both looked over to Mitt's hunched shape beyond the mast. They were both quite sure Mitt would want nothing more to do with them now.

The song stopped. Al drank the last of the arris. Then he stood up and staggered towards the well. Hildy and Ynen, both thoroughly frightened, pressed back against the stern and stared up at his swaying, grinning face. There was simply no knowing what Al would choose to do next.

'Funny thing, guvnor and little lady,' Al said slurrily. 'You look as though you seen a ghost. Another funny thing—I don't feel quite myself. Think I'll go and lie down.' He came off the edge of the roof and collapsed on his knees in the well. Neither Hildy nor Ynen could bear to touch him. They turned their feet sideways out of his way, as he floundered round and crawled into the cabin. After two attempts, he got on to a bunk and was shortly snoring.

'The gun's underneath him again,' Hildy said hopelessly.

They waited for Mitt to come back to the well. It

seemed the most important thing in the world that Mitt should come and be friendly with them. It had nothing to do with the fact that they were both sure Mitt was the only one who might get the better of Al. It was that if Mitt disowned them, then they were disowned indeed. But Al snored for two hours before Mitt moved. Old Ammet was as little help to Mitt's misery as Libby Beer had been, although Mitt reached out several times and pleadingly touched the stiff, salty straw of him. Mitt knew he would have to talk to someone. The only way he could think was aloud.

Wind's Road's movement altered. The dip and swing of her became shorter and stronger, though the wind was still the merest chilly breeze. Mitt knew they must be in coastal waters again. He jumped up, but there was still no sign of land. He hurried across the cabin roof to tell Hildy and Ynen what he thought, but when he looked at them, below him in the well, he wondered if he was going to be able to speak to them at all. Their searching expressions, and their very faces, put him off. Ynen's nose had blistered in the weather, but it was still Hadd's nose. Hildy's two pigtails were loose and puffy, and wisps of black hair blew across her narrow cheeks, but the sharp, tanned face was like Harchad's even so.

Hildy made an effort to talk about Navis. 'I know what you're thinking—' she said to Mitt.

'I'm no good at thinking,' Mitt said sadly. 'Not like you.' It sounded much nastier than he intended. Hildy took it for a snub and did not go on.

After that, none of them tried to talk about anything important, much as they all wanted to. The things Al had said were like a sore place none of them wanted to touch. This had a very odd effect. They found themselves chattering, and even laughing, about things that were not important, so that someone who did not know might

190

have thought they were three great friends. They got the pies out again and picked out the parts that were still good. The rest—more than half—they had to throw in the sea.

They had just finished eating, when Hildy exclaimed, 'Seagulls!' White birds were bobbing on the water behind, riding high and light like *Wind's Road* herself. Others wheeled above the well on big bent wings, each with a bead of an eye watching for more pie. Ynen looked at Mitt.

'Land,' said Mitt. 'Can't be too far off.'

They exchanged excited looks. Not only was the long voyage nearly over, but, if they could reach land while Al was still asleep, they had a real chance of getting away from him. Ynen tiptoed into the cabin and rustled all the charts there were off the rack above Al's bunk. Al did not move. He tiptoed back to the well with them. Most of the charts, naturally enough, were detailed maps of the water round Holand, but there was one which showed the whole curved coastline from Aberath in the far North to the sands round Termath in the South. Just above the middle of the curve, there was the large diamond-shaped block of Tulfa Island, about thirty miles out from Kinghaven. Below Kinghaven was the wicked spike of the Point of Hark, dividing North from South Dalemark waters. Below that again, much closer inshore, was a scatter of small and large blobs that were the Holy Islands.

'We should recognize that,' Ynen whispered, pointing to Tulfa Island, 'and I think we'd know the Point of Hark too. It looks like sheer cliff. I wish we knew how far North we'd come.'

'There'll be light on Tulfa, if—' Mitt began.

Al surged out of the cabin like a bloodshot bear. 'What's all this whisper, whisper, guvnor? Can't a man sleep?'

The three of them exchanged baffled looks. 'Seagulls wake you?' asked Mitt.

'You don't get charts out for seagulls,' said Al. He gave the horizon the benefit of his bloodshot look, and seemed as annoyed as they were at finding no land there. 'Fuss about nothing. Where's the food?'

They took pleasure in assuring him that all the pies were gone. There was, in fact, a hunk of cheesecake left, but none of them saw any reason to waste it on Al. Al annoyed them by taking the news philosophically. He said his stomach was not too good anyway, and turned to go back to his bunk.

It occurred to Ynen that if Al were this alert, the thing to do was to make use of him. 'How well do you know the coast?' he asked him.

'Like the back of my hand,' Al said, over his shoulder. 'Told you I'd been around, guvnor.'

'Then could you stay on deck?' said Ynen.

Al said nothing. He simply went into the cabin and back to sleep again.

But, as things turned out, they had no need of Al, nor of the charts, that day. The wind continued light. No land appeared. It was clear that they were in for another night of standing watches.

'We'd best turn due North,' Mitt said. 'We could run aground in the night on this course.' And again he settled to take the dawn watch.

Ynen called Mitt earlier than usual. The sky was hardly beginning to pale. But Ynen was horribly sleepy. He kept nodding off, and kept feeling that gentle nudge in his back from Libby Beer. The last nudge was not quite so gentle. Ynen jumped awake, into air that was chilly and muggy at once, and knew something was different. *Wind's Road* was riding in a high, jerky way. Ynen had not felt the like since the day they picked up Poor Old Ammet, and, for a moment, he was as terrified as he had been that first night, when there was space all round him and Mitt crying out in the cabin. He put his hand on Libby Beer to steady himself, and realized that the only thing to do was to wake Mitt.

'I think we must be in coastal waters,' he said to Mitt as he fell on to the warm bunk Mitt had just left.

Mitt knew they had been in coastal waters since yesterday. He got to the tiller before he was really awake. While he was furiously jerking the rope from the mainsail, which Ynen had tied in a manner Siriol would have given him the rope's end for, Mitt could tell *Wind's Road* was in alarmingly shallow water. He searched that paler side of the sky, but there was only misty darkness. Yet, while he searched, he could hear the roar and rumble of waves breaking.

'Flaming Ammet! That's a reef somewhere,' Mitt said. He wiped a sudden sweat out of his eyes and stared forward into the paling dark. He thought his eyes were going to burst out of his head with the strain. He could hear the waves clearly, but he could not see a thing.

The figure with flying light hair, half hidden by the foresail, was pointing right and slightly forward. Yes, but which? Rocks there, or go there? Mitt wondered frantically. The tiller swung firmly left under his hand. *Wind's Road* leant right, in the crisp wash and guggle of a current. Waves crashed over to Mitt's left, and he saw the dim white lather above the rocks she had only just missed.

'Phew!' said Mitt. 'Thanks, Old Ammet. Thanks, Libby. Though I don't know what call you have to keep on helping, with me and Al on board. I suppose you got Ynen and Hildy to consider. Thanks all the same.'

He heard the waves round more rocks ahead as he said it. This time, he did not hesitate to turn *Wind's Road* as

193

soon as he saw the light-haired figure pointing. He was pointing the other way almost at once. Waves crashed on both sides of *Wind's Road*, and the white spray showed whitish yellow in the growing light. Mitt found he was following Old Ammet's pointing arm through a maze of rocks it made him sweat just to think about. Once or twice, in spite of Old Ammet's care, *Wind's Road*'s deep keel grated, and she was snatched sideways in an undertow. Then Mitt would feel Libby Beer's strength on the tiller, pulling them to rights. Frightened as he was, Mitt smiled. The light was growing all the time. If this kept on, he was going to see them as they really were. Old Ammet looked more of a man every second. If Mitt pushed his eyes sideways, he had glimpses of a long white hand behind his on the tiller. It was worth the danger.

The last reef he saw clearly for himself. It was a welling and a milling of yellow water. It was nearly light. Then it was full day. The sun was up, making the sea look as if it was scattered with broken glass. The mainsail was cloth of gold; the island ahead was half golden, and the birds circling it were stabs of dazzling white; and the mist over to the right was a molten bank. The only sign of Old Ammet was a tuft of sunlit straw beyond the mast. Libby Beer was back to a coloured knobby thing, tied with string. And Mitt was so disappointed that he could think of nothing else.

Then he came to his senses. He bent down and whispered into the cabin, 'Island ahead! Come and look!'

Part 4

The Holy Islands

17

There were sounds of heaving and stumbling inside. To Mitt's disgust, it was Al who appeared, blinking and rubbing his bristly chin. Al glanced at the island. Then he calmly opened the locker and helped himself to the last hunk of cheesecake. Munching it, he surveyed the island again. Ynen and Hildy came out into the well. They looked first at the vanishing cheesecake, then at the island.

'That's Tulfa Island,' Al said, with his mouth full.

'Are you sure?' asked Ynen. 'I thought it was bigger than this.' The island was no more than a great rock, surrounded by drifting seabirds that kept up a long melancholy crying.

'Positive,' said Al. 'You want to turn into that mist there.'

'I'll try,' Mitt said doubtfully. There was little wind now, and that fitful. He put the tiller over and hauled in the mainsail. *Wind's Road* went dipping and swinging gently towards the mist that hid the land.

'Watch out!' said Ynen. 'The land's awfully close!'

It was, too, Mitt realized. It was a low green hump in the mist, only about a hundred yards off. He put the tiller hard over again. *Wind's Road* turned elegantly and leant along outside the mist. 'This must be wrong!' Mitt said angrily to Al. 'There's no land this close to Tulfa. Do you know where we are or not?'

'I've a fair idea,' said Al. 'Turn round again.'

To do that would mean tacking. Besides, Mitt did not

trust Al in the least. He hesitated, and looked over his shoulder, beyond Libby Beer. And he saw a tall ship gliding out of the mist. The sun was just catching her topsails and the gold on her many pennants. Mitt turned back again. 'What the—?'

The silence of Ynen and Hildy almost warned him. Al had Hobin's gun in his hand again. Mitt found himself looking into its six deadly black little muzzles. 'You do what I say,' said Al. He came a step closer. Mitt resigned himself to being shot. He felt, very fiercely, that it was a pity. He would never be able to sort himself out now. On the other hand, he supposed he deserved it. He was afraid it would hurt.

Then, most unexpectedly, Al hit him instead. A great blow caught Mitt hard in the stomach, and he sat down, hawking and gasping, hard on the lockers, feeling very angry, rather foolish, and quite helpless. *Wind's Road* yawed about in the douce breeze. Ynen put his hand out for the tiller, and took it back again when the fat little gun pointed his way. There was no danger. *Wind's Road* simply swung and creaked and drooped, rather as Mitt was doing.

The tall ship came gliding closer. They could hear the ropes of her many sails creaking, see the dew from the mist shining in drops on her canvas, and pick out every grain in the wheatsheaf carved on her prow. She stood over *Wind's Road* like a house, and took the last of the wind from her sails. Al grinned up at her tall side, highly pleased with himself.

'This has worked out wonderful,' he said. He jumped up on the cabin and ran along, shouting, 'Hey, *Wheatsheaf*! Hey, there! Bence! Is Bence aboard that thing?'

The tall ship turned. Her creaking sails flapped gently against the wind, until she and *Wind's Road* floated a yard or so apart. Mitt, holding his aching stomach, looked up to see a row of heads watching them, and a man on the highest part leaning over the rail to shout to Al.

'Al! Where did you take off to? There's been no end of askings and botherings and wanting to know where you were. Want to come aboard?'

Al laughed heartily. 'What do you think, Bence? I'm sick of this tub. See it gets stowed in harbour will you, and throw us a rope.'

'What about them?' Bence asked, moving his head towards Hildy, Ynen, and Mitt.

'They can come with their tub,' said Al.

Orders were shouted high above *Wind's Road*. Two small agile men came over the side of the tall ship and descended on ropes like two rapid white-headed spiders, until they landed lightly on *Wind's Road*. While she was still dipping and swinging, they handed their ropes to Al. He took hold of them and was hauled up, with a heavy scramble or so, until he reached the ship's rail, where a mass of hands reached out to pull him aboard. The tall ship turned at the same moment. Her sails creaked and filled. The air was loud with rippling for the few seconds it took her to vanish into the mist as quickly as she had come.

Hildy, Ynen, and Mitt were left bobbing in *Wind's Road* with the two small brown sailors. But they seemed to be rid of Al. They gave long breaths of relief about that, even while they were looking dubiously at the sailors. Ynen hurriedly took hold of the tiller. *Wind's Road* was his.

The sailors seemed in no hurry. They stood together by the mast, looking over *Wind's Road*, down at Old Ammet, up at the poor tattered pennant, over beyond Ynen to Libby Beer, and exchanging small singing murmurs. Quite suddenly, they came briskly to the well and swung themselves down into it.

'Will you move out and give us some room, little ones?' one of them asked cheerfully. He had a soft sing-song accent, the like of which none of them had heard before.

Ynen clenched his fingers round the tiller. 'This is my boat.'

'Then you must continue to steer her,' said the sailor.

'But you must be guided by us. The road has hazards,' said the second sailor. 'And will the other little ones go up before the mast to give us room?'

Mitt was so fascinated by the singing talk that he did not gather straight away that the men were asking him to move. He got up, holding his stomach, and saw that Hildy still had not understood. Mitt nudged her, and she jumped, feeling as if she had been dreaming. They scrambled stiffly on to the roof of the cabin. The sailors settled on either side of Ynen as naturally as if they sailed *Wind's Road* every day, and gave him gentle instructions what to do. Mitt and Hildy knelt on the cabin roof and stared, while *Wind's Road* turned and heeled softly into the now thinning mist.

They were little brown men with dark eyes and oddly light hair, as fair as light new rope. They felt safe, somehow. They were as warm and brown as the earth itself. Even Ynen felt lulled and peaceful with them. Mitt and Hildy could not shake off a feeling that they were dreaming—a good dream that they had dreamt several times before.

'This is a fine sweet boat,' one sailor remarked. 'Will you take in the foresails a fragment—Jenro will do it, little one. You steer left now.'

Jenro, the second sailor, put his brown hand to the ropes that led to the foresails. Ynen was a little shamed to see how much better *Wind's Road* sailed. 'Very sweet,' Jenro agreed. 'What is the name she goes under?'

'*Wind's Road*,' said Ynen.

The dark eyes of the two sailors met across him. 'Is it so?' said Jenro. 'Who comes sailing on the *Wind's Road*? What are the names of them?'

Ynen looked up uncertainly at the dreamy faces of Hildy and Mitt. There seemed no harm in saying. 'My name's Ynen. My sister's called Hildrida, and our friend's name is Alhammitt.'

Mitt blinked. Both sailors were looking at him, smiling warmly. He smiled back. They both made a little gesture, almost as if they bowed. Rather surprised, Mitt ducked his head back at them.

'This is Jenro, and I am Riss,' said the first sailor. 'Remember us in times to come.'

'Yes. Yes, of course,' Mitt said uncertainly.

Wind's Road had come gently past the green hump in the mist. The mist cleared steadily as she sailed. When Mitt looked away from the sailors' faces, he was astonished to find they were sailing among islands—more islands than he could count at a glance. Some were green and steep, with grey rocks standing above the green, and trees clinging to the rocks. Some were green and low. Some were quite small. Others, in the distance, were clearly several miles long. Mitt could see houses on nearly all of them, usually near the shore, as if the sea were their road and the island their farm or garden. Sheep and cows grazed in pastures that mounted above the houses. Smoke rose from the chimneys. The sea-space round them was so sheltered that it was warm and calm as a lake. Mitt could smell the salt of the sea mingling with the smell of earth, smoke, and cattle, in a close, queer mixture. He looked round, sniffing, warm and delighted, wondering why he felt so happy and so much at home, and everywhere he looked he saw the astonishing emerald green of more islands.

'Where *is* this?' Ynen said suspiciously.

201

Jenro smiled at him. 'The Holy Islands, little one.'

Hildy's head went up. The dreamy feeling left her, and left her feeling strained and rather sick. She retreated to the mast and knelt there by herself, nervously clasping her hands and gripping them with her knees. She seemed to feel better like that. Ynen looked dubiously at Mitt. This was not the North. Mitt still had to get away, and Ynen wanted to apologize. He was surprised that Mitt did not seem either annoyed or frightened. Mitt supposed he ought to be. But he was entranced, smiling and sniffing. Seabirds and land birds flew over, uttering their different cries. Jenro, with a mixture of pride and politeness, began to tell Ynen the names of the islands as they passed them, while Riss softly put in a word here and there about the steering. Their voices made Mitt feel as if this was a song he had heard a long time ago, which he had never managed to learn the words to.

'That was Chindersay, and there Little Shool. Big Shool is after. Then Hollisay and Yeddersay and Farn—'

'—to the right here, then left immediately—'

'—and Prest and Prestsay. High Tross there beyond. The large one is Ommern.'

'—your mainsheet out here, but with care. The wind gusts after Tross. And a sweet way to the right as you go—'

So *Wind's Road* threaded gently between tall emerald slopes and past low green humps, and Mitt listened and listened, trying to remember that song.

'Then you have Ommersay and Wittess, and we come out past lovely Holy Isle, the holiest of all. After, you will see Diddersay and Doen and the three Ganter islands—'

Mitt thought it was not quite a song he had in mind. It was the astonishing turfy smell of the islands, or a mixture of the two. Anyway, had he not once, years ago, thought he knew this place and set out to find it? Navis came into it somehow. Mitt was so pleased to remember this much that he scrambled over to Hildy and beamed at her. 'Hey, I take it all back about this place! You're going to love it here!'

He was rather hurt at the pale, haughty way Hildy looked. 'This,' she said, squeezing at her fingers, 'isn't the North.'

'Who cares?' Mitt said. 'I think I'll have a go at staying here myself. I wouldn't mind—I really wouldn't mind!'

'—left now—'

'—and there is Trossaver, with Lathsay beside—'

Wind's Road slipped between long high Trossaver and lump-shaped Lathsay and came into a wide space ringed with islands, where there was ship upon tall ship at anchor. One was just hoisting sail. Another was gliding in through a wide gap opposite, as if it were coming off patrol; but most were anchored, with bare masts. Among the anchored ships Mitt recognized the *Wheatsheaf*. She had no doubt sailed fast on wind above the islands that *Wind's Road* was too small to catch, but she was evidently so far ahead of them that Mitt suspected Riss and Jenro had sailed them on a tour of the Holy Islands. That suited Mitt, but he wondered why.

They sailed towards a long horseshoe-shaped jetty, with a host of little ships tied to it. Behind it was a small town of grey and white houses, with what looked to be the Lord's mansion rising above them at the back. The mainland was beyond again, as green and rocky as the islands, as if the town was also on an island.

'That is the Isle of Gard. The hardway to the land is behind,' Jenro explained.

'And a fine fleet in harbour,' Riss added proudly.

Hildy tried to unbend. 'There are more ships here than in Holand,' she said. She thought she sounded as condescending as her aunts. She saw Ynen wince a little. So she became angry with everyone and did not say any more.

As *Wind's Road* approached the jetty, Riss and Jenro sprang into sudden activity. Mitt had hardly had time to climb to his feet and offer to help, before the sails were down, ropes out, and *Wind's Road* was quietly nudging the jetty stonework, tied up and her long journey over. Mitt and Ynen stared at one another, tired, sad, and a little aimless. Riss, meanwhile, was out on the jetty, talking to a number of large blank-faced men who were standing there.

'Will you go with these?' he said, coming back to Mitt and pointing to the men. 'They are not of the islands.'

They were clearly not of the islands. They were dark and heavy, like a lot of men in Holand. But since they were standing in a line along the jetty, Mitt did not see he had any choice in the matter. 'I suppose so. All of us?'

'If you will,' said Riss. 'We shall see you.' He and Jenro both shook hands with Mitt, smiled warmly, and trotted away along the jetty. Feeling rather deserted, Mitt, Ynen, and Hildy scrambled out on the jetty too. The men closed round them to lead them away. It was alarming. But it was also very silly, because, for a minute or so, none of the three of them could walk. When they stepped forward, the ground was either unaccountably missing, or it came up and hit them before they were ready for it.

'Too long at sea!' gasped Mitt. 'You have to wait.'

The large men waited, silent and impatient, while Ynen fell into Mitt, and Hildy into both of them, and Ynen and Mitt shrieked with laughter, and even Hildy was forced to smile. None of the men smiled, even when they were able to set out through the town, rolling like old sailors and giggling as they went. They were not able to notice the town much, though Mitt did see that there were fields in it, confusingly, among the houses, with cows or wheat-stubble in them, and that, every so often, there was a short square-topped pillar about as high as his waist, where people had carefully laid flowers, fruit, and ears of corn. But they saw few people, because it was still early morning.

They came to the mansion, and were taken inside through a small door. Hildy relaxed a little. The small door meant they were probably prisoners, which must mean that nobody knew who she was. She was glad of that, because she could soon put that right. Mitt was not so sure. He had simply no idea what was happening. The only thing seemed to be to wait and see.

They staggered their way up a flat flight of stone stairs to a sunny stone landing. They waited, while one of the men went to knock on a door. Then—*Bang*! There was an explosion somewhere. All the windows rattled. All three of them jumped violently, and Mitt, at least, burst out in cold trickling sweat all over. He was nearly as scared as he had been in the storm. But the large man did not turn a hair and did not pause in knocking on the door. There was a voice-like noise from beyond it. The large man opened the door.

'They're here. Shall I show them in?'

'If you like,' said someone inside.

The man jerked his head. Hildy, Ynen, and Mitt trooped through the door into a long sunlit room smelling of food and gunsmoke—as queer a mixture, though less pleasant, as the mixed smell of the islands and the sea. The food-smell came from the table near the door. Al was sitting beside it, with his back to the table and Hobin's gun supported over the back of his chair. Another table was against the wall at the other end of the room. There was a row of bottles on it and cups balanced on the bottles. One bottle was smashed. Al fired again as soon as the door was shut. It was deafening. A cup jumped and shattered, and there was a great deal of laughter.

'Got the hang of this flaming gun now, Lithar,' said Al.

'About time,' said Bence, the captain of the *Wheatsheaf*. He was sitting on a chair by the window, eating an apple.

The third man said, 'Oh, Al! I *have* missed seeing you do that!'

Lithar's clothes were nearly as rich as Harchad's, but he looked nothing like so well in them. He had a mop of fairish hair over the brown face of a Holy Islander, and a long, long chin. He seemed quite well-built, but he sat in a strange hunched way which creased his clothes in all directions. When he looked towards them, Ynen, Hildy, and Mitt were uncertain how old he was, because his face was oddly lined, old and young at once. Like Mitt's face, Hildy thought, and she looked at Mitt to compare the two. But Mitt was young and undernourished, whereas—

With a horrible jolt, Hildy realized Lithar was a near-imbecile. It was as if her whole future, and her whole past too, fell away and left just herself—a small girl with untidy hair—alone in a sunny smoke-filled room. Hildy had not realized how much she had built on Lithar and the Holy Islands. She seemed to have founded on them everything which made her into Hildrida and not one of her cousins. It was not exactly her fault, but she had done the building. And it was all unreal. It had not even gone: it had just never been.

It was the same with Mitt. He took one look at Lithar, and one look at Hildy, and he knew that what was happening to Hildy now, had happened to him in Holand. But he had not admitted it. Everything he had thought of as being Mitt—the fearless boy with the free soul, the right-thinking freedom fighter—had fallen to pieces there, as thoroughly as Canden in his dream, or Old Ammet in the harbour, and he had been left with what was real. And it had frightened him to death. Mitt thought his face must be as yellow-pale as Hildy's. I hope neither of them are fools enough to say who they are, he thought. We better all make off North, quick.

'Who are you?' Lithar asked, with a surprised wag of his long chin.

Mitt and Ynen opened their mouths to begin on two separate false stories, but Al got in first. 'Little present I brought you,' he said, without turning round. 'Don't you like it?'

Lithar giggled. 'Well—not terribly, Al. Unless they do tricks. Are you acrobats, or something?' he asked them. 'Untidy children, aren't they?' he said to Bence.

Al hitched his chair round and leaned close to Lithar, in a way that could only be described as possessive. 'They're untidy because they've been at sea. Forgot to take their hair-brushes with them. But you know who they are? Who she is? She's your little betrothed. Harl's niece, from Holand. The brat with the long nose is her brother.'

Hildy said, 'How did you—?'

Al grinned at her. 'You sit on top of the cabin, little lady, boasting for half a day how you was betrothed to Lithar, and then you ask me how I know! Be reasonable!'

'I thought you were asleep,' said Hildy.

'Not me,' said Al. 'Too seasick. Well, Lithar? Aren't you going to thank me?'

Lithar, to help himself absorb what Al said, had put a forkful of food in his mouth. It looked like some of the tastiest sea-fry Mitt had ever seen. He and Ynen looked at it longingly. They were ravenous. Lithar chewed, wagging his brown boot-toe of a chin. 'I suppose she'll grow,' he said discontentedly, with his mouth full. 'But I don't want her brother.'

'Yes, you do,' said Al. He went back to eating sea-fry, too, but paused to wave his loaded fork at Bence. Mitt thought it was cruel. 'Here, Bence,' Al said. 'Tell us that news from Holand you gave me on the boat.' Bence raised his eyebrows and looked at Hildy and Ynen as if he did not want to say anything in front of them. Al angrily waved another forkful at him. 'Get on with it!'

Bence was the ruddy, hairy kind of man who looks strong-minded but is really rather weak. He was obviously well under Al's thumb. 'I just wondered—' he said. 'Well, the news from Holand is that the old Earl was shot some days back, and his sons had a set-to over the earldom. Harl, the eldest son, killed Harchad, the second son, and family. And Navis, the third son, and family, took fright and ran away. That's all I heard, Al.'

Hildy and Ynen stared desolately at one another, while Al laughed loudly and pointed his fork at Lithar. 'Understand?' Lithar nodded intelligently, and plainly did not understand. 'Harl,' Al explained, 'has come out on top. But Navis isn't dead, or not yet. You've got Navis's family here. You want the girl anyway. She's worth alliance, and bargains and a lot of money. But you want the boy too. He's a nuisance to Harl. Harl's got boys of his own, and he'll pay high to be rid of this one. And if the unexpected happens, and Navis comes out on top, then you've done him a favour instead, see? Don't worry about the girl. She'll grow.'

'Sure to. They all do,' Bence said heartily.

Lithar's lined face was riven with bewilderment, but he gave Hildy a formal smile, still with his mouth full, and Ynen a doubtful nod. Then he pointed his fork at Mitt. 'But who are you? Al keeps not talking about you.'

'I'm just a nobody,' Mitt said quickly.

Al tipped his chair back and looked at him. 'Don't be too sure of that. Murderer, aren't you?'

208

Lithar was delighted. 'Oh? Like you, Al?'

'No—though he flaming near got in my way,' said Al. 'I bear you a grudge for that,' he told Mitt. 'Harl's going to want him, too, Lithar. He had a go killing Hadd. It didn't come to much, but he'll make someone to blame—satisfy a crying need nicely, you might say. You offer to send him back for a price.'

Lithar cocked his long face intently. 'How much should I ask?'

Mitt wanted to say something, but he was in such terror that his mind was blank. How had Al known? He must have given himself away just as Hildy had, thinking Al was asleep, and his red and yellow breeches were on him to prove it.

Ynen looked at Mitt's face and knew exactly how he felt. Ynen felt bad. They had promised Mitt to take him North. Something Al had said came into Ynen's mind, and combined with the way those sailors had behaved. 'I don't think you should,' he said to Lithar. 'His name's Alhammitt.'

'Half Holand's called that,' Al said, swiftly and loudly.

But Lithar looked at him reproachfully. 'Now, Al. That isn't a name we take chances with in the Holy Islands. *You* should know that. I can't send him to Holand. I'm a godfearing man.'

'You're a superstitious ass,' said Al. 'You send him.'

'I can't,' said Lithar, and he smiled pleadingly, as if he wanted Al to forgive him.

Al's square face lost all its expression. He laid down his fork and picked up Hobin's gun again. It was empty. Al must have used all the remaining shots demonstrating it to Lithar. He grunted. Then he looked up in annoyance, because the door of the room opened. A little brown woman with white hair came in. She was a slim, upright person in a green-embroidered island dress.

'Clothing and food is prepared for the little ones,' she said to Lithar.

Lithar giggled. 'Little ones! A bit more respect, please, Lalla. You wouldn't believe how important they are! Shall I send them with her?' he asked Al. Al shrugged.

18

To Mitt's heartfelt relief, Lalla took them out of that dangerous room. A crowd of small brown island women were waiting for them outside, with beautiful dark faces and hair either snowy white or light-fair. No one could have been kinder or more concerned than these women. They hurried all three of them upstairs again to rooms where baths were waiting.

Hildy and Ynen, in spite of the situation, were very glad to have a bath. Mitt was hugely embarrassed. He was not used to baths. He was not used to being undressed in front of strangers. Two of the kindly women helped him, soaping and scrubbing and then drying him. Mitt was afraid he seemed unpleasantly dirty. And they kept shaking their heads distressfully over him, and talking about him in soft voices almost as beautiful as their faces.

'He is too thin, this one. Look at those legs on him, Lalla. But see the shoulders, and the span on them. There is the makings of a thick man, and the flesh of a sparrow to cover him.' Mitt writhed.

At length, feeling rather as if he had been put through the mangle in Hobin's back yard, Mitt tottered out into a long cheerful room with barred windows, where Hildy and Ynen were waiting to begin breakfast. Mitt hardly knew them. Hildy had been given a faded blue island woman's dress with white embroidery down the front, which made her look grown up and haughty. Ynen's black hair was wet and shiny and smooth. He had been given a second-hand suit so faded that it was the colour of blue-green distance. Mitt became very conscious of the good suit of new bottle-green they had given him to wear. He had never worn anything half so good. It gave him a feeling there had been a mistake somewhere, because it was certainly better than Ynen's.

They were left alone to eat breakfast. There were piles of smoking sea-fry, new bread, crusty outside and moist within, salty butter, and bunches of green grapes, smaller and sweeter than those of Holand. As Ynen said, it made a wonderful change from pies. But Hildy simply sat looking haughtier and haughtier and not eating.

Mitt found her very annoying. 'Do eat,' he said irritably. 'Keep your strength up.'

'I can't,' Hildy said, tight and toneless. 'Uncle Harchad's dead. And half the cousins.'

'So what? Good riddance, if you ask me,' said Mitt.

'Uncle Harl's a murderer,' said Hildy. 'He's no better than Al.'

'Well, you knew that before,' Mitt pointed out, 'and you didn't let it put you off your food then.'

'Yes, do eat, Hildy,' said Ynen.

'Don't you see?' said Hildy. 'Uncle Harl has probably killed Father too.' Two tears ran slowly down her narrow cheeks. 'Because we got away, people think he was with us.'

Ynen looked at Mitt, appalled. Mitt sighed rather. He felt he had enough troubles of his own, without sharing theirs. 'I always thought it was wrong somewhere,' he said, trying to think it out, 'what you told me about when you were coming away. Looks as if your Uncle Harchad may have been out to kill you.'

'You mean,' Ynen asked, 'that when those soldiers fired at us in the West Pool, it wasn't because they thought we were you, it was because Uncle Harchad had given them orders to stop us?'

212

Mitt nodded. 'Could be. Harchad or Harl. If you ask me, you were luckier than you knew, there.'

'Lucky!' exclaimed Hildy. 'You call us lucky, when Father's probably dead and Al's going to sell us to Uncle Harl!' Tears came down her cheeks in pulses. 'Lithar's an imbecile!' she said. 'And I boasted so! There's no such thing as luck. Life's horrible. I hate everything about it. I think I always have done.'

'You like sailing in *Wind's Road*,' Ynen said, rather hurt.

'With two murderers,' said Hildy, 'into captivity.' She bent her head over the pale oak table and sobbed miserably.

Mitt was offended. 'Stop that!' he said. 'If I hadn't had to get away, you'd be lying dead in Holand at this moment, and you know it! Ynen's worse off than you, and he's not crying. All this means is that we've got to get out of here and go North. So will you stop crying and eat something!'

Tears whisked over the table as Hildy raised her head and glared at Mitt. 'I don't think I've ever disliked anyone so much as I dislike you!' she said. 'Not even Al!' She snatched up a bunch of grapes and began to eat without noticing the taste.

'How can we get away?' Ynen asked anxiously.

Mitt got up and tried the door. It was locked. Rather dashed, he looked over at the bars on the windows. Somehow he had not expected the island women to lock them in.

'Iron bars,' said Ynen.

'Of course, stupid!' said Hildy. 'This is a nursery. The bars are to stop babies falling out.' Eating the grapes made her suddenly realize how very hungry she was. She began wolfing lukewarm sea-fry. 'Ye gods!' she said as she wolfed. 'I haven't been shut in a nursery for—for some time.'

Ynen and Mitt left her eating and went to look at the windows. They looked out on the mainland, rolling into green distance, and the shingly causeway which led to it from the back of Lithar's mansion. Little boats were drawn up to the causeway, nudging the shingle on either side. Immediately below them was a courtyard, with a gateway opening on the causeway. It was full of people, and people were walking backwards and forwards along the causeway too.

'We could get down,' Ynen said. 'Next window along. There's a drain that goes right down to the yard wall. We'd better wait till there are fewer people and then try.'

Mitt cautiously forced open the window over the drain and tried if he could get his head through between the bars. He found he just could. And, he knew from experience, where his head would go, the rest of him could follow, sideways on. Since he was bigger than Ynen, that meant that Ynen could certainly get through, and probably Hildy too. So they settled down to wait until there were fewer people about.

The time came about an hour later. Mitt put his head through, turned his shoulders sideways and shoved. He could hardly do it. He thought he must have grown. His stomach stuck. By the time he finally forced himself through on to the high sill outside, his stomach felt as if it had been pulled down near his knees. He turned round, hanging on to the bars, to help Ynen and Hildy through.

But Ynen could not get through. He was too well nourished. His shoulders were just too thick. He pushed and squirmed and squeezed, and Mitt pulled him perilously from outside, but it was simply no good. Ynen had to give up, bruised and miserable. Hildy was even worse. She was bigger than Mitt all over and could barely even get her head through. They stood unhappily against the window, while Mitt crouched outside with his knees aching from the strain, feeling both unsafe and obvious, wondering what they were going to do now.

'Do I come in, or what?' Mitt said angrily.

'Could you come back up and unlock the door for—' Ynen began to say.

'Oh, ye gods!' said Hildy. 'There's Father! Look!' Her face was suddenly bright red, and she looked as if she was going to cry again.

Mitt swivelled himself round on the sill to look. The man trudging along the shingle of the causeway was wearing farmer's clothes and big boots, but he was certainly Navis. Mitt knew him by the way he walked, and, even at that distance, by the face that was so like Harchad's and Hildy's. 'It is, too!' Mitt said. 'You lot have the luck of Old Ammet!'

'It's not lucky at all,' said Ynen.

'Mitt, go down and warn him, quick!' said Hildy. 'Tell him we're prisoners and it's not safe for him here. Quickly, before Al sees him!'

'But he'll know me,' Mitt objected.

Hildy shook the bars in her anxiety. 'He can't possibly— not in those clothes. If you won't go, I'll have to shout, and someone will hear!'

'All right, all right!' said Mitt. 'I'll tell him. I'll tell him to keep back on the mainland, and then I'll have a go at letting you out. Tireless Mitt does all the work again.'

'Oh, shut up!' said Ynen.

'And hurry up!' said Hildy.

Mitt made a face at both of them and slid down the drainpipe. Mitt to the rescue! he thought. He reached the yard wall without anyone noticing him at all. Nobody seemed particularly interested when he shot down from the wall and raced to the gate.

Navis was just about to come through it. Close to, Mitt saw that he looked tired and not very well shaved. The

215

big boots were caked with mud. But Navis took no notice of Mitt as Mitt darted out of the gate to meet him. That encouraged Mitt. Navis did not remember him. He could only have seen Mitt for half a minute on the day of the Festival, after all.

'Hey!' Mitt said to him. 'Don't come in here. It's not safe.'

Mitt had reckoned without two things. Navis had been a fugitive, living on his wits, for days now. And he had Ynen's memory for faces. Or perhaps not only for faces, for he recognized Mitt mainly by his build and the way he ran. And, since Navis had no reason to think Mitt would do him a good turn, he simply looked at Mitt as people do when they are surprised to find themselves addressed by a total stranger and walked past him into the courtyard.

Mitt was so annoyed by this haughtiness that he would have let Navis alone, had it not been for Ynen and Hildy watching from above. He ran after Navis and took hold of his sleeve. Navis shook Mitt's hand off and walked on. Mitt was forced to trot beside him, trying to explain.

'See here, it's not safe for you here. Lithar's wrong in the head, and the fellow who shot Hadd got hold of him and made him take Hildy and Ynen prisoner. They're up there, in that room with bars. Take a look.'

Since there were so few people about, Mitt risked pointing. But Navis would not demean himself to look. He trudged on, trying to decide why this murdering brat should spin him a yarn like this, and taking no notice of Mitt at all.

'Father's not listening!' Hildy said, with her head pushed against the bars. 'Isn't that just like him!'

'He may only be pretending not to listen, because it's safest,' Ynen suggested hopefully.

Mitt hoped Navis was pretending too. 'Hildy and Ynen sent me,' he explained, feeling sure this would convince

216

Navis. But Navis tramped through the main doorway of the mansion into a large stone room without appearing to have heard. The room was full of people. Mitt hung back in the doorway, wondering whether he dared follow Navis in. They were mostly island people. The sing-song of their talk rang round the room. Mitt decided that it was safe enough, and ran after Navis to make one more attempt.

'Do come out of here,' he said, dodging about near Navis's shoulder. 'They'll sell you to Harl to kill. Honest.'

Navis looked at someone beyond Mitt's head and called out loudly, 'Will one of you take this offensive child away, please!'

Mitt sensed a movement in the crowd and got ready to run. 'Can't you *listen* to me, you pig-headed idiot!' he said.

'Will you shut your unpleasing mouth,' said Navis. 'Guard! Remove this, will you!'

Mitt turned and ran. But the guard was nearer than he thought. Two big men seized him as he turned. Mitt lost his temper then. He kicked and struggled and called Navis a number of names he had learnt on the waterfront.

'Oh, him again,' Al said from behind Mitt. 'Not to worry, sir. I'll take care of him, sir.'

Upstairs in the barred nursery, Hildy and Ynen waited and waited. For a long time they were sure that, whatever had happened between Mitt and their father, Mitt would come and unlock the nursery door any moment. They had great faith in Mitt's resourcefulness. But when the island women came and brought them lunch for two, even Ynen gave up hope.

'I don't think Mitt was even trying to make Father understand,' Hildy said angrily. 'And now he's just forgotten us. His kind are all the same!'

'I don't think he would forget,' Ynen said.

217

'Yes, he would. He had a perfect chance to escape on his own, and he took it,' said Hildy.

'I thought he felt he owed us—' Ynen began uncomfortably.

'He didn't feel anything of the kind,' said Hildy. 'His whole idea was that we owed him everything, because of his rotten life in Holand!'

This was so exactly the kind of thing Mitt had said himself that Ynen could not argue any longer.

Long hours later, they were trying to play I-spy. Hildy was far too dejected to concentrate. 'I give up,' she said. 'There's nothing beginning with T in this room.'

'Table,' Ynen said drearily.

The door opened just then and Lithar shambled in. Hildy did not realize. 'How was I to know it was something as stupid as that!' she snapped, thoroughly bad-tempered.

Lithar stared at her, shocked. 'I don't think I want to marry you,' he said.

'That goes for me, too!' Hildy retorted. 'I hate the sight of you!'

Lithar turned plaintively to Al, who had followed him in. Behind Al came two of the large men, with Navis between them. 'Al,' said Lithar, 'I don't have to marry her, do I? She's not womanly.' Al laughed and patted him on the back.

'There, Hildrida. You have just received your first compliment,' said Navis. 'Possibly your last, too.'

'Where's Mitt?' Ynen said to Al. Al laughed and shrugged. 'You do know, don't you?' said Ynen. 'Have you killed him?'

Al chuckled. 'Say hello to your pa like a good boy.'

'Not until I've told you what a foul brute you are,' said Ynen.

'He's not very nice either,' Lithar complained. 'Let's go away.'

'After you,' said Al, and everyone went out of the room again, leaving Navis standing by the locked door.

Hildy and Ynen stared at Navis. He looked tired, dirty, and depressed. Hildy felt sorry for him. She was almost certain she was glad to see him. She went towards Navis to tell him so. But she did not quite dare, and stopped. Then she somehow ran at him without thinking and threw her arms round him. For just a second, Navis looked surprised. Then Hildy found herself being hugged, picked up and swung round, and her father looking more pleased and more upset than she had ever seen him. When Ynen came shyly up, Navis spared an arm for him, too, so that they all hung together in a bundle.

'Who warned you to get away?' said Navis. 'How did you manage in that fearsome storm?'

'Nobody. It was an accident. Mitt and Libby Beer and Old Ammet helped,' they said, and they tried to tell him about their adventures in *Wind's Road*. After a little, Navis let go of them and sat down to listen, pressing two fingers to the corners of his eyes as if he had a headache. They could not help noticing that he frowned and seemed to press harder every time they mentioned Al or Mitt.

'Why did you come here?' Ynen asked him at last. 'Was—is Al in your pay? I saw you talking to him in Holand.'

Navis looked up at Ynen in surprise. 'Of course not. You must have seen him the time he came to offer—for a large sum of money, naturally—to tell me of a plot against the Earl. You can't imagine how often people did that,' Navis said. He sounded very depressed. 'I found Al very uncongenial. But I mentioned the matter to Harchad, and, ironically, I remember Harchad telling me in return that he had put an agent in the Holy Islands to keep Lithar in line, in case the North attacked. If I had known it was this same Al, I would have stayed well away. I came because there are boats here—prepared to pay high for being taken North, and trying not to hope there might be news of you two. But it seems that Al has decided that Harl would pay more for us than I would pay for a boat—which I'm sure is true—so we are being sold back to Holand.'

There was a wretched silence.

'Wouldn't Uncle Harl let us go,' Hildy asked, 'if we all signed something to say we didn't want to be earls?'

Navis shook his head, with his two fingers lodged hard above his nose. 'He doesn't trust me. He never has. Besides, I kicked him in the stomach when he came to arrest me. He was so annoyed that he came out in the Flate after me himself, in spite of the storm. He nearly trod on me while I was lying in a ditch. By which I knew he wouldn't easily forgive me.'

Ynen laughed, though he was sure it was no joke. 'But didn't Mitt try to warn you?'

He saw his father's forehead crease. 'If Mitt is the boy who tried to blow up the Sea Festival—yes, he did. I thought he was lying and asked the guards to take him away. Al took charge of him after that. Is this one more mistake I've made?'

'Yes,' said Ynen.

'You didn't know,' said Hildy. 'I never trust Mitt either. His ideas are all in a muddle. But if Al's killed him, I'm going to call on Old Ammet and Libby Beer for vengeance.'

'I sincerely hope they answer you quickly,' said Navis.

But when, about an hour before sunset, Al came into the nursery with a number of the largest guards, he was as sturdy and carefree as ever, and rather more pleased with himself than usual.

'Up you get, sir,' he said, 'and you, guvnor. Bence is back from a little job I sent him on. The old *Wheatsheaf* is

220

all ready, the tide's right, and we're going sailing again. It's not what I'd have chosen, being a landsman and inclined to queasiness, but we reckoned you'd not be able to give us the slip so easy at sea.'

Navis stood up slowly. 'You mean you're taking us back to Holand.'

'Quick on the uptake, your pa,' Al remarked to Hildy. 'That's right, sir. We're taking you and the boy, and leaving the girl here.'

'Why are you leaving my daughter?' said Navis.

Al looked at Hildy. Hildy wanted to hit him, to scream, to make a fuss in every way she could think of, but she felt she could not when her father was behaving so calmly. 'Be reasonable, sir,' said Al. 'She's betrothed to Lithar. We've got to have a bargaining point. The money Harl offers has got to go up, and up again, and she'll be the reason. And if he won't offer enough, you may find we come sailing back here with you in a day or so. Look on the bright side, sir.'

'Oh, is there a bright side?' said Navis.

'For some of us,' Al answered genially. 'I'll trouble you to step along now.'

They said goodbye stiffly. None of them wanted to say anything important with Al there. Navis and Ynen were marched out by the guards. Hildy stood by herself in the middle of the room, with her hands clenched into useless fists, watching the door close behind them. She was determined not to cry till it shut.

The door opened again. Al put his head round it. 'By the by, little lady,' he said, 'something tells me that Lithar may suffer a little accident on the voyage. He would come with us, you know. Then there'll be a new Lord of the Holy Islands for you to marry.'

Hildy looked at that grinning face stuck round the edge of the door and was so angry that she shook all over. 'If

221

you mean it'll be you,' she said, 'I bet you have at least two wives already.'

Every scrap of expression went out of Al's face. 'Someone tell you their life-story, did they?'

'No,' said Hildy. 'I just know. You're just that kind of man.'

'Then you better keep that idea to yourself,' said Al. The door snapped shut and the key grated.

Hildy went on standing where she was, too miserable and frightened even to cry now. She knew she had been very, very foolish to say that to Al. But after all that had happened, it hardly seemed to matter. She thought she might as well sit down anyway.

She was just turning towards a chair, when she noticed that the door was swinging open again. Beyond, in the dark corridor, Hildy could see one of the little island women. She thought it looked like Lalla.

'Will you come out now?' asked the gentle island voice. 'It is time to be leaving, if you wish to go.'

'Oh, I do wish to go!' Hildy said, and hastened out to her.

Lalla turned and walked down the passage and Hildy walked beside her. It was so strange to be free suddenly that Hildy did not quite believe it. It felt like a dream. Dreamily, she went with Lalla down some stairs and along another passage.

'Where are we going?' she asked, as they came to more stairs and went down again.

'Out to the hardway. Riss is waiting there for you.'

Despite her troubles, Hildy was dreamily glad. Of the two little sailors, Riss was the one she had liked best. 'Where will Riss take me?'

'To the North, if you wish to go there.' They came to the end of the stairs and out into the big stone room where Mitt had made his last attempt to convince Navis. It was

222

empty now, rather cold, and seemed dim because there was such a blaze of evening light from the arched doorway to the courtyard. Their footsteps echoed softly from the stone. Among the echoes, Hildy heard Lalla ask, 'Will you be wishing to come back to the Islands again?'

Hildy thought about it, as they crossed the ringing stone floor. She would not have been surprised to find she never wanted to come here again. But she found she did. The Holy Islands had somehow taken her heart while she was sailing through them in *Wind's Road* into danger. 'I'd love to,' she said. 'But not if Al's here.'

'We can rid you of your enemies,' Lalla said, 'if you are prepared to trust Alhammitt.'

'Mitt?' said Hildy. 'Is Mitt all right?' Then she became embarrassed that Lalla knew how little she trusted Mitt, and wanted to explain herself. 'It isn't what he did. It's what he thinks, and the way he's been brought up. I mean, I know I'd probably be just the same if I'd been brought up on the waterfront, but I haven't. And I can't help the way I was brought up, either. I think mostly he annoys me. I suppose I annoy him. That's it, really.'

As Hildy said this, she came to the doorway and a blaze of orange sunlight. There was a bull in the courtyard beyond. It was a huge animal, almost red in the low sun. There was power in every line of it, in each stocky leg, and from its tufted tail and slim rear, to its great shoulders and blunt triangular head. It seemed to be loose in the courtyard, with no one to control it. Hildy stopped short and stared at it. And the bull raised two wicked horns growing out of a mat of chestnut curls, and looked at Hildy. Hildy did not care for the look in its large red eye. She turned uncertainly to Lalla.

The blazing low sun had dazzled her, but Lalla seemed taller than she had thought. In the dimness, her hair seemed not white but red, or brown. But it was the same singing island voice which said, 'It was only two things I asked you. Would you come again to the Islands, and would you trust Alhammitt?'

Hildy felt the ground shake under the weight of the bull as it trod nearer. It was unfair of Libby Beer to try and frighten her. 'What happens if I say *No* to those questions?' Hildy asked defiantly.

The lady standing in the dimness might have been a little surprised. 'Nothing will happen. You will go in peace and live quietly.'

Then Hildy found that it was important to her to answer both questions truthfully. She stood thinking, while the bull twitched its tail and paced heavily in the sunlight. 'Yes, I want to come here again,' she said. That was the easy part. 'And—and I suppose I do trust Mitt really. I did in the storm. It's just when I'm angry I notice the difference between us, but I don't think that's quite the same. Is it?'

She looked up to Libby Beer for an answer, but there was no one there. The stone room was empty. Shaken, Hildy looked out into the courtyard. That was empty too.

'Didn't I answer right then?' Hildy said. Her lonely voice rang round the room. Since there was no good to be done there, Hildy went out into the warm dazzle of the courtyard and walked over to the open gate. The damp scent of the islands met her there. The sea hurried to the shingle of the causeway in a myriad small ripples, setting the waiting rowing boat nuzzling at the stones.

As Hildy's feet crunched on the pebbles, Riss stood up in the rowing boat and smiled warmly. 'Will you thrust on the boat and climb in, little one? We will be stirring to your ship.'

Beyond Riss, *Wind's Road* was moored in the deeper water between the mainland and the causeway. Hildy

224

could see her swinging gently in the tide. She smiled at Riss delightedly.

'I think,' she said, as she kicked off her shoes on the shingle and tied a knot in one side of her Island dress to keep it out of the way, 'I think I've just been talking to Libby Beer.'

'That is not the name we use here,' Riss said. 'She is called She Who Raised the Islands.'

19

Al slung Mitt into a room which was probably a storeroom, and left him there while he went to attend to Navis. It was a very small stone room with a skylight too small even for Mitt to squeeze out through. Mitt sat with his hands behind his head, glaring up at it and hating Navis with all his heart. All his troubles went back to Navis. He felt as if instead of kicking a bomb this time, Navis had actually kicked him in the teeth. And Mitt had only been trying to help!

'That's the last time I ever do anything for that lot!' Mitt said to himself, and fell into a prolonged and fierce daydream about what he would like to do to Navis. He imagined himself as a powerful outlawed revolutionary with several hundred seasoned followers at his back. He imagined himself conquering a town full of terrified lords and ordering them all to surrender. Out they came, with Navis among them, cringing Harchads, quaking Hadds, dozens of Hildys and several frightened Ynens, all hanging their heads and shuffling, as the men from the North had shuffled through Holand. Mitt had them all killed, but Navis he saved till last for a truly frightful death.

It was most interesting. For years now, Mitt had been too busy with other things to do any daydreaming. He found he had been missing something. He did the story over again, with a larger town, and made himself more powerful and even more merciless. He began to see that he really had it in him to become such a revolutionary. He felt considerable respect for himself. He did the story a third

226

time, and conquered all South Dalemark, pursuing Navis ruthlessly until at last he caught him.

He was halfway through killing Navis very slowly, with great attention to detail, when Al came back again. Mitt jumped up and backed into the far corner of the small space. Al's face had its most blank and unpleasant look. Because of what he had been thinking of doing to Navis, Mitt knew rather well how much Al could hurt him if he wanted to.

But Al simply leant against the door and surveyed Mitt. 'You're a real nuisance to me,' he said, 'and I'm going to have to get rid of you quick. How many people know where you are?'

Mitt stared at Al uncertainly. He did not know what Al thought he had done.

'Out with it,' said Al. 'Or do I have to knock your head in? Navis knows you were the one with the bomb. Does Hobin know about that? Hobin must've given you that gun. I don't see you pinching one of Hobin's specials. He's too careful of them. Does Milda know where you are, too?'

Mitt shook his head and went on staring at Al. Out of the distant past came memories of Al's voice shouting that the cow had calved, and Al's square back marching away towards Holand to find work, but he could not bring himself to believe it.

'If you was anyone else,' Al went on bad-temperedly, 'I could send you back to Holand with the other two and good riddance! But I'm not having you tell Hobin about me. He'd have it round every gunsmith in the country, and without Harchad to back me I'd never get near a gun again. He's made it hard enough for me as it is. And all because I happened to drink a bit too much one day and let out to him how I bust up the Free Holanders. He said he was going to Holand to look after you and Milda, but I

227

know he did it just to spite me.' Here Al noticed the way Mitt was staring at him, and laughed at him. 'Say hello to your pa, then, why don't you?'

'Aren't you proud of me at all?' Mitt asked him. Al stared at him. 'Chip off the old block, and so on?' said Mitt.

At this, Al spat on the floor as Mitt remembered him often spitting in the dyke. 'Proud of *you*! I've got three kids in Neathdale, and the lot of them put together never got in my way like you do. First thing you ever did was get lost and put me under an obligation to Navis. Then you let the bull get at the rent-collector. Then you hang round my neck in Holand. Then when I thought I'd seen the last of you years before, you bob up dressed like a side of bacon and dump a bomb in front of Hadd just when I'd got my sights lined up on him! I don't know what good you thought that would do. Mind you,' said Al, 'I didn't know who you were then, but if I had known I'd have said it was Milda's fault. It looked just like one of her daft ideas.'

Mitt was not much given to blushing, but he felt his face going warm and red at this. 'It was my idea. So!' he said. He felt he had to defend Milda to Al. 'She's all right, Milda is. It's just she's not too clear about what's real. You know, always throwing her money about—' Mitt stopped. That was exactly the truth about Milda, and he had always known she was like that. Milda never looked to the future, whether she was buying too many oysters, or sending Mitt to be taken by Harchad. The fact was, neither of them had dreamt what it would be like. It was very painful to Mitt, the way Al was laughing about it.

'You don't have to tell me she's got no flaming sense!' Al said. 'She'd have ruined me if I'd let her. And you're just the same. Fancy making friends of Hadd's grandchildren!'

'They're not my friends!' Mitt said angrily.

'You could have fooled me,' said Al. 'Swap jokes on the cabin roof with your enemies, do you? Told them half your life-story, didn't you? And that Hildrida's no fool. If you say one word more to her, she's going to add it up with what I said and spoil all the plans I got for her. You finished yourself when you opened your big mouth, you did. You don't make friends with people like that. You batten on them.'

There were hurrying footsteps outside the storeroom door. Someone shouted, 'Al! Al, are you there? Lithar wants you.'

'Coming!' Al shouted back. 'I'll have to leave you to Bence to deal with,' he said to Mitt. 'Can't that gibbering fool manage for five minutes without me?' He banged out of the storeroom, muttering.

The bolts shot home. Mitt slid down into a heap in the corner. After a moment, he wrapped his arms round his head, as if that could keep some of his misery off him. But nothing could. The horrible similarity between himself and Al was clearly no accident. Like father, like son. And as Mitt hated Al so vehemently, he hated himself, if possible, even more. He had set out to be a brute like Al, and it had not been his fault if he had failed. Worse still, everything he had thought he was doing it for turned out to be a complete sham. Al had betrayed the Free Holanders, not the other way round. Mitt felt as if his whole mind was falling to pieces, like Canden in his dream. There seemed nothing left of him at all.

'One thing you might have done, Al,' he said from his corner. 'You might have put me out of my misery quick, instead of running away to flaming Lithar!'

It was some hours before anyone came to put an end to Mitt's misery. By that time, he was rolling groaning in the middle of the room. He barely had time to scramble up, and barely time to glimpse the little brown sailor,

Jenro, and another he did not know, and Bence standing in the doorway, before a large sack was pushed over his head and he was bundled head-down over Jenro's shoulder.

'Hey!' Mitt said, struggling miserably.

'Be silent, little one, and no harm will come,' Jenro said softly.

'Hurry up,' said Bence from the distance.

Mitt trusted Jenro and stopped struggling. The world began to bounce about as Jenro hurried somewhere with him. Mitt was uncomfortable with his head hanging down, but not badly so. After a short while, he was swung up, swung down, and lowered surprisingly gently on to boards that dipped a little. Mitt heard water slapping quietly under the boards and guessed he was in a boat. He felt the boat sway, bumping as the two sailors hitched on the oars. Mitt tried to see through the sack where they were. It was a hairy, porous sack, which tickled his nose rather. He could see very little light coming through, which made him suspect that the boat was under cover somewhere and whatever was being done with him was a secret. He would have yelled, but for what Jenro had said.

The movements of the two sailors stopped. Jenro's soft voice said, 'Then, Captain, you are settled that we must be stirring out to sea to throw this little one in?'

'Yes,' Mitt heard Bence say from above somewhere. 'And I'm coming with you to see it done.'

'Captain, there is no need to do that,' said the other sailor.

'Oh, isn't there?' The boat surged heavily as Bence landed in it. 'I know you lot. When you say no need, I start to get suspicious. Cast off there.'

The sailors said nothing. Mitt felt the boat move. The oars began a slow, sleepy *dip-creak-splash*, *dip-creak-splash*.

Shortly, bright sunlight fell across the holes in the sack. Mitt thought they must be out in the harbour. They went on steadily in the sun, *dip-creak-splash, dip-creak-splash*. It was so soporific that Mitt nearly fell asleep, in spite of his misery.

Then he heard the gentle voices begin again. 'Captain, throwing this little one in the sea is a thing we cannot do.'

'But you wait to tell me till we're past Trossaver,' Bence said from the distance. 'You'll do it.'

'Captain, there are two of us and one of you.'

'All right. You can watch me do it, then,' said Bence.

'But that is a thing we cannot do.'

'You'll have to put up with it,' said Bence. 'Al wants it done. You always do what Al wants, don't you?'

'We would not do this for Al either.'

Bence seemed really astonished. 'Not for Al!'

'No,' said Jenro. 'For this one came on the wind's road, with a great one to guide him behind and before.'

'What's that got to do with it?' Bence demanded. 'You saw Al come on the same flaming boat.'

'That matters not at all. The great ones contain multitudes.'

'Don't you throw your religion at me!' said Bence.

The voices stopped. The oars dipped slowly and peacefully. Mitt grinned to himself inside the hairy sacking and rubbed his itching nose. He suspected that Bence was more likely to be thrown into the sea than he was. He thought Bence knew it, too. Mitt dozed off, soothed by the sound of oars and glad to forget himself. Every so often he woke up to find the argument going on again.

'What am I supposed to do when two of my best men don't do what I say?' he heard Bence demanding.

'We will do what you say,' answered a gentle voice.

'Then I want this brat dumped in the sea.'

'But that is a thing we cannot do.'

Another time, Mitt heard Bence say, 'What do you think you're rowing all this way for, then? Are we just going to turn round and come back again, or what?'

'If you wish for us to turn round, Captain.'

'I do not! I want this brat dumped in the sea.'

'But that is a thing we cannot do, Captain.'

The next time Mitt woke, Bence's nerve had broken. 'I see,' he was saying. 'And if I lay a finger on him, it'll be me in the sea instead.'

'You would not force us to that, Captain.'

'Then what *can* I force you to?'

'If it is a thing that meets your mind, Captain, we can be stirring to an island and putting the little one on it. There are those where no mortal men live.'

'Bother meeting *my* mind,' said Bence. 'It won't meet Al's.'

'If you are not telling Al, we shall not be saying either.'

'Hm,' said Bence. After a pause, he said, 'Well, it's not so different from dumping him in the sea, I suppose, provided it's uninhabited. Which island is it to be?'

'Lovely Holy Island is nearby. There is none on her but She Who Raised the Islands and the Earth Shaker.'

'What's that supposed to mean?'

'No mortal soul lives there.'

'I thought there was supposed to be a mad old priest living there.'

'He does not live there. No mortal soul lives there.'

'Oh, very well!' said Bence.

There was a noticeable increase in the creak and jerk of the oars. Mitt could feel the boat shoving through the water. After barely a minute, the swing of the oars stopped. Shingle grated underneath, and grated again. Mitt could hear waves rattling the pebbles of a beach.

232

'Hurry up!' said Bence.

Mitt was lifted and carried by two people. Their feet crunched on sand, and then his own feet were placed tenderly on what felt like turf. Jenro pulled the sack off him and smiled at him.

Mitt had a feeling Jenro was going to say something, perhaps tell him something important, but, while Mitt was blinking and rubbing hairs from the sack out of his eyes, Bence was climbing angrily along the rowing boat at the sand's edge.

'Get back here,' said Bence. 'Or else.'

The two sailors smiled at Mitt, and Jenro certainly winked, though Mitt could not see why, before they trotted back to the boat. Mitt stood, blinking still, while they pushed the boat off, twirled it with a deft shove of an oar, and rowed smartly away, getting smaller and smaller against the green of the nearest island. He thought they were going at least twice as fast as they had come.

Mitt felt desolate. The nearest island was far too far for him to swim. Holy Island towered above him in a tumble of rocks and green grass. Little trees and heather hung far above his head. It was wild, uncultivated, and deserted. To judge from the fresh, peaty smell, there was water somewhere, but there was no food except berries. Mitt could not see why Jenro had winked. He was going to starve to death.

He tried to remember what Holy Island had looked like from the other side, as they sailed past in *Wind's Road*. He thought it had seemed lower and greener and—though he might be mistaken—he thought he remembered that the islands were nearer on that side. It was worth going to look, anyway.

Mitt set off round the island. There was no clear path. He was forced to wander up and down, between rocks and over slippery turf, sometimes almost down to the water's edge, sometimes quite far up the high hill, and, as he went, his miseries caught up with him again. He hated himself, and Al and Navis—everything—so much that he wished someone really had drowned him. He no longer wondered why Hildy had exclaimed she hated life. It was not worth living.

The sun was low. Mitt was hot and under a cloud of midges. And he found his way round the island barred by a huge block of granite. Grumbling dismally under his breath, he scrambled his way to the top of it. A green meadow spread beneath him on the seaward side, bright in the golden evening. Beyond it, the sea rolled and swashed in little waves. Mitt looked out over their golden ribbing and saw that the nearest two islands were only two hundred yards or so away. He could swim that easily. No wonder Jenro winked. Then he looked down at the meadow.

There was a bull in it. It was a huge animal, almost red in the low sun. Its great shadow stretched halfway across the meadow. As Mitt looked at it, the bull raised its triangular head, armed with wicked horns growing out of a mat of chestnut curls, and looked at Mitt. Its tufted tail swung. Keeping its red eyes on Mitt, it advanced towards the rock. Mitt could feel the granite tremble under the weight of it as it walked.

'Now what am I supposed to do?' Mitt wondered, crouching on top of the rock.

A woman came round the rock and looked up at Mitt. 'You'd better not go that way,' she said to Mitt, nodding towards the bull. She was wearing a green island dress with red embroidery, but Mitt thought she could not be an island woman. She was tall, and she had long red hair which blew round her in the sea breeze. Her face was very beautiful, and rather serious. 'Go up that way,' she said, pointing to the island above the rock.

Mitt looked where she pointed and saw a path of trodden earth climbing steeply this way and that among the rocks. He looked back at the bull, which met his eye unpleasantly. 'I suppose I'd better,' he said, and he stood up. Then it occurred to him that the woman was standing in the meadow, only a few yards from the bull. 'Are you safe there?' he said.

The woman smiled. It reminded Mitt of the way Milda smiled, when the crease went out of her face and the dimple took its place. 'Thank you. I can manage him,' she said.

As Mitt set off up the steep path, he saw the woman go towards the bull with her hand held out. The bull stretched its massive neck to nuzzle her fingers. Well, rather her than me! Mitt thought.

The path went backwards and forwards across the hill, diving between twisted trees and making hairpin bends over rocks. Mitt climbed with the rich smell of the earth and the sharp smell of turf in his nose. In his ears, the plangent plash and roll of the waves became larger, but more distant. Mitt wondered where he was going, and what good it would do when he got there. Then the path went round a rock with a tree growing out of it and entered a very small hanging dell, open one side to the sea, and greener than any of the islands. Mitt stood there to get his breath. There was a great view over the islands in the golden light, islands on one side floating green gold in blue-grey sea, and islands on the other side blue-black against the sun, floating in silver-gold, like clouds in the sunset.

Mitt, hot and breathless and miserable as he was, felt very bitter at the sight. Times out of mind, as a small boy, he had dreamed of such a place. Now he had found it, and what good had it done?

He turned away and went on into the dell. It was moist

and cool. To Mitt's pleasure, there was a trickle of water running down a rock. The sack had made him very thirsty. He put his hands and then his face into it and came out dripping. He noticed that beside him there was one of those stone pillars he had seen on the Isle of Gard. It was about as tall as a sundial, but wider. On it were two small figures, one made of green grapes and rowan berries, and the other of plaited stalks of wheat.

'Hey!' said Mitt. 'Here's Libby Beer and Old Ammet!'

He was stretching out a hand to give Old Ammet a touch of greeting, when he felt the dell tremble under the feet of a heavy creature. He whirled round, expecting to see the bull again.

A grey-white horse had stopped further down the dell and a tall man with flying light hair was dismounting from it. Mitt hastily brushed his wet face with his arm and backed against the short stone pillar. The man was Old Ammet. He came towards Mitt, smiling a little, with his long light hair blowing and swirling about his head and shoulders as if the wind were blowing half a gale in the dell. But there was no wind at all. He had a straight grave way of looking, which reminded Mitt a little of Hobin, though his face was nothing like Hobin's. It was like no face Mitt had ever seen. One moment Mitt thought Old Ammet was a grand old man, and the next, he seemed a handsome young one. And as Mitt saw these strange changes in Old Ammet, he was more frightened than he had ever been of any nightmare. With every step Old Ammet advanced, Mitt felt another wave of fear, until he was as terrified as he had been that time in Holand when he pretended to play marbles—right up to the moment when Old Ammet spoke to him. Then it all seemed perfectly natural.

'I was needing to speak with you, Alhammitt,' Old Ammet said. His voice reminded Mitt of Siriol's, though it was also quite, quite different. 'I have to ask you a question.'

'You could have talked to me any time,' Mitt said, feeling a little resentful. 'Why does it have to be now, when I'm all to pieces?'

Old Ammet's young face laughed, and his old face answered. 'Because there was no doubt till now what you would do.'

'What I want to do is get out of this place and go North,' Mitt said. 'What's so doubtful about that?'

'Nothing,' agreed Old Ammet, out of his grave old face. 'The men of the islands will help you go North.' Then his face blazed young and glad and eager, and he said, 'It is also quite certain that you will come back.'

'How did you know that?' Mitt asked. He knew it was true. He would have to come back to the Holy Islands. 'When do I come?'

'That is for you to say,' said Old Ammet, young and old at once. 'And when you do, it is laid down that we shall deliver these islands into your keeping. My question to you is: Will you take them as a friend or as an enemy?'

'As an enemy to *you*, you mean?' Mitt asked, highly perplexed by this question.

Again Old Ammet's young face laughed. 'We are not the stuff of enemies or friends, Alhammitt. Shall I ask this way: Will you come as a conqueror, or in peace?'

'How should *I* know?' Mitt said. 'What do you mean coming and asking me questions like that? What do you mean coming and pushing me around? It's my belief you've been pushing me around all the time, you and Libby Beer, and I don't like people pushing me around!'

'Nobody has pushed you around,' said Old Ammet. He looked as old as the islands. 'You chose your own course, and we helped you, as we were bound to do. We shall help

237

you again. All I needed to know was what manner of help we must give you in times to come.' And, as if Mitt had already told him the answer to that, Old Ammet turned away and went to his horse. The corn-colour of his clothes and hair caught the sun and seemed to melt into it.

'Hey, wait!' said Mitt. He felt very resentful and very disappointed in Old Ammet. He had expected more from him somehow. 'Well, what am I supposed to say? You might give me a bit of help over that at least!' he said, hurrying after the melting, hazy figure. Old Ammet turned round, melting back to a young man, and Mitt found he had to stop. 'Can't you give the Holy Islands to someone else? I don't deserve to get them,' he said.

Old Ammet shook his blowing hair and smiled regretfully. 'I'm not anyone's judge.'

'But you could be,' said Mitt.

'What good would that do?' said Old Ammet. 'What is your answer?'

Mitt was glad to find that he had not, after all, yet answered Old Ammet's question. He thought about it. The first thing he wanted to do was to ask Old Ammet to come back in an hour or so, to give him time to think. But Old Ammet stood there, old and patient beside the tall grey horse, and the horse cropped the cool green turf with drops of bright water falling gently from its mane, as if, for both of them, there was all the time in the world.

'I'm bad at thinking without talking,' said Mitt. 'I'm like Al that way. We both love to talk.'

'Then why not talk?' suggested Old Ammet.

But Mitt did not talk, because it suddenly came to him that he had it in him to be far worse than Al. Mitt, if he wanted, really could become the person out of his recent daydream, and go round the country putting people like Navis to death. Al did what he did for himself alone. Mitt would be doing it against people. Mitt looked up at Old

Ammet and caught his face as it changed to young. He looked as splendid as Mitt's daydream. Yet, beyond Old Ammet was the opening of the dell, and there lay the Holy Islands spread out between the evening sea and the sky. And Mitt knew he did not want to come back to them hunting people from island to island and putting them to death. It just did not fit. But if he came back as an enemy, he would. He had Old Ammet's word for it that he would come back. And it would be like destroying his own early daydreams.

He looked up at Old Ammet's face and caught it between young and old. 'It'll have to be friends,' he said.

Old Ammet, turned to old now, simply nodded gravely. It was no more than Mitt expected, but he was disappointed all the same. He had hoped Old Ammet would praise him, or at least reward him, for his decision. He was a very puzzling being, and, Mitt suspected, a very powerful one too.

'What's your name?' he said. 'It isn't really Old Ammet, is it?'

'Once,' said Old Ammet, 'it used to be the same as yours. But people have forgotten.'

Mitt thought he had known that. Old Ammet and Alhammitt did not sound so very different. 'And Libby Beer,' he asked. 'That's a silly sort of name.'

Young Ammet smiled at Mitt, dazzling him by the heave and billow of his bright hair and the brightness on his clothes. 'You can learn how to call both of us now you've decided. Go on up to our house and take what help you can from there. Remember to ask for our names.' He pointed to the end of the dell. Mitt saw the path went on there, up into the rocks. While he was looking, Mitt had a feeling Old Ammet walked dazzling out of the dell, leading the horse, into the sky. But he was not sure. He was only sure he was gone.

'Well, I've met him at last,' Mitt said, and he was wonderfully pleased now as he went on up the path.

It was not far, a short steep climb through the rocks. Then Mitt came to the very top of Holy Island, into a strong breeze, and found a little grey building which looked as old as the island. Standing in front of it was an old, old island man with long white hair and a wrinkled brown face.

'Hey!' said Mitt, remembering that Jenro had said there was no mortal soul on the island.

'You've had a hard climb,' the old man said in a gentle island voice. 'Come and seat yourself on the bench here and be breathing.'

'Thanks,' said Mitt. 'But I got to ask for their names first. That's what I come for.'

'Sit down first. That will be needing a quiet mind,' said the old man, pointing to a stone bench outside the house. Mitt went over and, a little impatiently, sat down. The old man sat creakingly beside him. 'Will you eat?' he said.

'Well, I—Yes—Thanks!' said Mitt. The old man was suddenly passing him a large bunch of grapes and a flat loaf plaited like an ear of wheat, and Mitt had no idea where he got them from. 'How about you?' he said politely.

'I am well, thank you,' said the old man.

Mitt supposed that meant he was not hungry. He was very hungry himself. The loaf was better even than the bread they had that morning and the grapes were sour-sweet, cold and juicy. He ate every scrap. 'How about those names?' he said, munching.

'The names of the Earth Shaker and She Who Raised the Islands are strong things,' said the old man, 'even the least of them. Spoken aloud by the voice, they are too strong, unless the speaker has right in the heart of him. And I must tell you that the names of the Earth Shaker are

240

cruel even then, as they are strongest. He who learns these names must never say them aloud, even sleeping, unless he wishes something perilous to follow. Will you still learn those names?'

Mitt was not sure. He did not like the idea that he might say something perilous in his sleep. He was about to tell the old man to forget he asked, when he realized that Old Ammet had indeed rewarded him for his decision, and this was to be the reward. Frightening though it was, Mitt saw he would have to take it, or he would be going back on his decision. And when he thought of himself conquering and killing among the people of the Holy Islands, he knew his decision was right. 'Yes, please,' he said.

'And who was it sent you?' asked the old man.

Mitt answered without hesitation. 'The Earth Shaker.'

'Then I will be showing you,' said the priest, 'if you have taken enough of their gifts.' He stood up as creakingly as he had sat down. Mitt brushed the crumbs off his suit and got up too. 'Can you read?' asked the old priest.

'Just about,' Mitt conceded.

The old man walked to the door of the house, but he did not go in. He signed to Mitt to go inside. 'Look under them in the sun,' he said. 'And do not speak what you read until you have true need.'

Mitt had to duck his head to get into the house. When he was inside, he was surprised to find it was not dark as he had expected, but light and warm and quiet. The late sun was streaming in through windows placed curiously low down, nearly at the floor. The red-gold light fell on the end wall, on two hollows in the stonework. In one hollow stood Libby Beer, and in the other Old Ammet. They were not as grapes and corn, but as queer old statues of themselves as Mitt had just seen them. Mitt knew that

241

whoever had made those statues had seen them, too. Libby Beer was carved smiling as she had smiled at Mitt, and Old Ammet was miraculously both old and young at once. Mitt wished he knew how to carve like that.

Look under them in the sun, the old man had said. Mitt took his eyes reluctantly off the statues and looked at the wall under the hollows. There was a mass of cracks there, as if something had hit the wall and all but smashed it. But, as Mitt looked, he found that the sun was lighting some of the cracks and not others, and that the lighted parts were forming letters. The letters fell together to form words, two words under each figure, and the words were names.

Mitt had always thought he could not read without saying what he read aloud. But he dared not do that now. It was one of the hardest things he had done, spelling out those words in his head. Three of them were such strange names, too, that he was not sure how to say them. Only one—the one immediately under the hollow where Old Ammet stood—was not so strange. It was almost Ynen, or like Ynen with an extra Yn to it. From this, Mitt gathered, though he could not say how, that the top name in each pair was the lesser name and went with the usual figures of Old Ammet and Libby Beer, made of corn and berries; and that the names below were the strong ones, and went with Old Ammet and Libby Beer as they really were. After that, he found them a little easier to remember. Even so, he walked to the door with his eyes up and his mouth moving, remembering hard.

'Will you let them stay easy? They will stay in you,' the old priest said kindly, seeing his trouble.

Mitt blinked at him. 'They will? They seem to get away every time I stop thinking them.'

'You will be saying them when you should not if you will not leave them lie,' said the old man. 'Now what you

242

must be doing is going down that way.' He pointed to the rocks on the landward side of the low grey house.

'But how can I get off the island that way?' Mitt said.

'The Earth Shaker will show you,' said the priest.

Mitt shrugged and looked over at the green hump of the nearest island, a good half mile away. Still, where the old man pointed, there looked to be an easy way down. Mitt turned back to thank him, and he was gone. Mitt knew he had not had time to hobble off anywhere. He was simply not there any more. Mitt could feel that the space by the house was empty somehow.

'And he felt like a real one, too,' Mitt said. 'I wonder who he was.'

20

*W*ind's Road heeled gently westwards in a peaceful evening breeze, threading her way among the islands. When the sun went red and gold behind High Tross and the misty green hump of Holy Island beyond that, Hildy began to feel chilly. Riss told her there were coats below. Hildy went into the cabin. There she found that not only had the cupboard been repaired, and the water-keg refilled, but the forward bunk held a pile of coats and seaboots to fit both men and boys. Puzzled by this, Hildy put on one of the coats and came out, intending to ask Riss about it.

A sweet haunting sound came to her. It seemed to be coming from Ommern. Hildy listened, enchanted, to a tune at once melancholy and filled with joy—at once a tune and at the same time only the broken pieces of a tune. Instead of coming from Ommern as she had thought, it came from the green hump of Wittess. But when she turned that way, the sound came from Prestsay to one side. 'Piping?' she said to Riss.

He nodded. 'The greeting of the great ones.'

Hildy leant over the side of *Wind's Road* listening until she thought her heart would break, but whether with joy or sorrow she could not tell.

They heard the piping aboard the tall ship *Wheatsheaf* too, as she tilted among the islands carrying Navis and Ynen to Holand. They were in Bence's stateroom, with Al, Lithar, and two guards. Bence was stamping about above in a considerable rage. It seemed that the *Wheatsheaf*'s sails

244

unaccountably kept losing the wind, and they were making very poor progress.

'Can't any of you trim a sail right!' Bence roared.

'It is the wind towards evening, and the islands taking the force from it,' explained a gentle voice.

'Teach your flaming grandmother!' roared Bence. 'You there! Stop sleeping along that yard and trim your sail!'

The piping came to Ynen's ears very sweet and fitful, sometimes like a melting song, sometimes as a wild skirling. He could not hear it properly for the roaring of Bence. 'I wish he'd be quiet,' he said to Navis.

From time to time, Bence fell into an exasperated silence. Each time, the piping came from a different quarter. Al wriggled his shoulders at it, as if it made him itch.

'I wish they'd stop that flaming piping! What do they do it for?'

'Nobody does it,' Lithar said, in surprise. 'It happens sometimes. Always near sunset, around suppertime. Shall we have supper?'

'If it makes you happy,' Al growled.

Bence's steward brought in cold meat and fruit and wine. Al did not eat much, though he drank the wine. The rest had supper and listened to the shouts of Bence and the piping in between. The steward cleared the meat away, and they were still among the islands and the piping still sounded.

Mitt heard the piping too as he swung down the side of Holy Island, galloping the occasional steep stretch. The sound seemed to come from the heart of the island beneath his feet. It was the wildest, most joyful music he had ever heard. Mitt felt so glad and confident that he would have sung, except that he was afraid of spoiling the music.

But when he came down with a steep rush to the shingly shore, and saw the well-known elegant shape of *Wind's Road* leaning past High Tross in the haze of evening, he nearly despaired again.

'They've got away! They've gone and left me!' he said. *'Wind's Road!* Hey, there! *Wind's Road!'* He jumped and waved and shouted, knowing they were too far away to see or hear him.

A sudden wave rose between Holy Island and green Ommern and travelled swiftly to the shore where Mitt was. It was so queer, all on its own, that Mitt stopped shouting and watched it. It rushed on, one lonely peak of water, and thundered down on the shingle beside Mitt in a mass of white water and the rubbly squeaking of pebbles. Mitt scrambled hastily out of range. Then he realized that the white foam of the wave was still standing high above his head. He found he was staring at one of the lovely white horses of the storm.

'Thanks, Ammet,' Mitt said, laughing a bit nervously. He had ridden a horse only when he was a very small boy, and that was a carthorse. He edged towards the horse. It put its nose down and blew salty breath at him. Nervously, Mitt grasped it by its rough wet mane, which it did not seem to like, and struggled on to its slippery back. The horse shook its head and rippled the skin under Mitt, but it did not throw him off.

'Can you catch that boat for us?' Mitt said to it.

The horse surged forward, joggled him, bounced him, and then seemed to be pure movement under him. Mitt found they were galloping across the sea itself, tossing spray, tossing the horse's mane, tossing Mitt. He fell forward and put his arms round the horse's neck. There were hard muscles in it, and it felt warm and cold together, like a hot day high on a mountain. Spray dashed into Mitt's face and the dark sea raced beneath. He could

246

only bear to watch it out of one eye. He tried peering forward for *Wind's Road*, but she had sailed behind Wittess.

Wittess was straight ahead. Almost there. Underneath him. The horse galloped straight across the island without checking. The only difference was that its hooves thudded deep and drumlike, and turf flew into Mitt's face instead of spray. Out of the corner of his eye, he saw several people, who all shaded their eyes to see Mitt against the sun. They did not seem particularly astonished.

'Must have odd things happen all the time,' Mitt said breathlessly to the horse, as it thudded down to the sea again. Among the sound of its hooves, he could hear the piping again, strong and wild. The sound changed to whipping water, and the horse seemed to splash wet sunset out of the sea. In the dazzle, Mitt saw the deck of *Wind's Road* just in time, almost underneath him, as the horse dissolved to a wave of grey foamy water.

Hildy turned round almost too late. She saw Riss smiling, a welter of disappearing water, and Mitt's feet landing on the cabin roof. 'You're not alive!' she said.

It was not very welcoming. 'I'm not a ghost yet,' Mitt said gruffly. 'Where's Ynen then?'

'With Father and Al on the *Wheatsheaf*,' Hildy said miserably. 'He's taking them back to Holand. They went hours ago.'

'Oh, well,' said Mitt. He was going to say it was a pity, and then forget about it, when he saw Riss was smiling at him knowingly.

'The *Wheatsheaf* will be between Yeddersay and the outer island,' Riss said. 'Jenro is seeing to that. They will wait until the sun goes down and the piping stops, when they will know you are not coming.'

'Oh,' said Mitt. This was too bad! It was not enough to decide to come back as a friend. It seemed to mean he

247

was expected to act as a friend, and to Navis of all people, here and now. Ynen, Mitt did not mind. But he did not want to see Al again, either. He shot a surly look at the bows of *Wind's Road*, where Old Ammet still lay, stiff and blond and bristly. It was all his fault.

But, while he was looking, Mitt suddenly remembered, for no reason he clearly knew, the time when he had first seen Old Ammet in his other, better shape, standing by the bowsprit as *Wind's Road* hung on the slope of that monster wave, trying to turn over and drown them all. For a moment he felt like *Wind's Road* himself. But at that point, he had already saved Ynen's life, by grabbing his ankle just in time. Mitt sighed. It seemed as if it was his way to make friends without knowing he had—just as he had with Siriol, or Hobin, for that matter. Perhaps even Hildy, or Navis, were friends too, deep down where it did not show.

'We better make haste to Yeddersay, then,' he said.

Riss looked dubiously up at the sail. He meant they were doing as much as the wind would let them.

'I'll see to it,' said Mitt. He clambered sideways along to Old Ammet and gently, politely, touched the image on its shoulder. 'Could you give us just a bit more wind, please?'

Hildy glowered after him. The pure annoyance on Mitt's face when he first realized what his decision meant made her feel anything but trustful of him. She saw the water ahead ruffle and darken. *Wind's Road* creaked. The sails tightened, and she heeled over with a much brisker rippling round her bows.

'Never fear,' Riss said, thinking Hildy was staring at Mitt because she was afraid of him. 'He has been on Holy Island.'

'I wish he'd stayed there,' Hildy muttered.

Wind's Road threaded among the islands quickly now,

accompanied by her own ruffle of wind. The sun was just touching the rim of the sea when she rounded Yeddersay, and there was Chindersay, and the piping came from Hollisay, loud and joyful behind them. And there, sure enough, was the *Wheatsheaf*, towering against the crimson sky, hardly moving at all, with her sails drooping and swinging about. They could have heard Bence bellowing easily on Hollisay.

'What are we going to do?' Hildy asked.

Mitt was not at all sure. 'There are four things I can do, I suppose,' he said. Then he had a bad moment, thinking he had forgotten those names. But, when he examined the inside of his head, they were there all right, safely stuck.

'Nothing, nothing, nothing, and nothing, I'll bet!' Hildy said scornfully. *Wind's Road* glided nearer the *Wheatsheaf*, and she saw that there happened to be two ropes dangling over her side, just where they would be within easy reach. Somebody trusted Mitt. 'I'm sorry,' she said. 'I've been having a horrible time, you see.'

'You're not the only one!' said Mitt, looking up at those ropes dangling over the steep side. Al was up there. Mitt was afraid the sight of him was going to drive those four strange names clean out of his head. It seemed to him that it would be as well to take precautions. As Riss was bringing *Wind's Road* up alongside the *Wheatsheaf*, Mitt hurriedly leant right over the side and came up again with his hand dripping wet. 'See here,' he said to Hildy, 'if I get in a fix, or you do, and if I don't seem to know what to say, shout this out.' And he scrawled with his wet finger on the cabin roof, big crooked letters: YNYNEN.

Hildy looked at them. 'But that's—'

'Don't say it!' Mitt said furiously. 'Just keep it in your head, will you!'

249

Hildy saw that if she did not trust Mitt in this, she would have lied to Libby Beer after all. 'All right. I'll remember.'

'Thanks,' said Mitt, and he swept his wet hand over the name, as *Wind's Road* gently scraped against the side of the *Wheatsheaf*. The ropes hung head-high. Hildy and Mitt each seized one. There was no need to climb. The ropes went up with them, hauled by a dozen men above.

'What's going on there?' bawled Bence.

One of the ship's boats went down past Hildy as she went up. Another splashed into the water beyond Mitt, as he reached the rail. As they both set their feet on the decking, helped by any number of smiling island sailors, a third boat was going down. Mitt saw Bence stare, and then make for the ladder down to the deck where he and Hildy were.

'This is your way,' Bence's steward said politely. Mitt and Hildy trotted beside him past masts and coils of rope, and past scores of sailors all busy getting down to the lowered boats, and arrived at the stateroom door just before Bence reached the bottom of his ladder. The steward opened the door for them and they went in. Bence suddenly saw what his crew were doing, and ran about shouting to them, instead.

Inside the stateroom, the lamplight was not yet as bright as the sky. No one quite saw who they were until they were fully inside. Then Ynen was unable to stop himself calling out, 'Mitt! Hildy, he's not dead!' Al jumped to his feet. Lithar recognized them both and said amiably, 'I wondered where you two had got to.'

'Bence!' bellowed Al.

'Mitt, I owe you an apology,' Navis said.

Mitt nodded at him as cordially as he could. He hoped that by keeping a friendly expression on his face he might make himself like Navis. But the one Mitt was watching was Al. Hobin's gun was in Al's hand, and Mitt kept one eye on it, with a name waiting on his tongue.

'Bence!' yelled Al.

Bence arrived in the doorway, angry and sweating. 'The flaming crew have got the boats out now!' he said. 'They're all rowing away.'

'Bence,' said Al, 'how did they get here? Him particularly.'

'I don't know!' Bence said, blustering a little. 'They were on that boat again—*Wind's Road*.'

'Then you can go by this road,' said Al. He brought Hobin's gun up, over his forearm, and fired at Mitt.

Mitt shouted out Libby Beer's lesser name as he saw Al's finger move.

With unbelievable speed, an apple from the table was in the air between Mitt and the gun. The bullet hit it. The apple burst all over the room, showering everyone with pulp, pips, and skin. The deflected bullet clanged into one of the lamps and broke its glass cover. Navis and his two guards put their arms up against a cascade of broken glass. After a stunned moment, everyone shook themselves and dusted off apple and glass.

Al looked from the gun to the broken lamp. 'What did that?'

'I did,' said Mitt. 'And I can do it as often as you've got bullets. We came here to fetch Ynen and his father away North, and you might as well let them come. You ready?' he said to Ynen and Navis.

Ynen and Navis were already standing up. They might have left then, in that shaken moment, had not Lithar cried out. 'Oh lovely! How pretty! You *do* do tricks then! Look at this, Al. Isn't it pretty?'

Everybody looked. It was irresistible. Lithar had a little apple tree growing on his knee. Its roots spread visibly over Lithar's trouser-leg, sucking up the moisture from the

251

apple-pulp on it. Its leaves turned from spring green to summer dark as they looked. There was another growing on the table, and several more coming up on the floor. Lithar was delighted.

'Do another trick,' he said. 'These are beautiful.'

Mitt almost agreed with him. Hildy agreed entirely. She leant over the tree on the table and watched it grow in astonishment.

'Very pretty,' said Al, giving Lithar's knee a cursory look as he passed. He took Hildy by her arm so suddenly and hard that she yelled. 'Now get out,' he said to Mitt. 'You and your tricks. I give you a count of five before I break her arm, and a count of ten before I strangle her. One—two—'

Mitt could see Al meant it. He could see Hildy was too frightened to say the name he had told her. He could see Bence standing aside from the door to let him go. He could see Ynen staring at him helplessly.

'Four,' said Al.

'A larger apple tree?' Navis suggested. 'Heavy apples?' Mitt looked at him and saw that he was as tense and helpless as Ynen.

If he's that fond of Hildy, why does he try to hide it? Mitt thought irritably. He said Libby Beer's great name, before Al could come to five. It was a name that rang and reverberated, and became more awesome after it was said. It swelled inside the stateroom.

The result was nothing like Mitt expected. The *Wheatsheaf* shook from stem to stern as if she had hit a rock. They all staggered. There was a creaking, and a hard rending. Bence, as soon as he heard it, turned and dived out of the door. The two guards hastily followed him, dragging Ynen and Navis with them. Lithar said, 'What's happening?' and ambled out past Mitt with his tree flapping on his leg. But Mitt had to stay where he was,

252

because Al, though he was hanging on to the table with one hand, still had hold of Hildy's arm.

There was a huge creaking, followed by the sound of planks snapping and splintering. The end of the ship with the stateroom in it tipped, so that Mitt had to hang on to the door.

'This ship's breaking up!' he shouted at Al, through the din. 'Let go of her!'

Al seemed to forget that he intended to strangle Hildy. He dragged her to the door and stared out. He, Mitt, and Hildy all ducked back as a mast as big as a tree, shrouds, sails and all, crashed down on their end of the ship. The ceiling above them began to cave in under it. Mitt took hold of Hildy's other arm and Hildy pulled. Al was so bemused that he let go of her. Mitt and Hildy struggled over broken decking to an amazing sight.

There was an island growing through the middle of the ship. It was a wet shiny hump covered with shells and weeds and smelling like the waterfront on a hot day, and it was growing steadily. Navis, Lithar, Bence, and the guards were all on top of it, being carried upwards as the island grew. Ynen was slithering anxiously down to them. Mitt stared round, weak with awe. The poor *Wheatsheaf* was in two shattered halves, on either side of the new island, and the surge and disturbance of its growth was rocking the ring of boats where the crew sat watching. Further off, *Wind's Road*'s mast beat to and fro.

'What's happening?' said Ynen. 'Hildy, what did he do?'

Grass was already springing on the wet hump. It grew faint and far apart at first, but it thickened as quickly as the apple trees had grown. The muddy mound grew greener as well as larger. Some grass seemed to be rooting on the timbers of the *Wheatsheaf* as well.

Navis shouted and pointed. Mitt and Hildy both turned round to find Al close behind them, in the act of grabbing for them. Hildy threw herself to one side and Mitt to the other, where Mitt sat down with a wet *smick* which reminded him nastily of the dykes by the West Pool. As he landed, he saw Al grab Ynen instead, and drag him by the leg down the muddy slope. The gun was still in Al's hand. Ynen put up a useless arm against it.

'Hildy! Help!'

'Mitt!' shouted Hildy. She pointed. She meant simply to shout that Ynen was in danger, but it came out with a stammer of terror. 'Yn—Ynen!'

The rough water round the new island spouted up into a point. A wing-shape of water whipped across Al and Ynen, knocking them sprawling. Hobin's gun was flung against Mitt. Mitt had barely time to pick it up, before the new island was a hurricane of wind and water. Huge yellow waves crashed over what was left of the *Wheatsheaf* and broke halfway up the newly green hump. One wave, sluicing down, left Ynen clinging to the grassy mud between Mitt and Hildy. Though none of them could hear, or even think, Mitt hung on to Ynen, and Hildy leant over him screaming, 'It's all *right*!' until her throat was sore.

Then it was over. The sea was rippling and calm. The island had gone on greening in spite of the waves, and it was now as green a hump as the Ganter Islands. There was little of the *Wheatsheaf* left—just a few spars floating nearby. Nor was there any sign of Al. But where he had been there was a curiously shaped patch of green corn, growing and ripening, and crackling like fire with the speed of its growing.

The crew of the *Wheatsheaf* called remarks to one another and began rowing in to look at the new island. Navis stood shakily up at the top of the mound and shouted through the twilight to know if Hildy and Ynen were there.

Mitt shook the water out of his eyes. Ye gods! he thought. What happens if you say his big name?

A desperate thrashing in the water just below him caught his eye. He slid carefully down to look. Lithar's young-old face looked up at him imploringly. Mitt knelt on the salty turf, holding out a hand, and Lithar struggled towards it.

'You should learn to swim,' Mitt said, catching hold and heaving him to land.

'Never could,' said Lithar. 'No more tricks, please.'

The nearest boat arrived then, and Jenro leant out of it. 'I will stir you over to *Wind's Road*, you and the two other little ones and their father.'

'Thanks,' said Mitt. 'And then you take Lithar home and look after him for me.' He looked at Lithar, but Lithar was not attending. He was looking woefully at his knee. His apple tree had gone. 'He's a bit in the head,' Mitt explained.

'We know that he is,' Jenro said, without expression.

'Do what I tell you,' said Mitt. 'You look after him. You. And don't let anyone else get at him.' Jenro still looked expressionless. Mitt was exasperated. 'You've got to have someone until I come back,' he said. 'And he needs looking after.'

'Until you come back,' said Jenro. He smiled. 'Very well. Will you all five climb in and I will stir to the *Wind's Road*.'

Riss leant down to help Navis, Ynen, Hildy, and Mitt aboard *Wind's Road*. As soon as they were up, he slid down into his own rowing boat and untied it.

'I think I'd better take first watch,' said Navis, rather wearily, looking at the three tired children.

'You do that,' Mitt said. He felt exhausted. He had barely strength to wave to Jenro and Riss.

They waved back. 'Go now on the wind's road and return sevenfold,' said Jenro. The island men sat in their boats and watched *Wind's Road* lean away North in the brown tag-end of sunset, carrying Libby Beer behind and Old Ammet in her bows.

A GUIDE TO DALEMARK

Adon, the last king of Dalemark before the country split into two, about whom many stories were told.

Al, the most common short form of Alhammitt, the commonest name in South Dalemark. The name of a castaway picked up by *Wind's Road*.

Alda, the wife of Siriol, and an alcoholic.

Alhammitt
  1. The true name of the Earth Shaker.
  2. The most common man's name in South Dalemark.
  3. Mitt's full name.

Ammet, a straw image thrown into the sea every year at the Sea Festival at Holand, which was said to bring luck to the city. Smaller images were made and sold for luck. Even greater luck was supposed to come to any boat that found Ammet floating beyond the harbour and brought him aboard. The name is a corruption of Alhammitt. See also **Poor Old Ammet**.

Andmark, the earldom in the centre of South Dalemark which was probably the wealthiest in the whole country. Henda was Earl of Andmark until he was killed in the Great Uprising a year after the main events in this book.

Armour was different in North and South Dalemark. The South used breastplates with exaggerated curves designed to deflect bullets, while the North, where guns were scarce, still used chainmail.

Arms Inspectors were employed by all the earls of the South to keep strict watch on gunsmiths, armourers, and weaponsmiths, who were not allowed to work without the Inspectors' seal on their equipment. The earls rightly feared that the craftsmen might otherwise sell weapons to common people and make weapons for the earls that were deliberately flawed. Despite the Inspectors, many armourers seem to have done both these things.

Arris, a rough spirituous liquor brewed throughout South Dalemark from discarded grapes and sprouting corn. There are only two things to be said for it: it was cheaper than wine and tasted slightly better than gley, brewed further north out of leftover cider pressings.

Autumn Festival, called Harvest in the North. The feast that celebrated the gathering of crops.

Autumn Storms, a regular feature in Dalemark. In historic times they reached as far north as Gardale and could be very severe. The worst lasted for days, with gales swinging from north-west to south-west. With a shorter storm the winds tended to gust stronger but not veer so much. If the gale was southerly, the storms came repeatedly for several days.

Bad luck gave rise to similar superstitions all over Dalemark, some very old. Those needing explanation are:

1. Giving. It was considered disastrously unlucky to start to give a thing and then withhold it. This is why the stall-keeper in Holand had to give Mitt the image of Libby Beer.

2. Festivals, feasts, and ceremonies. Enormous bad luck was incurred if anything interrupted one of these. Both Mitt and Al interrupted the Sea Festival, and both were unlucky.

3. Speaking a falsehood to one of the Undying was even more unlucky. Mitt and Hildy both narrowly escape doing this.

Beat the water. People pretended to do this as part of the Holand Sea Festival, using garlands of fruit and flowers. Maybe the idea was to subdue the sea for the following year.

Beer was drunk as a cheaper alternative to wine.

Bence, Captain in Chief of the Holy Islands fleet and commander of the *Wheatsheaf*. Bence was not a Holy Islander and despised the customs there. He was born in Wayness in the earldom of Waywold.

Big Shool, one of the larger of the Holy Islands.

Bull, the most usual form in which the Earth Shaker appears. This is why bulls' heads were carried in the Holand Sea Festival, although it was said the bull only appeared in the Holy Islands.

Canden, the younger of two brothers from Waywold, devoted to freedom fighting. He moved from Waywold to Holand, where conditions were much worse, deliberately to stir up rebellion. In Holand he joined the secret society of the Free Holanders and shortly proposed the group should fire one of the earl's warehouses. The older Free Holanders refused and stayed at home, while Canden led the younger and more hotheaded ones to the warehouse. There they found they had been betrayed and that soldiers were waiting for them.

Canderack, the earldom on the west coast of South Dalemark, where the best wine was grown. Until the reign of Amil the Great, Canderack owned a fleet that was a rival to Holand's.

Canderack Head, south of Canderack Bay, a headland that was an important landmark for shipping.

Chindersay, one of the outer ring of the Holy Islands, notable for the dark colour of its rocks.

Cruddle, one of the traditional instruments played at the Holand Sea Festival, a sort of triangular fiddle with three gut strings. The player held the cruddle under his chin and scraped the strings with a loose horsehair bow. Cruddlers were seldom musicians. Their sole aim was to make as much noise as possible.

Dalemark, the fifteen earldoms of Aberath, Loviath, Hannart, Gardale, Dropwater, Kannarth, the North Dales, the South Dales, Fenmark, Carrowmark, Andmark, Canderack, Waywold, Holand, and Dermath, together with the so-called King's Lands (the Holy Islands, the Marshes, and the Shield of Oreth) make up historic Dalemark.

Dermath, the earldom in the extreme south-east of South Dalemark.

Diddersay, one of the Holy Islands.

Dideo, a fisherman of Holand, one of the few older members of the Free Holanders who knew how to make a bomb. Dideo put this knowledge to use, first for Mitt and again in the Great Uprising, where he had a hand blown off by one of his own bombs, but he survived this and ended his days as a respected member of the City Council of Holand.

Dropwater, the earldom immediately north of the Point of Hark in North Dalemark, and the richest after Hannart. It possessed a good harbour. Before the Great Uprising that brought Amil the Great to the throne of the combined kingdoms, there was much smuggling done between Dropwater and the Holy Islands.

Dyke End, the birthplace of Mitt, farmed by his parents for the first six years of Mitt's life. The name comes from the situation of the farm and nearby village at the end of the great Flate Dyke, quite near where it runs into the sea ten miles west of the port of Holand.

Earl, the aristocratic ruler of one large segment of Dalemark. In the old days, prior to the reign of the Adon, earls held their places as officers of the king, but when Dalemark ceased to have kings, each earl became a little king in his own right. Many misused this power, some brutally, and all went to great lengths to keep it.

Earldom, a division of Dalemark ruled by an earl. It was said that the earldoms came into being when King Hern in prehistoric times divided his kingdom into nine and set nine men in charge to govern under him. These divisions were then called marks. Later, six more marks were added after Hern conquered the lands in the south. The system worked well provided the king was strong. The common people traditionally regarded the earls as merely the officers of the king, and continued to think this way even when there were no more kings.

Earth Shaker, the title of Alhammitt, one of the elder Undying, who had become the god of corn and of the sea. The title might describe the sea, but it also refers to what happens when any of the Earth Shaker's secret names are spoken.

Enblith the Fair, Queen of Dalemark in early historical times, said to have been the most beautiful woman who ever lived. She was said to be a daughter of the Undying. The musician-magician Tanamoril found Enblith living as a pauper in the woods and tricked the king into marrying her.

Farn, most southerly of the Holy Islands.

Fishmarket, a broad thoroughfare in the town of Holand, where fish was sold until the days of Amil IV.

Flags in historic Dalemark were nearly taboo. This seems to go back to the fact that in prehistory, flags were only flown for religious ceremonies. In Mitt's time, they were only flown at Midsummer Fairs and by ships at sea. No earls and few kings dared to fly flags, until Amil the Great designed the royal standard of the crowned wheatsheaf.

'Flaming Ammet', an oath peculiar to Holanders and a favourite of Mitt's. Since Ammet was an image of the Earth Shaker made of straw, the notion of it on fire amounted to blasphemy.

Flate, the general name for the flatlands below sea level surrounding Holand. These had all been reclaimed from the sea, but most of them had been let go back to marsh or heathland.

Flate Dyke, the main drainage ditch for the lowlands around Holand. It was wider than most roads and ran dead straight for nearly fifteen miles, the water in it flowing like a river to an outlet ten miles west of the port of Holand.

Flate Street, a street in a poor but respectable district to the west of Holand, where Earl Hadd provided Hobin the gunsmith with a house and workshop.

Flind, a non-existent person given a fairly common name as part of a password arranged by Siriol.

Flower of Holand, the boat belonging to Siriol, part of the fishing fleet that sailed regularly from the port of Holand, on which Mitt served his apprenticeship.

Free Holanders, one of many secret societies of freedom fighters in the city of Holand, the one to which Mitt belonged from the age of eight. Its members were mostly fishermen who, though they believed ardently that they should free South Dalemark from the tyranny of the earls, could seldom agree how this should be done. However, when the Great Uprising finally came about, all the Free Holanders were active in it, both in the fighting and in the reshaping of the government afterwards.

Ganter Islands, a cluster of three islands among the Holy Islands.

Garlands of apples, corn, grapes, and flowers were worn by all those taking part in the Holand Sea Festival and afterwards thrown into the sea.

Great Ones, a term for the Undying on the Holy Islands.

Great Uprising, the term for the countrywide revolution in Dalemark which brought Amil the Great to the throne. This took place roughly a year after the main events in *Drowned Ammet.*

Guilds were organized companies of craftsmen and merchants throughout South Dalemark. Most guilds were formed at the time of the Adon, when many tradesmen were shrewd enough to see that South and North were becoming increasingly estranged and the earls ever more powerful. Almost every trade, including the Singers, took hasty steps to obtain protection from the law, usually by petitioning to the Adon for a Royal Charter, so that in after years the earls could not easily disband them. The guilds generally kept a low profile all over the South, looking after members and the widows and orphans of members, training apprentices, founding schools and saving money. All paid taxes promptly. The earls of the South suspected the guilds of quietly financing the various uprisings, but could never prove this.

Guns were invented in the time of the Adon, but never much used in North Dalemark, probably because iron was scarcer there. The South used guns extensively, although they were forbidden to all but earls, lords, and their hearthmen. Early guns were clumsy, inaccurate and used mainly for sport, until Hobin invented the rifled barrel, with a spiral groove down the inside that caused the weapon to fire far more accurately. There was then a rush to buy guns. Waywold and Canderack both made a lot of money smuggling guns to the North.

Gunsmiths' Guild, to which Hobin belonged, along with all other gunsmiths, was a sober and respectable body of men who, in fact, spent the majority of their meetings laying careful plans for the Great Uprising.

Hadd, the angry and tyrannical Earl of Holand who, after a lifetime of injustice, quarreling with Henda and other earls, terrorizing his family, and overtaxing and suppressing his subjects, was murdered during the Sea Festival by an unknown marksman.

Ham, the partner and mate of Siriol aboard *The Flower of Holand*. Ham's full name, like so many in Holand, was Alhammitt. He was a large, good-natured, unintelligent man who was killed during the storming of the palace in Holand at the start of the Great Uprising.

Hammit, a South Dalemark name, one of many abbreviations of Alhammitt.

Hands to the North, an unknown group of freedom fighters in Holand. They were quite possibly invented by Harl Haddsson as cover for his attempt to assassinate Earl Hadd or by Harchad Haddsson as an excuse to pull down buildings to give *his* assassin a clear shot at Earl Hadd.

Hannart, the chief earldom of the North and the most hated in the South.

Harchad, second son of Earl Hadd of Holand, head of Hadd's secret police and master of his spies, said to be the cruellest man in Dalemark.

Harilla Harlsdaughter, eldest girl cousin of Hildrida and Ynen, betrothed at an early age to the lord of Mark by her grandfather Earl Hadd.

Harl Haddsson, the eldest of the Earl of Holand's three sons, a fat and seemingly indolent man, who became Earl of Holand following the death of Hadd. Holanders took to saying he was worse than Hadd. Harl was killed when a mob stormed the palace at the start of the Great Uprising.

Hearthmen, a privileged band of soldier companions sworn to a lord or earl and personally responsible to him alone. They formed a private army when need arose.

Henda, Earl of Andmark in central South Dalemark, a violent and paranoid man, who spent much of his time quarrelling with the Earl of Holand. He lived in constant dread of plots from the North and rebellion in the South. He was so cruel and so much disliked that he was beheaded by his own hearthmen during the Great Uprising.

High Mill, a village twenty miles north-east of the port of Holand, on rising ground towards Dermath. It was well known as a beauty spot.

High Tross, one of the islands of the Holy Islands, so called from its high and rocky outline.

Hildrida Navissdaughter, one of the company who sailed north to Aberath in the yacht *Wind's Road*. She was granddaughter to Earl Hadd, who betrothed her at the age of nine to Lithar, Lord of the Holy Islands. Hildrida was noted, throughout her life, for her fierce temper, inherited from her grandfather.

Hildy, the pet name of Hildrida Navissdaughter.

Hobin, the elder of two brothers from Waywold, whose family seems to have been secret hereditary guardians of the kingstone. Hobin was a brilliant and innovative gunsmith, highly respected by his guild and much in favour with the earls of Holand, Waywold, and Dermath. Hadd valued Hobin's skill so much that he arranged for Hobin to transfer to Holand, where the earl supplied him with a house, a workshop, and a good salary. Here Hobin met and married Milda, mother of Mitt, by whom he had two daughters. Hobin was secretly as much of a revolutionary as his brother Canden, but he bided his time and planned, unlike Canden, until the time was ripe for the Great Uprising, when he earned the name of Bloody Hobin for his extreme revolutionary ferocity.

Hoe, a village on the rising ground west of Holand.

Hoe Point, the spit of ground next to the village of Hoe, which was the second major landmark for ships sailing out of Holand.

Holand, the leading earldom of South Dalemark, situated on land at or below sea level in the extreme south of the country. Holand was a sizeable city and a flourishing seaport with a fleet second only to that of the Holy Islands. It was the seat of Earl Hadd, whose residence dominated the city.

Hollisay, one of the Holy Islands, supposedly named from the number of holly bushes growing on it.

Holy Islands, a scatter of islands in the large bay between the Point of Hark and Carrow Head, famous as a haven for shipping. They were home to a strange, fey people, thought to be descendants of the earliest inhabitants of Dalemark, and full of legends of the Undying. The Holy Islands are part of the King's Lands and not strictly under the rule of any earl, but at the time of this book, during the long interregnum between the death of the Adon and the crowning of Amil the Great, the islands were considered part of the South and their fleet at the service of any earl of the South who could arrange an alliance.

Holy Isle, the centremost island of the Holy Islands and rightly named. Only those who are meant to go to it can find it.

Horsehair drums, traditional crude drums made of horsehide with the hair still on it, beaten loudly and arhythmically at the Holand Sea Festival, possibly because Old Ammet was thought to govern the wild horses of the sea.

Horses of the sea were white and said to belong to Old Ammet. They appeared galloping in the sea around a doomed ship.

Irana Harchadsdaughter, one of Earl Hadd's many grand-children, cousin of Hildrida and Ynen, betrothed at an early age to Agnet, third son of the Earl of Waywold.

Island people, the inhabitants of the Holy Islands, who are something of a separate race, being small and brown-skinned, with dark eyes and very fair hair. Their sing-song accent is unlike any other in Dalemark. They are said to be descendants of the first peoples ever to settle Dalemark and they retain detailed beliefs and customs concerning the Undying that are no longer known in the rest of the country.

Isle of Gard, the ruling island of the Holy Islands where the Lord's mansion and the main fleet are.

Jenro, a Holy Islander, coxwain aboard the flagship *Wheatsheaf.*

'Jolly Holanders', a sea shanty that was known and loved all over South Dalemark.

K, at the beginning of a name was only used in North Dalemark. In the slurred and softer dialect of the South a *K* becomes a *C* (pronounced CH) or *H*. For instance, the Southern form of the name Keril is Harl.

Kastri, the Adon's son by his first wife and ancestor of Earl Keril of Hannart.

Keril, Earl of Hannart, descended from the Adon and generally considered the most influential man in the North. In his youth, Keril had actually taken part in an uprising in the South and was rumoured to support all freedom fighters there. This made him the earls of the South's most hated man.

Kialan, younger son of the Earl of Hannart and later his heir.

Kinghaven, in the earldom of Loviath in the North, the main port city of the North, notorious for brewing bad lager.

Konian, the elder son of the Earl of Hannart, executed in Holand after a travesty of a trial, along with his ship's company.

Lagan, villainous half-brother of the Adon, who tried to murder him.

Lalla, housekeeper of Lithar's mansion on the Isle of Gard and an aspect of Libby Beer.

Lathsay, one of the Holy Islands.

Law of the Sea, was largely unwritten, but held to throughout Dalemark waters, by both North and South, and felt to be much more binding than any written law of the land. Among other things, the law stated that all ships near enough to help must go to the assistance of any boat in trouble.

Libby Beer, the name of the image largely made of fruit that was thrown every year into the harbour at Holand during the Sea Festival. The name is a corruption of one of the secret names of She Who Raised the Islands, one of the Greater Undying. Libby Beer is mother of fruitfulness and wife of the Earth Shaker.

Lithar, Lord of the Holy Islands. Lithar was of special value to the earls of the South because he was lord in his own right of part of the King's Lands and therefore not the subject of any earl. His fleet was the largest and best in the country. He was betrothed to Hildrida Navissdaughter when he was twenty and she was nine years old.

Little Flate, a coastal village on the slightly rising ground south-west of Holand which was the first landmark for ships out of Holand. Boats gave it a wide berth because of the shallows just offshore of it.

Little ones, the name Holy Islanders give to those under the special protection of the Undying.

Little Shool, one of the Holy Islands, barely yards from its neighbour Big Shool.

Lord of Mark, holder of the northernmost lordship in the South, a plump and middle-aged widower who was betrothed to Harilla Harlsdaughter when he was thirty-eight and she was ten years old.

Lovely Libby, one of the big merchant ships sailing out of Holand. Like most of the tall ships of Holand, she was named from the Sea Festival for luck.

'Luck ship and shore', the ritual reply to the traditional greeting 'The year's luck to you' at the Holand Sea Festival. Only Holanders say this.

Lucky ship, any ship sailing out of Holand that found and retrieved the image of Old Ammet after it had floated out to sea from the Festival. The yacht *Wind's Road* was doubly lucky from having brought the image of Libby Beer along as well. Anyone noticing this fact had to be a Holander.

Lydda, Siriol's daughter, a plump, good natured girl who married a sailor from the merchant fleet of Holand. Her husband later took over Siriol's boat and business.

Marks, the old name for the divisions of Dalemark instituted by the prehistoric King Hern. These later became the earldoms.

Marriage by proxy, a custom among the earls of holding a wedding with the bride not there. Her place would be taken by a woman who was married already. The practice may have originated to save the nobly born bride the trouble and expense of a journey to the wedding, but it was widely used in the South when the bride was unwilling, or a child, or both.

Milda, mother of Mitt and later wife of Hobin the gunsmith, who was the father of her two daughters. Sadly, neither Milda nor her daughters survived the violence of the Great Uprising. The most probable theory is that they perished in the confusion when the earls of Dermath and Waywold sacked the city of Holand in revenge for the storming and burning of the Earl's palace there.

Mitt, short for Alhammitt. Mitt was born at Dyke End in the earldom of Holand on the day of the Sea Festival at the farm that had been in his father's family for generations. He moved to the city of Holand as a child, where he became a freedom fighter until he was forced to escape to the North to avoid arrest.

Navis Haddsson, third son of the Earl of Holand, a brilliant and efficient soldier who was allowed to play no part in the affairs of Holand after the death of his first wife. After the murder of Earl Hadd, Navis escaped to the North by a different route from that of his two children, Hildrida and Ynen, where he played a prominent part in the Great Uprising and was eventually made Duke of Kernsburgh.

New Flate, the drained flatlands some miles west of Holand. It was very fertile farmland but was never prosperous until the reign of Amil the Great because of the ridiculously high taxes imposed by the earls of Holand.

North, the seven earldoms of Hannart, Gardale, Loviath, Aberath, Dropwater, Kannarth, and the North Dales, naturally split from the Southern earldoms by a range of mountains between. It was the earliest part of the kingdom of Dalemark and very mountainous, which meant that, though poorer than the South, it was a far freer place. The laws there governed the ruling earls as well as the common people. Most ordinary people in the South thought of the North as the place of freedom and of magic.

Northern Cross, the most noticeable constellation of stars. Sailors valued it because it revolved around the true north. Other well known constellations are Enblith's Hair, the Flatiron, Hern's Crown, and the River. At this time only sailors studied the stars. Proper astronomy only began in the reign of Amil the Great.

Old Flate, the flatland towards Waywold, west of Holand, a part of the earldom which had once been drained and farmed but which had been allowed to return to sea-marsh because of ruinous taxes. It became the haunt of snakes, criminals, and disease.

Old Man of the Sea, a seeming priest who appeared to certain people on Holy Island, who was really an aspect of the One.

Ommern, the greenest of the Holy Islands.

Ommersay, one of the largest of the Holy Islands.

Palace, of Earl Hadd in Holand. Most earls, even in the South, lived in humbler mansions, but Earl Hadd, partly from pride and partly because he insisted on all his family living with him, enlarged and renamed his dwelling. This palace was largely destroyed in the Great Uprising.

Piper, from the time of the Adon onward, the name most often used for Tanamil of the Undying, one time lord of the Red River. It was said that after being released from bondage, Tanamil went to the Holy Islands, where his piping may still sometimes be heard on calm evenings.

Point of Hark, the high rocky peninsula that divides North from South Dalemark waters.

Poor Old Ammet, the full name of the image made of plaited wheat and decorated with fruit, flowers, and ribbons, which was yearly thrown into the harbour at Holand during the Sea Festival. Nobody knows whether this ritual echoes some sacrifice of the Undying or is simply a charm for good luck and an improved harvest. Any boat that picks the image up at sea after it has floated out of the harbour is assured of good luck ever after, but this is rare: tides and currents have to be exactly right. Usually the image sinks in the harbour.

Prest, one of the Holy Islands, large with high crags.

Prestsay, a small rocky island among the Holy Islands.

Proud Ammet, a big merchant ship based in Holand, where Earl Hadd's assassin seems to have been when he fired. Like all tall ships of Holand, this one was named out of the Sea Festival for luck.

Rattles, rotating wooden rattles, where the noise is made by a wooden flange meeting a ratchet, which are traditional at the drowning of Old Ammet in Holand. The rattle users are always small boys in half-yellow, half-red suits.

A Reader for the Poor, a book designed to teach working people to read. It was written by a lord's clerk in Carrowmark who had little imagination. A typical page begins: 'Ham beats the cask. He knocks in five nails. Will that make it hold water?'

Riss, a seaman aboard the flagship *Wheatsheaf* in the Holy Islands.

Scarnel, a pipe made of pea or bean stalks, hollowed and varnished, traditionally played at the Holand Sea Festival by any number of amateur pipers. The sound is indescribably horrible.

Sea Festival, called Autumn Festival elsewhere in the South and Harvest in the North, this is peculiar to Holand. Two images, one of straw and one of fruit, are carried in a noisy procession of men and boys clothed in red and yellow and wearing garlands and peculiar hats, accompanied by discordant music on traditional instruments and by other, lesser images. At the harbour, a strange form of words is said and then the two large images are thrown into the sea. This is followed by feasting and holiday.

Sevenfold, a merchant ship from Holand that had once the good luck to pull Old Ammet out of the sea. Every man aboard was said to have made his fortune later. *Sevenfold* herself was sold when she became old to a merchant in Waywold, who renamed her *Fair Enblith* and was not particularly lucky with her.

Sevenfold II, a merchant ship sailing out of Holand, given this name when the earlier *Sevenfold* was sold. Her cockboat was found by the yacht *Wind's Road.* Like most ships in Holand, both *Sevenfold*s were named from the Sea Festival.

She Who Raised the Islands, the most common name for the lady of the Undying who, as wife to the Earth Shaker, has power nearly equal to his, but more benign. As Libby Beer, she provides fruit and nourishment, but in her stronger aspects, she is the earth itself and the only power able to control the Earth Shaker. She is adored particularly in the Holy Islands, where she takes the shape of a beautiful red haired woman dressed in green.

Siriol, the owner of *The Flower of Holand,* a fisherman and a prominent member of the Free Holanders, the society of secret freedom fighters to which Mitt also belonged. Mitt was apprenticed to Siriol until Hobin bought out his indentures. Siriol was prominent in the Great Uprising and afterwards became semi-permanent Mayor of Holand.

South, the eight earldoms of Dermath, Holand, Waywold, Canderack, Andmark, Carrowmark, Fenmark, and the South Dales. This part of Dalemark has a warm climate and fertile soil, and would have been highly prosperous but for the greed of the earls. At the time of this book, the South was in places poorer than the North and much more oppressively governed. The North regarded the South with disgust. The people of the South had mixed feelings about the North: on one hand they thought of it as the place of freedom and magic; on the other, they thought all Northerners brash and stupid. The South was certainly noted for virtues not found in the North, such as efficiency, coolheadedness, and perseverance, together with a strong sense of humour.

Specials, guns made secretly by Hobin in Holand which he sold only to a chosen few. Each gun had some unusual feature, and all were better than any weapons he sold in public.

Square rigging, the old type of sail which is simply a sheet of canvas slung between two yards across the mast and swivelled to catch the wind. The South very early gave this up for a more efficient fore-and-aft rigging, but the North still clung to the old square rig right up to the reign of Amil the Great, when Ynen Navisson reorganized the national fleet and introduced the first steamships.

Square-topped pillar, a waist-high primitive altar, only found in the Holy Islands.

Stirring, Holy Island dialect term for rowing a boat.

Tears, a potent magic. When Mitt weeps on Libby Beer, he unknowingly invokes her protection.

Termath, the southernmost port in Dalemark, the seat of the Earl of Dermath.

'The year's luck to you', the ritual greeting between Holanders on the day of the Sea Festival.

'To tide swimming . . . ' the ancient charm of invocation to the Earth Shaker and She Who Raised the Islands, spoken as part of the Holand Sea Festival. Any who doubt that this is indeed a charm should note that the words *go now and return sevenfold* are repeated three times in it.

Tross, one of the largest of the Holy Islands.

Trossaver, another of the Holy Islands, said to be the most beautiful.

Tulfa, the Southern spelling of Tulfer Island in the bay off Dropwater.

Undying, have the status of gods, but seem once to have been human.

Waywold, the earldom next door to Holand on the south coast.

'Welcome aboard, Old Ammet, sir!' the traditional greeting of the crew of a boat lucky enough to find Old Ammet floating in the sea, which shows proper respect to the Undying.

West Pool, the second harbour of Holand, shallower than the main harbour and protected by walls and gates, where the rich always kept their boats. Harbour dues here are still very high.

Wheatsheaf, the flagship of the Holy Islands fleet.

Wheatsheaf crest, the badge of Holand and much feared, because Harchad Haddsson gave each of his spies a gold button with this crest on. Later, surmounted by a crown, it became the Royal Crest of Dalemark.

Wind's Road
1. An archaic term for the sea, used in spells and invocations.
2. The name of the yacht owned by Ynen Navissson.

Wine was made all over South Dalemark, but the best came from Canderack. Since the worst came from Holand, it is probable it was Canderack wine aboard *Wind's Road.*

Wittess, one of the Holy Islands, low and green.

Yeddersay, one of the outer ring of Holy Islands.

Ynen, son of Navis Haddsson, one of the company who sailed North in *Wind's Road*. Ynen, as Amil's chief of shipping, later became as famous as his father Navis.

Ynynen, the lesser of the Earth Shaker's two secret names. Readers are strongly advised not to say this name beside the sea or in a boat.

Other books in the Dalemark Quartet

Cart and Cwidder
ISBN 0 19 275279 0

Clennen and his family earn their living as musicians, travelling the lanes of Dalemark in their colourful cart. With warring earls and spies all around, few people move between the North and the South, so they often carry news, and sometimes a passenger.

One such passenger is Kialan. But who is he? And is there any connection between him and the sudden violence that overtakes them on their travels? As Moril tries to discover the mysterious powers of the cwidder it seems as though the fate of his family is somehow tied to Kialan as they become bound together in terror, flight, and music.

This is the first book in the best-selling Dalemark Quartet by acclaimed author, Diana Wynne Jones.

The Spellcoats
ISBN 0 19 275280 4

When her father is killed whilst at war with the Heathens, Tanaqui and her brothers and sister are left to fend for themselves. But the people in their village quickly become suspicious of their Heathen looks and godless ways and soon they are forced to leave.

As they begin a terrifying journey down to the sea Tanaqui realizes the important part she has to play against the evil Kankredin, who is bent on destruction and waiting for them at their journey's end . . .

This is the third book in the best-selling Dalemark Quartet by acclaimed author, Diana Wynne Jones.

The Crown of Dalemark

ISBN 0 19 275277 4

For Mitt, North Dalemark seems just as full of spies and tyrants as the South, and it's not long before he himself is blackmailed into carrying out a murder. The intended victim is Noreth, a young girl who has proclaimed herself the rightful heir to the crown of Dalemark.

Soon Mitt and a small band of followers set off with Noreth on a journey to ride the royal road, collect the Adon's gifts, and claim the crown. But all the time they are unaware that the evil forces of Kankredin are among them . . .

This is the final book in the best-selling Dalemark Quartet by acclaimed author, Diana Wynne Jones.